FIRE IN THE HOLE

BOOK YOUR PLACE ON OUR WEBSITE AND MAKE THE READING CONNECTION!

We've created a customized website just for our very special readers, where you can get the inside scoop on everything that's going on with Zebra, Pinnacle and Kensington books.

When you come online, you'll have the exciting opportunity to:

- View covers of upcoming books
- Read sample chapters
- Learn about our future publishing schedule (listed by publication month *and author*)
- Find out when your favorite authors will be visiting a city near you
- Search for and order backlist books from our online catalog
- Check out author bios and background information
- Send e-mail to your favorite authors
- Meet the Kensington staff online
- Join us in weekly chats with authors, readers and other guests
- Get writing guidelines
- AND MUCH MORE!

Visit our website at
http://www.kensingtonbooks.com

RICHARD S. WHEELER

FIRE IN THE HOLE

PINNACLE BOOKS
Kensington Publishing Corp.
http://www.kensingtonbooks.com

PINNACLE BOOKS are published by

Kensington Publishing Corp.
850 Third Avenue
New York, NY 10022

All Kensington Titles, Imprints, and Distributed Lines are
available at special quantity discounts for bulk purchases for sales
promotions, premiums, fund-raising, and educational or insti-
tutional use. Special book excerpts or customized printings can
also be created to fit specific needs. For details, write or phone
the office of the Kensington special sales manager: Kensington
Publishing Corp., 850 Third Avenue, New York, NY 10022, attn:
Special Sales Department, Phone: 1-800-221-2647.

0-7860-1709-0

Pinnacle and the P logo Reg. U.S. Pat. & TM Off.

First Pinnacle Books Printing: September 2005

10 9 8 7 6 5 4 3 2 1

Printed in the United States of America

For Benjamin C. Bruce, with admiration

Chapter 1

A sharp pain stung Dink Drago's left foot and shot up his leg. A vicious pain exploded in Dink's nostril and bloomed in his head. He stirred. Something was pinning him down. He couldn't move a limb. He was cold.

He felt something move on his chest and then the weight vanished. The stars whirled above him. His head ached. He didn't know where he was, but he had never been so cold. Another sharp pain, like the stab of a knife, stung his foot, but he couldn't move it. A giant weight held him.

Nothing worked. His limbs had quit him. Then, slowly, he took stock. He was lying in a dark alley. There were rotting snowbanks around. He heard a fiddle and some stomping. An icy breeze rocked a red lantern up a ways.

Then he remembered. He was in Skeleton Gulch, Montana Territory. He was probably lying in the muck behind Traveler's Rest Saloon. And he knew what had caused the pain. He turned his head slowly and saw them.

Rats. Dozens of them, waiting.

He knew all about rats. These were black rats, and they were waiting for another chance. A bold one had bitten his nose. Others had taken some meat out of his feet. His Wellington boots were missing and so was his coat. If he didn't get up soon he would freeze to death. And if he didn't escape the rats they would eat him alive, his feet and face first, and then the rest.

He lacked the strength to get up. But the rats were waiting. He could see them now, twenty or thirty in sight, more down around his feet, and who knows how many others? Waiting for some meat.

Dink knew he didn't have much time. He was cold deep down inside, cold where he shouldn't be cold, cold around his heart.

His lungs were still working. He sucked in cold air and pushed it out, and again and again, hoping to get some strength, some clean air in him. It helped even though he was colder than ever. He kept sucking air, thrashing his arms and then his legs, keeping the rats at bay—for a moment.

A Mickey Finn.

He had arrived in Skeleton Gulch that evening, put up his wagon and old nag at the livery barn, and headed for a likely saloon to warm up, have a drink, and find a place to stay. He was a little guy, not much over four feet, and that's how he came to be called Dink. His real name was Tom, but he had answered to Dink for years.

The bartender had surveyed the stranger, slid some chloral hydrate into his whiskey, rolled him, and tossed him into the alley to live or die as fate decreed.

Some town, Skeleton Gulch.

He felt a rat bounce on his chest, try for another bite of nostril, miss, and pop away. Dink knew the wetness around his lips was blood. His feet were wet with blood too. He might get rat-bite fever, but he doubted it. He had been bitten too many times and was somewhat immune. Rats were his business, and he had heard that Skeleton Gulch had more rats than any mining camp in the West.

He had to get up and get away, but the Mickey Finn all but paralyzed him. He had to; he had no choice. He dragged himself up until he was sitting, suddenly nauseous, while his head banged and throbbed. But he refused to lie down again. Get up or die.

He could see his stockinged feet and the holes in the stockings where the rats had chewed the fabric away. The rats hadn't quit him. These were a bold and hungry lot, and sometimes the wavering light of a lantern glowed in their eyes. They had backed off a little and one of their gang leaders was upraised, scolding him.

"You're dead," he said.

That was his business, or at least one of them. He was the best rat catcher in the world. He could clean a camp in a few weeks. There were cellar rats and attic rats, and he knew how to nail them all. He specialized in all kinds and species of rats.

He forced himself to his feet, and was immediately engulfed in nausea. He wanted to unload everything in his gut, except there was nothing in his belly. He hadn't eaten since dawn. Shakily, he hunted for his purse, a small doeskin bag he kept in his pocket. It wasn't there. He didn't expect it to be there. They had seen Dink walk in, fed him the Mickey, and pitched him into the icy night.

The livery barn was down the slope somewhere. Skeleton Gulch didn't have an inch of level ground in it, but few mining camps did. If he could get to the barn, he might get a night's rest in the hayloft. And he might find some spare clothing in his wagon, if that hadn't been pillaged too.

But getting to the livery barn was a problem. He faced an alley full of broken glass, smashed bottles, tin cans with jagged edges. One thing about mining camps: The alleys were the lower intestines. He would be better off on the main drag. That meant walking through the Traveler's Rest. He stepped gingerly toward its rear door, which opened onto the alley. A rude and rank outhouse stood there, but no one bothered to use it. The rats scattered, but not far, and he saw them congregate just out of reach, waiting greedily, ready to chew anything. If live flesh wasn't available, they would eat whatever was at hand, garbage, trash, cloth, leather.

Dink felt the ground squish under his bare feet; the urine hadn't quite frozen, but would soon. His own blood would mix with the sludge. He opened the door and saw light and warmth. The light hurt his eyes and started his head to throbbing. He walked past a small storage room and stood at the back of the saloon. A potbellied stove threw heat into the room. Three oil lamps cast pale and fetid light over the place. A dark quietness pervaded the saloon. The fiddling had come from next door, not here, where men's music took a darker tone. There was almost as much slime under his bare feet here as out in the alley. He hoped there would not be broken glass.

No one was noticing, not yet. Dink didn't want trouble. He was still woozy, barely able to stand. He needed a night's sleep to get the knockout juice out of his body. The narrow saloon stretched a long way to the street, and there were plenty of big galoots bellied up the bar. There was nothing to do but try, so he worked his way toward the street, unnoticed at first.

But then the barman, a keg-shaped brute with hair parted in the middle, yelled.

"Hey, we don't let rats in here." He was grinning, looking for more sport.

He was the one who had poured the Mickey for Dink.

Dink ignored him and worked toward the door. But someone tripped him and he sprawled, landing on the foul planks of the floor. Someone else grabbed a fistful of Dink's shirt and lifted him up.

"What we got here?" the oaf asked, shaking Dink as if he were a dog.

"It's a rat terrier," yelled someone.

Little did the man know. Dink tried to extricate himself, but he had no strength and was on the verge of vomiting.

"He's barefoot. We don't allow barefoot in here," the saloon man yelled.

Dink quit struggling, too sick to resist. But he did take stock. This was probably the worst dive in Skeleton Gulch; Dink had been fooled by the name, which invited quiet comfort and safety.

"What should we do with him?"

"If he ain't got money, he's a vagrant," the saloon man said.

Dink knew who had his purse. When he had sipped the Mickey Finn, he had dropped to the floor, out cold. The barkeep and some of his cronies had no doubt lifted him up and dragged him outside and dropped him in the alley. And snatched his purse, his boots, and his coat.

Dink knew he was in trouble again and utterly unable to defend himself. Best just keep quiet until they lost interest. What bullies wanted was response, any sort of response.

He was right. They bantered back and forth, and then someone dragged him out the double front doors and threw him into the muddy street. That suited him fine. He heard a crackle of laughter within. He slowly staggered to his feet, filthy, still bleeding, nauseous, half-frozen, but alive. He would catch rats another day.

He headed down the gulch toward the Howdy Livery Barn at the base of the street. His feet were so numb he wondered if they were frostbitten. But then he spotted a pile of steaming horse apples and remembered an old farmboy trick. He headed straight for the pile, stuck both feet into the middle of it, and let the hot moist apples warm his feet for a minute.

Skeleton Gulch was a town that never slept. Up above, the headframes of the gold mines poked the night sky.

Scattered below them was a gaggle of mercantiles, a tenderloin, and miners' cabins.

When the apples were no longer supplying heat, Dink walked the rest of the way down the grade to the livery barn and found the hostler dozing on a bench.

"Mind if I sleep in the loft?" he asked.

The hostler, a wiry little man like Dink, looked him over. "Two bits," he said.

"I got a wagon and mules here."

"Yeah? Where your boots?"

"I got rolled."

The hostler laughed. "They all get rolled. All right, but the loft's full of attic rats. You'll get bit."

Dink knew the score. Attic rats liked high places. They were bigger and lighter-colored than the black cellar rats that nested in burrows. The attic rats, Norway rats, were just as mean, just as hungry, and just as dangerous.

"I'll make room in my wagon," Dink said.

He had slept in the small, canvas-topped wagon many times, and if his war chest hadn't been stolen he would find a bedroll and some spare moccasins. He washed at the horse trough and climbed into his wagon. Tomorrow he would start catching rats—if Skeleton Gulch would let him.

Chapter 2

Daylight filtering through the canvas stretched over the bows of his wagon awakened Dink Drago. He felt sick. Slowly, he took stock. The rat bite that nipped his nostril stung mercilessly. The others, bites in both feet, stung less but ached. Nausea consumed him and he dreaded getting up.

The Mickey Finn had almost finished him. It was probably enough to flatten a big man and way too much for a little man like Dink, scarcely a hundred ten pounds. It was sheer good fortune he was lying here, safe in his wagon in the livery yard, rather than lying in that alley, a bunch of bones stripped of flesh by hundreds of black rats.

Maybe that barkeep had wanted to kill him. Dink would never forget that beetle-browed brown-haired skunk splashing booze into crockery and shoving the drink in Dink's direction. The keep had wiped his hands on a grimy apron and waited. The whole place had waited. Dink had been puzzled by the sudden silence. He had sipped, coughed on the rotgut, sipped some more, and then a giant sledge smashed into his head. Or so it seemed as he found himself tumbling to the slimy floor.

Now he lay in his bedroll, barely able to keep the contents

of his belly inside him, the last traces of the Mickey still threatening mayhem. He knew rats carried all sorts of diseases, including the plague, but they mostly got lumped together into one name: rat-bite fever. He ached, but he didn't feel hot or feverish. Maybe he would escape. He'd been bitten enough before to give him some resistance.

He realized he didn't have a dime; when they rolled him they made off with everything in his pockets, including the cash to get along until he returned to Denver. He would have a tough time of it buying breakfast, paying the livery bill, getting some new boots.

He fought his way to a sitting position, not much feeling like it, and pulled his moccasins over his feet. It was just as well he had some soft moccasins because he couldn't put boots over those swollen feet. Not for a while. He would let his chin stubble grow; his nose hurt so much he didn't even want to touch his face. The nostril must be the worst of all places to get bitten.

Dizzily, he slid down to the livery yard and made his way into the barn. A new hostler was there. This one was squat, square, half-bald, and not looking any too bright.

"I'm looking for work," Dink said.

"That means you can't pay. You got until noon to get your wagon and stock out of here."

The liveryman was brighter than Dink had given him credit for.

"And if I don't?"

"Then you ain't gonna see your stock until you do."

"You own this place?"

"What's it to you?"

"Just curious. A man wanting some business usually smiles a little."

"Listen, punk, I could squash you with one hand."

Dink nodded. He'd heard about Skeleton Gulch, and everything was proving to be true. He'd heard big men threaten him all too often. It was as if being short, thin, and wiry invited bullies to strut.

He headed back to his wagon, pushing one leg and then the other, and pulled a handful of flyers from his trunk. He was in the rat-catching business so he ought to get at it and worry about a meal later. In his wagon were fifty wire-cage traps specially designed by Dink, as well as a hundred or so of the usual jaw traps that would snap over a rat's neck and break it. And in a small chest were several poisons, including an arsenic salt that he preferred not to use, and some strychnine-laced barley in canisters. He preferred West African rat's-bane, a shrub whose seeds were fatal to rats. The seed was hard to get so he kept it for bad cases. Like Skeleton Gulch. He backed out of the wagon, noticed the bulky liveryman staring, and handed the man a flyer.

"This town's full of rats," Dink said.

The man stared at the flyer, his lips moving, and Dink realized the lout couldn't read.

"It says I can clean the rats out of town. I can charge by the rat, or bulk, your choice. It says I guarantee my work and when I'm done you won't have a rat problem. At least not right away. If you don't take measures, you'll get them again."

"A rat catcher! You look like a rat."

Dink had heard that too. Actually, his skinny short frame was helpful. He could squirm under buildings, into crawl spaces, and set traps in rat runways. He could crawl into cramped attics, lower himself into sewers, set traps wherever rats nested.

"Skeleton Gulch has its share," Dink said.

"Wait! How much to clear rats out of my hayloft?"

"Two cents a rat."

"I'm not gonna pay two cents a rat."

"Then let them eat your feed and lose your two cents a rat that way."

"You pay me by noon or you ain't staying here."

The man wasn't so bright after all. Dink headed into the morning to take the measure of Skeleton Gulch and start his sales campaign. He always pitched his trade when he arrived in a town, lined up what business he could.

Skeleton Gulch nestled under some high peaks that blocked the setting sun but provided abundant water and firewood for the mining town. It was as far from anywhere as a town could be in the territory of Montana. The capital, Helena, was maybe eighty miles away as the crow flies, but it might as well be five hundred. No law or order or taxation ever visited Skeleton Gulch from those in authority. At least that was what Dink had heard.

Up toward the edge of a high bench were the gold mines, half-a-dozen headframes poking into the bold blue sky. Rough mine buildings occupied the slopes below them, a scatter of toolsheds, powder bunkers, equipment bins, and a thundering twenty-stamp mill. In every direction the slopes had been denuded of the thick pine forest that once clothed them, but in the distance dark green slopes vaulted upward into snowy mountain ridges. A huge glacier filled a distant valley with white.

The hillsides were speckled with stumps, and even now the heavy rains were cutting gullies and running muck into town. A mining camp ate wood and didn't care where it came from or how the scenery looked after the virgin forests were slaughtered.

The town itself was a huddle of weather-stained wooden buildings, some of them nothing but rough-sawn plank covered with rotting tarpaper, others, the fancier joints, sheathed with board-and-batten siding. Most of the buildings sat on log foundations, which would swiftly rot out from under the structures. The place wasn't built to last. No one had spent an extra cent. Dink had never seen such a dark and sullen little town, a sinister wound in the mountains, oozing evil. Even the creek ran yellow, carrying away the foulness of the rotten little town. No wonder it was rat heaven. For every human, there probably were a hundred rats, and most of them breeding five or six litters a year.

He could smell rats. That ability came from years as a rat catcher. Others swore rats didn't smell, but Dink knew the dull, sour smell, knew that Skeleton Gulch had more rats than any place he had ever been, black rats, big Norways, stowaways that arrived in crates and wagons hauled by teamsters from the Missouri River port of Fort Benton, or up from the railroads far to the south. Rats came with humans, and the two lived together, rats and humans.

It wasn't all bad. There was not a scrap of rotting garbage or waste food fouling the whole town. But the rest was bad. They could gnaw through anything except solid metal, and were no doubt pillaging the town's precarious food supply. And they could kill people.

He peered up at the mines. Their boilers were spewing sinister yellow smoke, lit to smoky gold by the early light filtering into the valley. Once in a while a vagrant breeze whipped the choking yellow smoke into town. The clatter of one-ton ore cars reached his ears along with the sudden roar as one car after another unloosed tailings into a growing heap of them that someday would engulf Skeleton Gulch. Dink saw not a bird in the sky.

He hefted his flyers and headed for the main street, which was nameless as far as he could tell. No one had bothered to give Skeleton Gulch street names or honor the town with avenues, places, or parks. There weren't even proper streets. A hodgepodge of buildings and shacks nested everywhere, blocking traffic. What sort of dump was this? He already knew. He had received his welcome last night.

He headed for the Skeleton Gulch mercantile, the

place most likely to suffer from rats. This weather-stained place was as bad as, or worse than, the rest of this miserable dump, and looked ready to blow away, or rather, burn up. A half-hour fire would reduce Skeleton Gulch to good clean earth.

SKELETON GULCH STORE, the hand-painted sign said. There were grimy double doors leading into an unlit cavern of a building sheathed with planks. A tired mustard-colored canvas glued over the plank walls kept the wind out. Windows were expensive, so there was only one in front.

Dink studied the interior, letting his eyes adjust to the gloom. He had soaked his moccasins getting there, and his feet were hurting. This place charged pirate prices: Eggs were a dollar each, potatoes fifty cents.

He spotted what looked to be the proprietor, a bald, chinless, stooped geezer, and approached.

"You want something and can pay?" asked the man. It wasn't exactly a welcome.

"I'm a rat catcher. I'll clean the rats out of here, plug up their holes, and you'll save money."

"Rats? How do you know I got rats?"

"I know. This place is loaded with them. Here." Dink handed the man a flyer. "You hire me, and in a few days you won't have rats. I'll get under the building, set up traps in their runways, nail sheet metal over their entries, and you'll save plenty. I charge two cents a rat, or a flat rate, whichever you want. Guaranteed for three months."

"No rats in here," the man said.

He seemed oddly frightened, as if Dink Drago posed a menace.

Wordlessly, Dink pointed to burlap sacks with jagged holes and missing contents; potatoes that had been pillaged, flour sacks broken open, barrels of hard candy that had been gnawed into sieves. There were rat turds all over the floor.

"You're losing hundreds of dollars a month here. You need a rat catcher."

"I ain't the man to talk to," the bald man said.

"You own it?"

"No, Victor Mines owns it. They own everything."

"Who runs it? Who do I talk to? I'll have a little visit with him."

"It ain't a him," the old gent said. "And she don't mind rats."

Chapter 3

Next door was Kilgore and Son City Mortuary. Dink thought that might be a good place to sell his services, and headed in. An acrid smell engulfed him at once.

He waited while his eyes adjusted to the darkness, and found himself in a cramped room piled with yellow pine boxes. A few more elaborate ebony caskets stood on sawhorses at the rear. And there were half-a-dozen barrels and casks lying about, which intrigued him.

A thick-lipped gent sporting black sideburns emerged from a red velvet-curtained doorway, wiping his tattooed hands on a towel.

"I am so sorry," he said. "I'm Hap Kilgore. How may I console you?"

"Actually, I'm in the extermination business."

Kilgore stared. "I have all the business I want," he said carefully. "But if you want us to pick up someone, we will do it."

"Rats. I trap rats. Did you know that rats can produce five or six litters a year? That rats spread disease? Like the black plague? That in three or four months a female rat can be bred?"

"Oh, rats it is." Kilgore's lips formed words that never emerged from his throat.

"You have a rat problem," Dink said.

"How would you know that?"

"I know. There's rat offal on the floor. I see toothmarks and gnawing on some of those boxes. You have a serious problem here."

"The whole town does, sir. What is the name?"

"Dink Drago. I'm a rat catcher. I trap rats, poison them, block their runways, destroy nesting areas, rat-proof buildings with sheet metal, protect food supplies, and advise clients about the ways to keep the rat population under control."

"I have no need."

"Certainly you do. Now I'll just have a look back here and advise you."

Dink pushed through the black velvet drapery into a workroom that featured a plain table with a sheet-metal surface. An unclad male body rested on it, fish-belly white. A swarm of rats under the table fled instantly. Black rats, small and mean and bold.

Another table held a heap of bones, once a skeleton, but the rats had reduced what was left to chopsticks and hair. This undertaker plainly had his own unique system of embalming.

"They save you money, eh?" Dink said.

"Out. You don't belong here."

"What do you do when someone wants an open-coffin visitation and service?"

"You don't belong. Leave at once."

"You use one of those lead-lined coffins, I imagine. Rats will eat most anything but lead."

"Out!"

"I can catch these rats, destroy their nests and breeding areas, block their passageways, set traps for any that come after I've left, clean the rat droppings, and freshen the air. Two cents a rat or bulk rates."

The undertaker softened. "There are a lot of rats."

"These are black rats. *Rattus rattus,* in Latin. They hug the ground. There are also attic rats, bigger, lighter, and you no doubt have those too. The whole town does. These bones here on the metal table. Rats have cleaned off everything."

Kilgore stared pensively at the charnel heap. "That's how we found the body. Pile of bones. The constable called us. Bones in the alley. We're hoping for a name. God rest his soul."

"I see. A man is thrown into an alley and within hours no one can identify him."

"Oh, we usually do. Someone is reported missing. Often there's some hair, or clothing. . . ."

"What are you going to do with these bones?"

"Oh, stuff them in a barrel, I imagine. No one has claimed them."

"Does this happen often?"

"Mining town, sir. Often enough. It's quite common."

"You have a lot of business?"

"So many poor souls don't survive in the mines, Mr. Drago. We're here to serve."

"How many on the average per month?"

"Oh, how could I say? A dozen maybe."

"A hundred forty-four a year. That's a lot of dead people for a town this size. One might expect fifteen or twenty. Who pays for these piles of bones that are unidentified?"

"The mining company. Victor Mining. They have given me a generous contract to deal with bones of vagrants."

"This is a vagrant, this here?"

"Well, sir, no one has been reported missing, so it must be. They drift in, you know."

"How many vagrants come to Skeleton Gulch?"

"All the time, sir, coming to work in the mines or sell things to merchants, or try to live on free lunches in the saloons."

"Ten a month, twenty?"

"Oh, we bury that many, yes. They drink too much, stumble into the alleys, and the rats finish them. You know how mining towns are, attracting the dreamers and schemers, most of them without a cent in their pockets, and half of them unable to live a sober life. I tell you, there's something about mining towns that attracts the lowest of the low."

"I imagine some go to the Traveler's Rest for a friendly drink."

"Oh, yes, that's where we pick up most of the poor drifters. They seem to gravitate there."

"You been here long?"

"Ever since the boom started four years ago. I was one of the first to arrive in this fine town, seeing the need for my services. People have been most kind. I have no competition."

"This your place? You have a son in the business?"

"Alas, sir, I lost my son to rat-bite fever. I carry on alone."

"Then surely, Mr. Kilgore, you'll want to rat-proof this building. Let me show you their runways. I can see a dozen just by peering about, and there must be many more. You must have three or four hundred rats in here."

He sighed. "I don't own it. Just rent it. You'd have to talk to the owners."

"Who are?"

"Victor Mining Company."

"They own much of the town?"

"Nearly all, sir."

"Do they own all the mines too?"

"All, I take it. And now they're interconnected. What started as five mines is now all the same mine."

"Where's the cemetery?"

"Downslope about a mile, then left. There's no land up here with any soil on it, and it's crowded anyway, so we must carry the deceased some distance."

"I suppose Victor Mining owns that too."

"Actually, yes, and as a public service they ask nothing of the families of the deceased. The plots are free."

"Very kind of them," Dink said.

"I, ah, don't think I'll employ you, Mr. Drago. The rats tidy up my business."

"I imagine they do," Dink said.

He headed into a chill day, knowing it never warmed up much at these altitudes, and hiked the nameless street toward the cemetery. This moiled and muddy thoroughfare was lined with unpainted false-front stores weathered brown by sun and snow. He passed a harness maker, gunsmith, and an array of dowdy saloons. Only the saloons showed any signs of trying to lure trade. Some took imaginative names: the Golden Hind, which featured the image of a lady in a large bustle; the Bunkroom, which gave no hint what sort of bunk lay within.

At the Silver Queen, a steerer lurking in front of the door caught Dink's arm. "In here, pal."

"Sorry."

"I says in here. In you go." The big bruiser literally dragged Dink through the double doors and into a smoky saloon and gambling emporium, strangely crowded for mid-morning.

"Spend it here, pal. Everything for every taste."

The bruiser let go and headed to his post on the street. Dink surveyed the odorous place, spotted a rear exit that opened on the alley, and headed for it, passing roulette tables, keno, poker layouts surrounded by perspiring miners, a side-parlor with red drapes and rouged ladies and the sound of an untuned piano, plus a few tightly closed doors. No one stayed him. He opened the rear door and was smacked with the stench of urine, but headed down the alley without being waylaid by man or rat. These saloons were a little too friendly.

He cut back to the main street and reached the lower edge of town, mostly the domain of cordwood dealers, wagon yards, livery barns, and storage sheds, and continued downslope, finding a little fresh air at last. The turnoff to the cemetery was plain and he took it, walking another two hundred yards to a dismal flat overgrown with weeds and alder brush. No one cared for the place or for the dead. Trash littered the whole place: old wagon wheels, Hercules dynamite boxes, broken glass, some scraps of faded cloth, rusty cans, and in the midst of all this, the first of spring's bright blooms.

He found a single row of graves, six in all. Only one headstone; the other markers were painted headboards that would last a few years and then tumble into dust. That intrigued Dink. Six identified graves for a mining town of three thousand, in which the mines took their weekly toll? Dink studied the place, smelled rats, and discovered a few rat holes around the graves. Not even the dead escaped those gnawing little snouts. Dink knew that if he exhumed any of those caskets, there would be only a few bones, scraps of hair, and bits of cloth within, and most likely, some of them would be fine nesting and breeding dens for the rat population of Skeleton Gulch.

There had to be more. In a corner he found a series of circular dents in the yellow soil, all unmarked, with a few rat burrows as well. This was where the barrels and casks of bones went. None of these graves was identified. He guessed there were thirty or forty barrels buried there.

Dink had a hunch he ought not ask Hap Kilgore about these. The dead were there, all right, bones stuffed into kegs and casks and lowered into round holes. He guessed it would take the loose bones of three or four mortals to fill one keg. It was an odd thing: A large and bustling mining town had scarcely any identified graves. He made note of it, and of the rats populating this trash-filled corner.

Skeleton Gulch had plenty of rats, all right, and they were eating the evidence.

Chapter 4

Dink Drago studied the shingle, AMOS P. CUTLER, ALLOPATHIC MEDICINE, and went in. He was instantly confronted with a reek he couldn't identify, but he smelled something else he could identify, *Rattus norvegicus*. He swore he could tell the difference, even if no one else could. Here in the anteroom he found clean benches, a swept floor, and windows that had recently been massaged.

The good doctor operated without assistants, and plainly had a patient in the consultation room behind the blue-velvet curtained doorway. Dink settled on a bench.

"No, not an enema," a male voice bellowed. "Anything but that."

"You're packed tighter than a Baltimore cigar."

"I don't care. Give me a pill."

"All right. A purgative then. I'll give you two. Old Dr. Barton used to call them Thunderclappers. Take one before bedtime. Get some spare linens ready. And keep a chamber pot within two feet. And a Sears catalog or a dozen corncobs or three issues of your favorite newspaper. Came back if you don't get purged."

Dink heard a muffled agreement, some grunts, and a moment later a burly bearded miner bolted through the blue curtain and out the front door. A discreet twenty seconds after that, the doctor emerged, wiping his hands on a towel.

He stared at Drago through rimless spectacles. "Take your shirt off, your boots, and wash your hands in that bowl over there. You can tell me your name and what ails you and whether you intend to pay," Cutler said.

Drago found himself staring into bold blue eyes. They were startling eyes, emitting light, or maybe piercing straight through him. He couldn't quite say, but he felt that the doctor had assessed him in two seconds, diagnosed him in five, and was ruminating the cures.

"I'm not sick. I'm a rat catcher."

"A rat catcher, are you? Then you're risking trouble. People here like rats. What did you say your moniker is?"

"I'm Dink Drago, new in town. I provide the most advanced rat-catching techniques known to science."

"You look ill. Take off your shirt and tell me about rats while I examine you. I'd say you recently were bitten on the nose by a rat, that you are slightly nauseous, have rat-bite fever, and you have not yet recovered from whatever floored you yesterday, probably a Mickey Finn."

It was Dink's turn to stare.

"Usually I get a half-eaten corpse, or Hap Kilgore gets a pile of bones. You're a rarity, a live one. Off with the shirt now. Where else were you bitten?"

"I'm selling a service. That's what I'm here for."

"Let's have a look at your feet. Rats go for toes. I'll do what I can and trade it for some professional rat catching. I don't know where you're from but you came to the wrong place. We love rats. Skeleton Gulch is the Rat Capital of the World. Population three thousand humans and fifty thousand rats."

Dink surrendered. His feet had swollen so much he could barely pull his moccasins off.

The doctor sat on a stool, grabbed the first available foot, and studied it.

"I thought so," he said. "I have a carbolic salve. Lister's work, you know. After Pasteur found out that infections were caused by invisible organisms, Lister began experimenting with dilute carbolic, great success. Killed the little buggers. He could cut on someone and have it heal up. Now look at this. The rats got a few good nips, didn't they? That big toe isn't going to be so big anymore."

The doc gently laved the wounded and befouled feet and spread a salve over the wounds. Then he tackled Dink's nostril, which Dink endured but just barely.

"I know it stings, but all rat catchers are brave and stoic. More nerve endings around the nostrils than anywhere else except maybe the fingertips," the doc said. "But maybe we can do something about that infection. Now, young man, I've done everything I can think of to stop the rats, but they still get in. Look at that base molding. Solid sheet metal, clear around. There's rats in the crawl space under here, and I've trapped them, but they're there. Wherever there's tin on the floor, that's where I fought rats."

"You've got attic rats, Doc. They live in the rafters. They're bigger than the other kind. They don't come up from the floor."

"Attic rats? Rats in my belfry?" He laughed. "Show me."

Dink spotted a hatch leading to the low attic, and pointed. It was ajar. "Norwegian rats, big rats, like upstairs life. Your attic's full of them. They've taken up residence."

"Well, damn. How do I get rid of them?"

"I'll see what they have for runways. We'll block those and trap and poison what's up there."

"Attic rats!" Cutler shook his head. "This burg's got rats of all shapes. Next you'll tell me there's bedroom rats and parlor rats and kitchen rats and outhouse rats."

"All of those, Doc. You're the first person I've talked to who wants to get rid of them. You own this building?"

"I do. I bought the lot and raised the structure. The Skeleton Gulch Town Lot Company tried to jump this lot, but I told them I'm as good with lead pills as I am with powders, and they backed off."

"I don't suppose the town lot company's owned by the Victor Mining Company. . . ."

"Well, that's a good question. Same crowd anyway."

"And who might that be?"

"You're new in town, that's for sure."

The doc was suddenly wary.

"On the average, how many deaths are there per month? How many do you see?"

"Not many," Cutler said dismissively.

"Are you the coroner?"

"There's no coroner here. Skeleton Gulch chases away anyone that pokes around. Like you."

"I'm just a rat catcher."

Cutler laughed suddenly, and Dink let him.

"You treat the miners?" Dink asked.

"Some. I get the traumas, the busted heads and mashed toes, and Hap Kilgore gets the rest."

"Including the rat-killed?"

Cutler's humor vanished. "He gets the dead or co-matose, men without names. Males, rarely female. Unknown people, their wallets gone, their faces eaten, nothing left in their pockets, if any pockets are left."

"Murdered."

"I'm not going to answer that."

"This town kills and hides the evidence. Kilgore fills barrels and casks with bones and buries them. Six marked graves in your cemetery. Lots of round dimples in the sod with dirt thrown over a big barrel. The coffins are rat nests, by the way. You wouldn't find much in them except a lot of fuzzy stuff and hundreds of baby rats and some needle-nosed mamas."

"You've been around town, Mr. Drago."

"I've hardly started. Who wants the rats around?"

"I can't answer that; Victor Mining Company is a mystery."

"Why are you here, practicing medicine in Skeleton Gulch, Montana?"

Cutler shrugged. "I didn't plan to stay once I got the idea of how things are. But they need me. I'm the only physician. The nearest one is in Helena. Victor Mining figures it's cheaper to heal up an experienced miner than lose its personnel, so the company pays me now and then. They have hiring problems. A lot of men quit; too many to make the mines profitable."

"Quit or disappear?"

Cutler seemed to pull into himself. "Who knows, Drago? You won't find any parish records in the local churches because there are no churches."

"I almost died. A Mickey. Out in the cold. Rat bites in an alley. I woke up just in time. Homicide, Doc."

"Think what you want, Drago."

"Rats are like an innocent verdict. No evidence left. Have I got that right?"

Cutler smiled, and eyed the windows.

"And if I clean all the rats out of town, crime will have no place to hide. Have I got that right too?"

Cutler stared at him, those bold eyes peering through and through. "Count on me to patch you up," he said. "If you last more than two or three days."

"I will count on you. Are there any others I can count on?"

"A few. But none of the saloons or gambling halls or cafes. They'd just as soon pour a Mickey into your coffee as into your rotgut booze."

Dink nodded.

"Buy your chow from groceries and cook your own meals."

"Who else can I trust?"

"The teamsters. They're mostly on the road and out of town. Some mining engineers. Oh, I'll supply names, when I know you are who you are."

"Who do you think I am?"

He paused and then spoke in a monotone so low Dink could barely hear him. "I wrote the Rocky Mountain Detective Agency in Denver two months ago."

Dink peered through the window into a bright blue sky where the universe was cleaner than in Skeleton Gulch. "I'll take care of your attic rats now, Doc," he said. "They're getting into your chambers."

"There are rats high up the ladder," Cutler replied. "First you heal up that foot. My rats can wait until you're feeling better."

"No, I'll get started now," Dink said. "I'll get some stuff from my wagon and fix you up. You might want to close up the shop while I crawl around in your attic."

"If no one needs me, I will."

Dink pulled moccasins over tender feet and headed into the smoky street, marveling that the sky could be so bright and blue, and this bleak thoroughfare so sullen and grim. He dodged the hostler who would be wanting money, dug out a trap, bait, sheet metal, a bottle of arsenic trioxide, hammer, and roofing nails, all of which he packed into a burlap sack, and headed back to Cutler's chambers.

The work didn't take long. He sealed the offices, cleaned out nests, baited one of his box traps, which lured rats into them, and finally dropped through the hatch and into Doc's study.

"It'll take a couple of days," he said.

"It seems I'm to have the first rat-free building in Skeleton Gulch."

"Temporarily. They gnaw their way in again."

"That sounds like the human race," he said. "What did you say your name is?"

"Drago, Dink Drago."

"I'll remember it," Cutler said.

Chapter 5

Skeleton Gulch, in the bright light of noon, seemed subdued and serene except for the yellow smoke drifting through town. Dink Drago stood in the unnamed main street, seeing little foot or horse traffic. The town slumbered by day, crackled to life at sundown. He was still nauseous and growing acutely hungry. He needed work fast, not only to feed himself but to pay off the hostler. If he didn't come up with some cash, the livery man would confiscate his rig or his great old nag until he coughed up something. The prospects weren't good.

Up on a flat several hundred yards from the main drag stood a rectangular, solid building of mortared mine rubble, more substantial than any other in town, and relatively fireproof. He had noticed it at once last evening. An unlit red lantern hung beside its door. It stood apart from a district consisting of cribs and two-story board-and-batten boxes, all catering to off-shift miners. The town's leading lights wouldn't have to brave the footpads and hooligans of the sporting district. And also wouldn't be seen by their employees.

Drago debated whether to pawn his shirt for a one-bit bowl of gruel or just endure if he could. Maybe he could talk a sporting lady out of two bits, enough to stuff some-thing, anything, into his starving belly. Things were get-ting rough. Cutler's salves weren't doing a thing for his nausea or the infected toes and nostril.

He hiked wearily toward the big and well-manicured structure, the only such building in all of Skeleton Gulch. Above town, the mine boilers belched sinister yellow smoke, and the rattle of rock sliding out of cars into tail-ings piles offended the peace. The only sign of life in all of town was the fevered activity along the ridge where mines hauled up ton after ton of high-grade gold ore and the stamp mill pulverized it with a steady earth-shaking thump of its massive hammers.

He climbed a shallow grade to the veranda, sensing that the denizens of this house hated daylight, hated sunny af-ternoons, hated blue skies. He opened a massive door and found himself in a hushed dark foyer draped in red velvet and flocked orange wallpaper with fleurs-de-lis. He smelled rats. A nymph du monde appeared instantly, looked Dink over dubiously.

"I don't think so," she said.

"I'm not buying, I'm selling."

She tittered. "No takers," she said. A chippy joined her and tittered too.

"I'm a rat catcher. That's my trade. I can tell the place is full of rats. I'll get rid of them for you, do it fast, and charge very little."

That met with utter silence. The first nymph, who wore a pink kimono, perhaps to advertise her vaguely Ori-ental wares, frowned. Dink wondered what he had said that might evoke such heavy silence.

"You better leave," said the other nymph, a skinny and consumptive one with a hyperactive tongue that found no peace in her blistered mouth.

"You've got rats here. I can see some runways. I can

smell them. I'll clean 'em out. Two cents a rat, or maybe bulk rates. I'll get rid of them all, clean their nests, block their paths. You'll save money. Your kitchen won't lose food. You won't get sick all the time. You won't wake up with a rat sitting on your coverlet. You probably got bit more than once and I can stop that. There's ground rats and attic rats and I trap them all."

It was odd how his spiel seemed to frighten them both. As if he was touching on a tabooed subject.

"Here's what you do. You go get the owner and I'll talk to her. Maybe she's in the market for some extermination."

"She's asleep," said Pink Kimono.

"Here's my card. I'll be back," Dink said. He passed it to the consumptive one, who stared dumbly at it. She obviously couldn't read.

"Get Bruno," she said, waving the card as if it were a fan.

"Get him yourself," Pink Kimono shot back.

"What's your name, sweetheart?" Dink asked.

"You better get outa here before Bruno comes, and you don't mention rats. He don't like to hear about rats. If we talk about rats, he . . . he . . ."

Whatever she intended to say, she didn't say it.

"Lend me a buck," Dink said. "I just got into town and I haven't gotten any business yet. I'll pay you, first job I get. That's for certain."

She shook her head and clutched the kimono tight over her ample breasts, causing sudden lust in Drago.

"Why are you afraid of a rat catcher?" he asked. "I'm here to help out. I can make this a good place to be. You've been bitten plenty of times. I can see the scars. That's what I'm here for, to stop that."

"Go! Leave at once!" she cried.

A giant figure parted red curtains and Dink beheld a man twice his size, bald and bullet-headed, poker-faced with a dead man's eyes.

"You heard the lady," he said, never pausing in his trajectory toward Dink.

"I'm a rat catcher. This place is full of rats and I can clean 'em all out, stop their breeding."

Bruno laughed, a guttural roar, and shook his massive frame. One whack with one paw would send Dink careening across the parlor.

"Here's my card," he said, handing it to Bruno, who took it, much to Dink's surprise. But Bruno grabbed Dink by the scruff of the neck, as if he were a sparrow, and propelled him toward the door. Dink felt himself being lifted by a locomotive of a man, and didn't resist.

"What's the trouble?" This from another woman, who stood a good six feet tall herself and towered over Dink. She too wore a kimono, white silk with yellow roses embroidered over it. Her jet hair framed a coarsely handsome face. Agate eyes bored into him.

"I'm a rat catcher," Dink said as he was being propelled out the door. "I'll clean out every rat in Skeleton Gulch."

The woman raised a hand. Bruno stopped mid-step.

"You the proprietor?" he asked.

"I am the Yellow Rose." She said it in a way that suggested Dink should know the rest.

"I just arrived. I came here to offer my services," he said, handing her his last card. "I can fix up this place and the whole town."

"Usually it's the other way around," she said. "We can fix you up. We have no rats here and no need for your services. And there are no rats in Skeleton Gulch. I'm sure you understand."

Dink thought better than to dispute her. No rats in Skeleton Gulch. The two nymphs had drawn back and seemed ready to flee. Their anxious gazes told Dink that he was in the presence of a forceful woman.

"Two cents a rat, or bulk rates. Guaranteed for three months. I clean out nests, block passage, rat-proof kitchens."

"What rats?" she said.

Bruno started to haul him out the door, but Yellow Rose stayed him with a wave of the hand.

"Mr. Drago," she said. "Leave Skeleton Gulch. Don't come back."

"Why?"

She didn't reply, but nodded to her goon.

Bruno shoved him toward the door, and then out.

The nymphs followed, wailing.

The massive door slammed behind him. He stumbled and righted himself. Lying on the planks of the veranda was a dollar bill, slowly flipping along under the breeze.

Pink Kimono's dollar bill. He plucked it up. Fifty cents for the livery man; two bits for a cheap meal. Two bits for breakfast.

Pink Kimono's face and arms had been covered with small scars, the sort of scars that might be visited upon someone tied up and plunged into a rat parlor. The sort of scars visited upon a prisoner in a rat-infested dungeon. The dollar wasn't a loan; it was a plea for help.

He dusted himself off. The warm sun lifted his spirits, along with the promise of food. High above, a mine whistle shrilled. Yellow-gray smoke belched from the mine and mill boilers and then lowered over town, a trick of the mountain winds. In a moment, the sun vanished and a thick yellow haze cloaked every building and turned every pedestrian into a ghostly figure. Drago coughed and headed for a cafe. The air would be better inside. With luck he'd get a bowl of stew without waking up two hours later in an alley.

He found a humble joint that touted a MINER'S LUNCH, TWO BITS from its weathered shingle. The air was better in there. The wheezy proprietor slapped a bowl of stew in front of Dink, made honest change, and Dink found himself staring at a gray and greasy meal. The meat could have been anything from gopher to badger to rattlesnake. But with a little salt it was edible, and Dink slowly slurped down the entire miner's portion. At least the joint didn't skimp.

It was an odd time of day to be eating, and he found himself alone in the dump. There were rat droppings all over the floor. Maybe he had eaten fillet of rat.

He caught the old man as he limped from the kitchen. "I'm a rat catcher. You want me to clean out the rats? Two cents a rat, or bulk rates, you choose."

The cook laughed. "That's my meat," he said. "Me, I'm a busted-up miner, so I do this."

"I'll clean out the place, seal it up, and you won't lose food. Guaranteed three months if you follow my instructions."

"Ain't my building," the man said.

"I suppose it belongs to the Victor Mining Company. They going to object if I clean out your rats?"

The busted-up miner gimped over to Drago. "You could try, or you could die," he said.

"I clean you up. No more rats in here. What would happen?"

"It'd be the last time I lay eyes on you, pal."

"Who's the Yellow Rose?"

"Who's God?"

"What does she do?"

"She runs Skeleton Gulch. Now don't ask me no more."

"What does she own?"

"She owns the rats," the man said, snapped a dish towel, and retreated into his kitchen.

And maybe the Victor Mining Company, Dink thought.

Chapter 6

Dink lay abed in his wagon with the hostler appeased for one night and some foul food churning his belly. He was edging toward nausea again and his bitten toes ached. At least here in the livery barn yard he could enjoy the honest, acrid smell of horse manure. The stench rising from every building and alley in Skeleton Gulch was enough to sicken the heartiest and healthiest soul.

Everything had turned out to be true.

A few weeks earlier, General David Cook, head of the legendary Rocky Mountain Detective Agency in Denver, had summoned him. Drago had entered the anonymous door and found himself in the familiar and austere anteroom. There wasn't another soul in the silent room. Then the general opened a pebbled-glass private door, smiled, and beckoned Dink into the inner sanctum. Cook was built in rectangles, with a rectangular head and jaw and torso, rectangular hands with squared-off fingers, even rectangular brows and eye sockets. There were more sharp edges to that man than to any other man Dink had met.

"I've a job for you if you want it. You probably won't when you hear me out. It's the most dangerous assignment I've ever given and your life won't be worth two cents."

"That's the price of a rat," Dink replied.

Those rectangular eyes crinkled. Cook had an odd humor, given his profession.

"Ever heard of Skeleton Gulch, Montana?"

"Gold town."

"Full of rats," Cook said.

"They'll want my services."

"No, they won't. That's the point. They won't want you at all. You still interested?"

"Less than I was ten seconds ago."

"We think Skeleton Gulch is the most vice-ridden and murderous town in the West."

"That's a mouthful."

Cook nodded. "It's worse than that. We've been hired to find out who the vice lords are and what can be done about them. And so far, we've been unable to prove anything. What little information we have is rumor and gossip. It's the most secretive town on earth. We don't even know who owns the mines. They're hidden behind layers of holding companies. The Victor Mining Company. That's the only name we know, the only name on the real-estate records. You interested?"

Drago nodded.

"I hardly know where to start," Cook continued. "The mines, I guess. At first there were five independent gold mines, all rich. The owners of three vanished; the owner of the fourth sold out and then disappeared. Now all five are owned by Victor Mining Company. It also owns most of the town, the lots, the buildings, the waterworks. It owns the Skeleton Gulch Town Lot Company, which has been known to jump lots it had already sold, drive out merchants it didn't want around.

"The Victor Mining Company has a bad safety record. Several small cave-ins, plenty of injuries, some toxic gas problems, ruined lungs, all of that. To keep operating, it pays four dollars a day, a dollar more than the going rate for mining labor. But it gets the extra dollar back in a dozen ways. It owns every saloon and dive and gambling parlor and opium den and brothel in town. It charges pirate prices for water. Rents for its miners' cottages are sky-high, and there's nowhere for a miner to go. It owns all the lots and all the land for miles around. It operates a debt treadmill; miners get so far behind they can't escape.

"Now get this: The Victor Mining Company is owned by a holding company, Skeleton Gulch Properties, but we don't know who owns that. There's a few front men listed, but the real ownership is well hidden behind walls of paper. Whoever owns the mines and all the town properties doesn't want it known.

"But that's just part of it. The whole place is overrun by rats. More rats, I'm told, than any other place on earth. These rats have a way of destroying certain evidence, such as the identity of a body. Such deaths are recorded as 'party unknown,' or 'vagrant,' or not recorded at all. Let a drunk stumble into an alley to sleep it off, and he's a skeleton by dawn. That interest you?"

Dink nodded.

"It gets worse. The scarlet women are captives. Most of them are widows of miners who died suddenly in the mines. When they're fixing to leave the gulch they get kidnapped and stuffed into one of the cribs, or the big parlor house if they're halfway pretty, and if they protest they disappear."

"Why?" asked Dink.

"Someone, and I'll get to that, likes to control everything. It's not just money. She could skin money off miners and whores and cash her gold mine dividends without killing a soul. There is something like a local terror going on there, and I need to know what it is, and why, and how to bring her to justice."

"Her?"

"The Yellow Rose, name unknown but rumored to be several women. I'll get to that later. She's mistress of the big parlor house, and has a network of well-paid pugs enforcing her will on the whole town, some of them in constable uniforms, others in black broadcloth suits. And I guess she may be responsible for anywhere from fifty to a hundred fifty murders. If that's true, and I can't say for sure, she's the worst killer in the United States." He paused. "This could be mostly nonsense. All I have is rumor."

"And maybe she'll add me to the list."

Cook smiled cheerfully. "She likes rats. She won't like rat catchers."

"Why send me then?"

"We've sent two male operatives and they vanished. We sent a woman and she vanished and is presumed dead. We sent a man posing as a whiskey drummer and he got run out of town the moment he asked a question or two."

"How do you know as much as you do?"

"Correspondent."

"Who is he?"

"I'd endanger him by telling you."

"What did he want?"

"Justice."

"Why hasn't the territory moved in?"

"In Helena they tell me it's all rumor. There hasn't been a murder in Skeleton Gulch since it started up."

"No lawman there?"

"The place is located in the western mountains, end of the road, cut off from everything, especially in winter. There's supposed to be a sheriff's deputy and three or four town constables. But there isn't a deputy and the constables don't arrest anyone, and that's another thing for you to find out about."

"Where do I get support?"

"You don't. You'll be on your own."

"Tell me about the saloons."

Cook smiled cheerfully. "Worst lot of lowlifes ever collected on this continent. Not a square gambler in the lot. The barkeeps would as soon turn you upside down and shake the coin out of your pockets as serve you a rotgut drink. The bars are thick with pickpockets and sluts who fondle your purse out of its nest. There are steerers in front of every joint, and their task is to shove the miners inside and not let 'em out until they're broke or dead."

"Why do the miners head for the saloons then?"

"What else is there to do in a little mining camp a hundred miles from anywhere?"

Drago pondered it. "I don't think so. You need the militia."

"You're the best choice. A rat catcher. Who'd think you're an agent? Little fella. That works for you."

"You may think so. I think I get pushed around by everyone who's a foot taller."

"Exactly," said Cook.

"Damn you," Drago yelled.

Cook laughed.

"What do you want and what do you pay?" Drago asked.

"You're going to clean the rats out of Skeleton Gulch. And you'll get paid at your usual rate of two cents a rat."

"No rewards?"

"When has RMDA ever shelled out? We're all volunteers, except maybe expenses. But there'll be two hundred waiting for you here if and when you succeed. Fifty a month for four months. That's what we figure. And we'll pay transportation."

"Do I get expenses?"

"Catching rats is your living. You'll earn your expenses at your trade. Why should we pay you? All you have to do is use your eyes and ears and pay your own way."

"If I live. No, General, I don't like it."

"I wouldn't like it either, but you're on your way."

"What else do I need to know?"

"There's a joker in the deck."

"There always is."

"This one is called Vanishing Jack. That's not his real name. Once in a while he shows up in town with a couple of mules loaded with the best quartz gold ore anyone has ever seen. He hauls it to the stamp mill, takes his pay in cash, buys more supplies, and heads out. A hundred pugs and miners and con men and crooks have tried to follow him, but he always shakes them off and disappears. He evokes greed in every bosom in Skeleton Gulch, and the Yellow Rose has offered a fat purse to anyone who can track him to his mine or ledge, or whatever he's got that yields bonanza gold. The whole town's primed. Vanishing Jack rides in; a hundred crooks throw their kits together to follow him. How he slips out is the mystery."

"Why does he come to Skeleton Gulch at all? He must know it's a skunky little town."

The general shrugged. "You know as much as I know."

"You think he's a part of the mob?"

"Not likely."

"Any name you can give me? For Vanishing Jack, for the Yellow Rose? For anyone I should meet?"

Cook's face broke into a rectangular smile. "I knew you'd accept. Try a certain doc there. He might spill a few beans. I think the name's Cutler."

"And what do I do when I get to Skeleton Gulch?"

"Clean up the rats, Drago, clean it up."

"I haven't said yes."

"Find out who owns what. Who's profiting from the mines? Find out who owns the saloons. Find out whether there's a conspiracy here that's murdering anyone or anything in the way. Find out how many bodies. How many people are missing. Find out whether the bartenders are just freelance killers, rolling whoever they feel like and tossing the bodies to the rats. Find out who's stealing what. Find out who the tinhorns are and what sort of reputations they've got, and what their cut is from the saloons. Find out how many miners and whores and children and innocents are slaves, trapped by debt. Find out what sort of law enforcement—I use the phrase loosely—there is, and whether the constables are in with the criminal crowd. And then when you know the whole story, report to me. Or clean it up."

"Just like that."

"Some rat traps break rat necks."

"Just like that."

Cook wheezed happily and fired up a Tampa stogie. "Here's train fare. Third-class coach. The wicker seat will be hard on your skinny ass. Your rat wagon goes express freight, along with your nag. You'll end up in Corinne, Utah, and head north from there into the territory. Keep me posted, my usual Denver box and alias. You'll be Fat Boy. I thought that up myself. Sign your letters Fat Boy. Don't wire collect; I won't accept."

"I want more pay."

"I knew you'd get around to that. Nobody does anything for the good of the world anymore. Fifty a month, five for expenses."

"Thanks for the generous offer."

Cook smiled, sucked his Tampa, and waved Drago out the door.

That was it. One skinny rat catcher who was to tame a town. One little rat catcher against an army of pugs, black suits, goons, sharpers, hooligans, whores, and confidence men. One skinny rat catcher against an army. Just like that.

Dink drifted off to sleep, still hurting. Skeleton Gulch was all as General Cook had said, only worse. He wondered why he was risking his life. He wondered why he bothered. It couldn't be for money; there were safer venues for exterminators. Maybe it was for justice. Rats had a way of following humans. But rats were always most plentiful around vice. Maybe if he could set a few female slaves free, return stolen money to victims, and put the mob of crooks out of business, it would be worth the effort. If he lived.

Chapter 7

Dink Drago's first stop was Dr. Cutler's chambers. He dropped from his wagon, set the wagon brake, and headed inside.

Cutler was attending a patient.

Dink didn't wait; he headed for the rear, where there was an outdoor access to a crawl space, and wiggled in. He heard the usual swift rustle even before his eyes adjusted to the gloom. His two box traps had caught ten black rats, which tumbled violently over one another when he lifted the cage. He pulled the traps out, replaced them with two fresh-baited ones, and studied the gloomy cavern, lit by countless chinks in the loosely mortared foundation. He could see rat burrows, nests of heaped-up debris, and well-worn trails crisscrossing the whole area. He could not rat-proof a porous space like that.

By the time he was done with that chore, the patient had departed, and Cutler met him at the curtained doorway.

"Ten black rats in the traps," Dink said. "But there's no way to keep rats out of there, not with a loose sandstone foundation. All you can do is keep them from gnawing into here. And I can catch them as fast as they invade."

"Well, that's ten less rats. How do you dispose of them?"

Dink didn't much care to impart the details. "Drown them," he said shortly. "That's fastest and cheapest."

He clambered up a homemade ladder into the attic, and collected two wire cages up there, both heavily laden with chittering rats that whirled inside the trap. He discovered, off in a far dark corner, that the rats had gnawed a new passage into the doctor's kitchen ceiling, having been barred by Dink's tin patches elsewhere. Dink nailed more tin in place and descended, carrying his two traps.

"Twenty-seven," Cutler said. "I didn't know I had so many damned rats."

"They cut a new hole into your kitchen. They'll keep on until you seal the outside of this building."

Cutler was grinning. "And how do I do that?"

"You can't unless you want to install armor plate. Not now. After I kill another ten thousand, maybe you can slow them down. Let's look at your kitchen."

Cutler led the way. Dink pointed to fresh rat droppings on the counter and floor. He opened a wooden cupboard and scraped away a pile of dry droppings next to a sugar bin, then pointed to a neatly gnawed round hole at the back. "Right into the larder," he said.

"My God, man, what am I to do?"

"Keep all food in tin canisters. And even then some rats will work through the metal."

"Thirty-seven rats and three humans last night," Cutler said. "Two men, a woman, and no identification. Piles of bones in three different alleys. A son, a father, a mother, a daughter, who knows? Gone. Gone the dreams and hopes. And nobody has a name. You catch rats, catch them all, and fast, and count on me."

"Did they call you?"

"No, someone got Kilgore. Why call a doc for a pile of bones? He shovels them up. Big scoop shovel, like a coal shovel. He doesn't like to touch what's left, and puts on gauntlets. He's killed a few hungry rats just by braining them with that shovel."

"Are there records?"

"There's supposed to be."

"A coroner?"

"Sure, the chief constable, who shall remain nameless."

"Does anyone here have a name? Does the Yellow Rose have a name?"

"Drago, if there's no names, there's no crimes and no deaths, see? No perpetrators, no victims. No court proceedings, no verdicts."

"Is there a court? Even a justice of the peace?"

"Sure, Harry Tampa, a vice president of Victor Mining."

"Well, a name at last."

"Yeah, except he lives in Helena, where he bribes the legislature with fifty-dollar bills and whores. Now let me see your feet. You nostril's infected, red as a cherry. How are you feeling?"

"Fevered, but I'm not going to sit around and wait."

"Why not wait? You're sick."

"It's who I am, Doc. Maybe it's being half the size of anyone else."

Cutler led Dink into his examination room, stuck a thermometer into Dink's mouth, applied his carbolic salve to the reddened toes and nose, and checked his waiting room for patients. He found none.

He screwed the cap onto his salve and sank into his swivel chair.

"By my private count that's forty-two bodies this year. A handful of regular recorded deaths, two wives, three injured miners. The rest unknown, off the record. I thought the hair on several of the women looked familiar, one had been a dark blonde, nothing but a few strands of it on a rat-cleaned skull. She'd been a miner's wife and ended up in the cribs. Someone threw her into the alley. I couldn't prove it. I can't prove anything."

"I'm just a rat catcher," Dink replied.

Cutler laughed and slapped Dink on the shoulder. "How much do I owe? Two cents times thirty-seven?"

"Nothing. You're treating me."

"The hell with that," Cutler said. "Here's a buck."

Dink didn't argue. "I'll be back tomorrow. I don't want to charge you for the black rats. Fast as I catch them, there'll be more under there."

"It's sort of like crime, isn't it. You catch a few and a dozen take their place."

"Why don't the miners walk away?"

"They can't. They're all in debt, or so the company says. And the ones that walk away are never seen again. Anywhere."

"Who's Vanishing Jack? He walks away."

"Wish I knew. Some say he's related to the Yellow Rose. If that's the story, there's been a little family trouble. The Yellow Rose put a price on Vanishing Jack's head."

"For what?"

"For escaping her control."

"Why does he hang around here? He could take his ore anywhere else?"

"Find out the answers, Drago. I'm as curious as you are."

Dink headed into the bright sunlight, looking for customers. The Skeleton Gulch Bakery caught his eye. The facade was brightly enameled in cream and green. That outfit would have a rat problem for sure. He stopped the wagon and peered in through clean and clear windows. These people were making an effort, unlike most of the businesses in town.

An enormous rosy-cheeked woman greeted him.

"Vass iss?"

"I'm a rat catcher. You have rats?"

"Oh, rats! Carl, come. This man catches the rats!"

A skinny and long-whiskered gent in a chef's white bib emerged from a back room.

"Rats, Carl. This man catches."

"That's my business. I can tell you've a problem. I can see the calling cards on the floor. I can smell them."

The skinny man rolled his eyes. "Pray Gott we could be free of rats! They are everywhere, fouling our pastries."

"Two cents a rat, and less for a bulk purchase. I destroy their nests, plug their runways, trap them, seal work areas."

"How is it you catch?" said the massive woman.

"Box traps, sometimes spring traps, poisons."

"No poisons here. This is bakery."

"I would have suggested the same. You want me to have a look?"

The pair looked at each other, as if communicating something beyond Dink's ken.

"We are Carl and Gerta Hohenzollern," he said. "And vass iss?"

"Dink Drago. Rats are my business."

"You work for Victor Mining?"

"No, I am a private contractor. It'll take a while, but I can clear out every rat in here."

"We would like that. It iss rat pellets in the Dakota flour, ruined bread, pastries, my Gott, nibbles off the sides, rats in the ceiling, under the floors. Everywhere."

"The ones up in the attic, those are the big Norway rats."

"Ach! Gerta, like I always say: Never trust a Norwegian. They brought the rats, did they?"

"It's just a name. I don't know where the rats came from. It's a type of rat, that's all."

"Norway rats. And what's under the floor, eh?"

"Those are black rats, Mediterranean rats."

"Ach! Italian rats."

"No, not any country's rats. The black rats populate all the countries around the Mediterranean."

"French rats, ya?"

"Black rats have traveled in boats all over the world."

"Spanish rats?"

"Just rats. You need help. Do you want it?"

"Two cents? How can we pay two cents? You will make thousands of dollars and we can't pay."

"One cent a rat, and you give me pastries and bread each day, all right?"

"One cent a rat! We are disagreeing!"

"You give me whatever bread and pastries I need, and forget the cash. That will include a loaf of day-old bread for my old nag. He's one happy nag when he gets bread."

"Ah! Now you make sense."

Dink set to work. A trapdoor allowed access to a foul cellar. The acrid odor was choking. For a while he considered a scarf over his nose, but he ignored his instincts and studied the hellhole. There were several breeding nests, angrily defended by females. Heaps of ancient dung and debris were spread across the dirt. Like most of the buildings in Skeleton Gulch, this one's foundation was too porous to seal. He would do better catching what he could, sealing the bakery, and helping the Hohenzollerns keep flour and sugar and other staples in tight metal bins.

He baited four box traps, destroyed a number of nests, hammered tin over several access points, and plugged some chinks in the foundation.

That done, he tackled the foul attic, which was alive with the big northern rats. They collected angrily, defying him to crawl around in their empire. There were so many avenues to the bakery he doubted he got them all, but by the end of the afternoon he had plugged most and baited several big box traps.

"I'll be back tomorrow," he told Gerta, who beamed and

pushed a sack full of tarts his direction. It would make a fine supper.

He stepped into the late afternoon and was suddenly collared by a big brute in blue.

"You was supposed to leave town today. Now git, and don't come back," he said, shaking Dink until his jaw rattled.

Dink handed the man a box trap full of rats. The whole lot were crawling over each other, making the trap hard to hang onto.

"Take these and drown them," he said.

The constable stared at Dink, at the rats, and laughed. "The Yellow Rose won't like it," he said. He shoved the trap into Dink's arms. "Come along with me. And bring the rats."

Chapter 8

The thick and leering constable pushed Dink along toward one of the side streets and into a grimy antechamber. Then he opened a massive wooden door and shoved Dink into a tiny cell, lit only by a slit of light just below the ceiling. It stank of urine. A bench and a pail were the sole furnishings.

"What am I here for?"

"Vagrancy. Pull out your pockets."

Dink did. Doc's dollar bill fluttered down.

"Hand it to me. You see? You have no visible means of support."

"I have a trade and I was practicing it, and I was making a living."

"So I noticed. What's the name? Nah, don't bother. I'll put down vagrant in the book."

"When do I see a judge?"

"Oh, maybe never, far as I care."

"How long do I stay here?"

"You was told to get out of town and you didn't."

"A woman tells me to go. What has that got to do with it?"

The constable laughed.

"I'm new here so you'd better explain it," Dink said. "A woman doesn't want a rat catcher in town, so what's that to anyone? The law, for instance?"

"You ain't gonna be here long so it needs no explaining."

He swung the door shut. It thudded and he heard the bar drop. But then it opened again and the constable yanked the trap apart and spilled rats into the dark room. The rats ran in all directions and began circling the walls.

The constable chuckled and slammed the door again.

Dink grabbed the half-filled sheet-metal pail of urine and splashed the foul stuff over a congregation of rats. Then he pulled his legs up. The pail was the only weapon he had and he would use it.

The rats stayed on the floor, circling endlessly, pausing at the door where a crack of light shone from underneath. Dink concentrated on breathing. It was hard to find a breath of fresh air. He thought that this tiny jail room might be his tomb.

It had come to this then, and much faster than he had imagined. Skeleton Gulch didn't fool around. He settled into the hard, clammy bench and waited. He suspected he might wait for days, slowly dying of thirst.

But to his surprise the door swung open in an hour or so.

"Come outa there," the cop said.

Dink found himself facing a red-nosed smiley drunk.

"Vagrancy, resisting arrest, despoiling public property, one thousand or a hundred days."

Dink didn't say a word.

"Pay up."

Dink shook his head.

"Then we'll take your wagon and your horse. You walk out of town starting now. Let him go, George."

The constable beckoned. Dink stepped into clean air. An hour in that hole was a lifetime.

He saw his wagon parked outside, DINK DRAGO, RAT CATCHER painted on its enameled sides. The wagon, traps, harness, horse, and gear were worth more than a thousand. And they well knew it.

He said nothing. They were waiting for him to say something so they could throw him back in there. A few rats had braved the light and were spreading into the front room.

He nodded, heading through the door and into the muddy street, walking slowly, deliberately, carefully, away from there. He didn't know where to go except to get out of sight as fast as possible. He was a little man and well versed in the ways of slipping into small spaces that might hide him. He could vanish fast. But for now, he headed slowly down the street, turned on the unnamed main street, and headed downslope.

About the time he reached the wagon yards on the lower end of Skeleton Gulch he made up his mind.

What was he running from? Not the constable and the slimy city magistrate, but the mysterious woman called the Yellow Rose, whose word was law in Skeleton Gulch. If he left town he would eventually report to General Cook that he had failed. Dink hated to fail. Let some big galoot fail if there was failing to be done. If being a little fella meant he had to work twice as hard and be twice as daring, then he would do whatever it took.

He washed at a horse trough in a wagon yard, rinsing the stink and slime of that hellhole away, and then turned back toward Skeleton Gulch. The sun shone blandly, melting the last of the snows on the mountaintops, baking juniper until it perfumed the air. Skeleton Gulch lay in a clean sweet cleft of the western mountains, and Dink drew his strength from those quiet eternal slopes. For the moment at least, the yellow smoke drifted straight into the sky.

He had become a rat catcher because of his size. What else could a little man do well? But that wasn't a noble occupation, not like what he might have achieved if he had set his sights higher. He grew up in cities, one after another, tagging along because his father was restless and moved from town to town, always looking for the end of the rainbow, and always finding little joy in clerking in dry-goods stores, or hardwares, or grocery shops, or men's clothiers. Dink had never known his mother and his pa had brushed off all talk of her; there was only his pa, drifting from place to place, and Dink, the sole son, lonely, ripped from friends as fast as he found them, without sisters or brothers. And yet it wasn't all bad. His pa had always cared for him, tempering his wanderlust enough to keep his boy clothed and fed.

Little did his pa know how starved Dink was for other things, such as a home, pals, a neighborhood to call his own, a family. He could scarcely remember the places. Shaker Heights, North Tanawanda, Upper Arlington, Covington, Cicero, Chelsea, Upper Darby, West Mifflin, Webster Groves . . . He couldn't even remember the places. They all had rats. The rodents fascinated him. He took to studying rats. Maybe every sizable city in the country had rats. And taller people never saw them.

Then one day when he was fourteen, his pa died of cholera and he was alone, without friends, without family or roots. All he knew was rats. He headed west as boys often do, working for wagon trains, railroads, teamsters, making up for the skepticism of his employers by toiling twice as hard. He learned about life then, good people, mean people, righteous people who were mean, rascals and wastrels who were kind and generous. He was so small no one noticed him except one girl once, who treated him as a boy doll and explored him cheerfully.

By the time he ended up in Denver, at age seventeen, he had drifted into his strange life profession. It wasn't one he liked, but it made him a living. Maybe someday he would be something else, do something he liked. It couldn't be a lonelier trade. Whenever he mentioned that he was a rat catcher, women fled and men eyed him suspiciously. No one wanted to think about the rats in the alleys and basements and attics.

One day General Cook of the famous detective agency spotted him cleaning rats out of a gambling parlor, and one thing led to another. From Cook's point of view, Drago had the perfect profession to gain access anywhere and listen anywhere and report what he had seen and heard. And that was how his life was spinning out now; he was the top man for the shadowy and powerful detective agency, the man they sent when no one else could crack a case.

If the Yellow Rose owned Skeleton Gulch, then maybe he should talk to the Yellow Rose. It was turning dusk, the lady would be up and about, and maybe a direct approach would get him somewhere. He hoped it would not be that foul cell once again. And he damned well wanted his horse and wagon and gear back.

It was easy to hike back through town in the evening traffic. He dodged the strong-arm gents who yanked customers off the street and jammed them into the saloons and parlors. Little Dink Drago hiked along invisibly, almost the child as far as anyone could say, not much over four feet, and a wraith. From open double doors, the sound of sour fiddle music lacerated the night, while dime-a-dance girls stomped with their miner partners. Stale beer fumes caught Dink's nose, and other darker odors, sour and acrid and sometimes the smell of rot.

Sometimes, when he veered close to the narrow rubbish-filled spaces between buildings, he saw and heard furious scurrying. The rats were out and looking for supper. This street had no name, and neither did the main street. He was, by God, going to name them. He would give names to each street and cross street. Just why, he couldn't say, but it had to do with curbing crime. Putting names to things would be the beginning of order. He would call this street of saloons and dives Yellow Rose Street. He would call the main street, which bisected the town and was lined with merchant establishments, Middle Street, because it cut Skeleton Gulch in two.

He climbed the grade toward Yellow Rose's rectangular parlor house, noting that two lamps lit the doorway. He paused, thinking he had chosen the one sure way to put himself into the worst trouble of his short life, and then rejected that notion. Audacity had its uses.

He pushed the door open and found the place humming with customers, noise, laughter. He absorbed the shine of glass, pond ice, good whiskey, women in diaphanous gowns that gauzed over lush breasts and silky limbs, men in black broadcloth and paisley cravats. To the left was a bar, well populated with males who had never lifted a pick or shoveled rock in their lives. To the right was a small red parlor, dimly lit and discreet. Bruno the bouncer was nowhere in sight, at least for the moment. The Yellow Rose probably thought he was bad for business and kept him away.

Dink headed into the soft-lit red parlor, and instantly a nymph emerged from a curtained area, looked him over doubtfully, and shook her head.

"No, we prefer that gentlemen be properly attired."

"I want to talk to the Yellow Rose is all. She knows me. We met this afternoon."

"She's busy. If this is a business matter, tradesmen are welcome each afternoon at the rear door."

"No, I have no business with her."

"Then why—oh, you're the one Genevieve talked about. The little rat catcher."

"I'm out of the business," he said. "I thought maybe she'd stake me to a new one."

She had a pretty smile that revealed even white teeth. "Tomorrow."

"I won't be here tomorrow."

"That's right, he won't," said the Yellow Rose. It didn't surprise Dink that the towering woman had been absorbing every word.

She beckoned Dink into her inner sanctum and Dink wondered if he would ever come out alive. He followed her down a gloomy hall and into a chaste office with oil portraits in gilded oval frames on the walls and a musky perfume masking the odor of the rat-infested halls.

"Maybe I'll bed you," she said. "I enjoy novelty."

Chapter 9

Dink eyed the towering woman, who was fitted out in cream velvet with blue piping, an outfit that somehow transformed her harsh features into something softer.

Her office, lit by twin green-shaded coal-oil lamps, was elegant and tasteful, but somehow bellicose in its affluence in spite of the care she had taken. The gilded frames of the portraits glowed softly.

"Who are those, your parents?" he asked.

It surprised her. She glanced at one of them, an oil of a man as harshly made as herself, with dark saturnine eyes, a long sharp beak, and hair drawn back and tied into a queue in the old fashion. There was a family resemblance.

The other portrait, probably her mother, was of a cruel woman; none of the artist's softening devices concealed the curl of her lip or the disdain in her eyes.

"You resemble them," Dink added. "They were tall, I suppose. You're the tallest woman I've ever seen. Over six feet. It gives you advantage in the world."

"A little man wanders in here and starts in on my family," she said.

"You're tall through no art or fault of your own; it's how

you were born. I'm short through no failing of my own. It was what was handed to me by life. I've had to overcome it."

"You came to see me even though I told you not to. What do you want? It had better be good. This is my busy hour so be quick."

"Those are handsome cats," he said, eyeing two huge toms that curled about her feet, rubbing themselves against her velvet skirt. One lacked an eye. The other, a striped yellow, arched its back and lashed its tail back and forth.

She softened, if only for a moment. "They protect me," she said.

"From rats."

"From loneliness. I am not in the world to make friends so I have acquired two. They never talk back."

She was trying to make something sharp out of it, but failed. She loved her big tomcats.

"Well?" she asked.

"I want my wagon and team and traps back. Those are my means of making a living. I perform a service, earn my way, protect the health and comfort of those I serve, but now I am turned loose with nothing. What is your purpose?"

"Why should I talk to you? What am I supposed to know about a wagon? Who took it and why?"

"You took it, or saw to it that it was taken. I want it back."

"Am I the law? What are you talking about?"

"Yes, you are the law in Skeleton Gulch."

She smiled suddenly. "I am merely the keeper of a house of ill repute. Now are we done?"

"Where do I pick up my wagon and team?"

"Come back at eleven. I've a mind to entertain you. Maybe I'll give you your wagon back, rat catcher, maybe not. If you amuse me, I might."

"My name is Dink Drago."

"It fits."

"And what's yours?"

"I have none."

"That fits too."

She waved him off. On her finger was a ruby that flashed a sinister red in the lamplight.

"I don't sell myself," he said.

She wasn't amused. "Don't come back. Life is short in Skeleton Gulch."

"Do you have brothers and sisters?"

"What? What are you talking about?"

"I'm interested in your family. A family with no names. A town with no street names."

She suddenly loomed over him, her cats flanking her like imperial guards. Her breath was foul.

"Out." She waggled that gem-burdened finger.

"A rich family. You don't need to run a parlor house but you do. You are an interesting woman."

She pushed straight into him, her formidable bosom crushing into his face. He felt himself being shoved backward. Strong as he was, he was no match at all for this dreadnaught.

Her jeweled hand caught him by the scruff of the neck and propelled him out of the study, through an anteroom, and into the parlor where the nymphs met their clients.

"Take your pick," she said suddenly.

He wasn't surprised.

"How about the bar?" he asked.

"You don't like women?"

"At the bar I'll sit and drink good bourbon and listen to the gossip about you and find out everything you declined to tell me."

She stopped dead, released him, and laughed. She had the strangest laugh, a throaty, cynical laugh that actually sounded more like a sob to Dink.

"On the house," she said. "And then maybe we'll try something different. We'll see whether the rats like you."

The warning chilled him. Only once in all his years of tracking down rats had he come across a true rat hole. That was in a Chinese quarter of San Francisco. Tong lords, or maybe simply fat slavers who trafficked in Canton girls shipped in machinery crates to California, would toss a disobedient or sullen or weepy girl into one and shut the trapdoor above her, and listen to the screams and sobs and whimpers and groans, and then the silence. In a little while, there would be nothing left, nothing at all, not even much bone. Death by rat bite was perfect murder.

That was all the warning Dink needed. He had spotted rat bites on the Yellow Rose's nymphs. One minute in a rat hole would do it. One minute of screaming. He drifted into the bar, wondering whether he'd survive another Mickey Finn.

"A whiskey and water," he said. "On the house."

"I know," the cadaverous bartender replied.

Dink wondered how he knew. He watched carefully. The barkeep poured from a bottle he had just used to refill someone else's glass and Dink saw no hanky-panky in any of it. He took the chilled glass in hand and looked around. A quiet crowd, all male, all dressed in the black broadcloth uniforms of success, conversed at tables. Dink guessed that every one of these gents was an employee of the Yellow Rose.

He didn't trust his drink and took the smallest sip, waiting to see its effect on him. It was fine whiskey; smooth and silky. He was the only male in the place in workmen's clothing, and he didn't doubt that his rough attire was drawing stares. But maybe he could put that to use. Here he was, where he wanted to be, in the heart of Skeleton Gulch, and with any sort of luck he would learn much.

The gent next to him looked him over and eased away.

Dink was certainly not of the managerial class. A space opened around him. Suave, amused men drifted away, studied the fat nudes on all the walls, propelled by the odor from Dink's work clothing, which not long before was scraping the ground in foul crawl spaces under buildings.

That left the wall-eyed bartender, who eyed him curiously.

"I'm new. The town has no street names. Why's that?" Dink asked.

"Actually, on the plats of the town lot company, east-west streets are alphabet, north-south streets are numbers. They just never got put up, is all. But they got names."

"You make a good drink."

"Tell it to her. She don't pay me but tips and a free lay now and then."

"Who are these gents?"

"Her managers mostly. Run the mill and the mines and the counting house."

"Just the two classes? Managers with money up here, and the stiffs stay in town? That's how she wants it?"

The barkeep smiled uneasily and started to turn away.

"That her family, those oils in her parlor?"

"That's them, all right. The old man bought stock in the Victor. When he died, she and her brother got it. But he vanished a few years ago, big fight, she won, he disappeared."

"Sounds familiar. Nothing like an estate to start the siblings fighting. Tell me this. How come she started this place up? The mines are worth a fortune. Why this?"

The wall-eyed bartender grinned darkly. "Some women, give 'em some money, and they do whatever they want."

"What's her name?"

"I heard a dozen names, and don't know and wouldn't tell you if I did, because this job's worth something."

"And so's your life."

The bartender stared sharply, whirled away, poured

some good whiskey for a gent down in the corner, and returned.

"I didn't get your name," he said.

"Dink Drago. I'm a rat catcher."

"You catch rats? Like, you go in and wipe them out?"

"That's what I do. Two cents a rat, or bulk rates."

"How come she's talking to you, eh?"

"Because I told her the town's full of rats and needs cleaning out. And also because I got picked up by her private constable, and next I knew I was fined a thousand for vagrancy and my rig was confiscated and I was told to get out. I wanted my rig and horse and equipment back."

The barkeep stared at him, shook his head, and drifted away. Dink knew he wouldn't get any more out of that one, but what he did get was valuable. The Yellow Rose had a brother who inherited half of the Victor Mining Company and then vanished. And she started the parlor house after she got rich.

That was enough for one night. It was nearing eleven and he didn't want to hang around for whatever sport the lady had in mind. The crowd had thinned. Half those men in black suits had drifted into the bedchambers. Dink polished off the last of his whiskey, slipped quietly out of the bar, and through the front door.

"I knew you'd quit me," the Yellow Rose said. She was smoking a cigarillo in the chill June night. "Well, Drago, if you hang around Skeleton Gulch, I'll jail you again. Your wagon's right there."

Chapter 10

Dink climbed into his wagon seat and took the lines. The leather was frosted and it chilled his hands. In the dim light he could see his traps under the canvas-covered bows. His blankets and gear were all there. She had returned everything but the dollar.

He watched her draw on her cigarillo and exhale, while dull yellow lamplight lit half her face, making a mask of the other half. Then she turned and went back inside. It was black and cold and quiet. He slapped the reins over his old dray horse and steered the wagon down the sharp grade into Skeleton Gulch.

The night was very dark and as cold and mysterious as Yellow Rose's soul. He didn't know where to go. He hadn't a cent to pay the livery man. The horse would need attention. He felt the wagon creak and groan as he eased it down the slope. He felt the tongue push against the harness, hurrying the nag.

She was toying with him. He was used to it. Women sometimes did that to little men. But this was different. One moment she was telling him to leave town. The next she was inviting him into her bed. The next she was hinting of a dire fate if he hung around Skeleton Gulch, such as being eaten alive by rats. One moment she was denying she was anything but a madam; the next she was returning the wagon confiscated by her constables and corrupt city magistrate, tacitly exposing her power over everyone and everything.

None of it made much sense.

If those were her parents in the oval gilded frames, she probably came from a powerful and rich family. If they weren't, she was a fraud. By all accounts she had acquired the mines first, consolidated them into the Victor Mining Company, one of the richest gold properties in the United States—and then had become a madam. That's what obsessed him. She didn't need to become a madam. Why turn to a such a life as she was living now? What had driven her? Surely not a need for money. Nor a need for lovers. In some rough way, she was breathtaking. She would have her pick of men.

She was a mystery as dark as this night. He could barely see his way, and was helped only by the lamplight tumbling from the saloons and dives along what he was calling Yellow Rose Street, one saloon after another, dives that never slept, never dimmed their lamps so long as there was one miner or one sucker who could be shaken out of a few dimes.

He spotted the burly steerers out in front of some joints and feared they would spring out, grab his reins, and force him into their dives. There wasn't a one who didn't top two hundred pounds.

He slapped reins over his nag until it stumbled into a trot, and he rattled past the three blocks that catered to all known vices, and found himself on the lower end of town in thick impenetrable darkness. No stars or moon lit his way. He slowed the horse and let it pick its way. Yellow Rose eventually fed into Middle Street, as he was calling the main one, and he found himself ghosting along the wagon yards of the shipping outfits that kept Skeleton Gulch supplied.

That would do, he thought, if no one objected.

He found his way into a yard, past the high-walled hulks of big freight wagons. A patch of open sky helped him. He found a likely place, stumbled around until he located a horse-watering trough, pumped water, broke some ice in the trough, unharnessed his horse and watered it, and tossed it into a pen. He supposed there would be hell to pay the next day, barging into a company yard like that. But he was too weary to care and moments after he pulled his bedroll around him, he was sawing wood.

He awakened to sunshine and shouts. Light poured through the canvas above him. Something was stirring teamsters out in the yard. He pulled on his high-top moccasins and laced them, braved the fresh and frosty air, and found some burly, bearded teamsters gesturing and gossiping around a big freight wagon with the name Starr and Son stenciled on its sides.

Dink joined them. They stared at him.

"Who are you?" a tall one finally asked.

"Dink Drago. I'm a rat catcher."

"Oh, you're that one. Little enough to wiggle under floors." But as soon as the big one said it, he looked stricken.

"It doesn't bother me any," Dink said.

"Well, you have a big spirit," the teamster said by way of expiation.

"We was just saying that Vanishing Jack showed up this morning and got plumb away as usual," a tall smooth-shaven gent explained. "You know about him?"

"Not much."

"Well, he's a legend. They don't know his name but he answers to Jack, and he comes to town now and then, different hour each time, never regular, with one or two mule-loads of the best quartz ore anyone has ever seen. Gold busting out of it. He takes it to the mill, collects what's owed him from the previous visit, buys what he needs, and high-tails out."

The boss teamster chuckled. "There's a few hundred people around here who would like to know his secret. Half mean to kill him, half mean to steal his mine. They jump on horses and follow him every time he comes, but he always shakes them off. These pugs here hardly know the front end of a horse from the rear. He just vanishes, and that makes people just plain ornery. No one can just vanish. But Jack does. They don't even find mule tracks."

The teamster was clearly enjoying himself. He plucked some Bull Durham from his pocket.

"The hounds chase that fox for miles, up canyons, over ridges, into forests, out on glaciers, through rivers, up creeks, and then he's gone. Just plain vanished and gone, until a month or so goes by, and he's back in Skeleton Gulch, maybe midnight, maybe dawn, maybe dusk, maybe the middle of the day, no one knows, and does his business at the mill while the mob saddles up and starts after him."

The big lean man looked vaguely familiar to Dink, but he was sure he had never met the gent in his life. He was slim, hawkish, with a long hatchet of a nose, burning black eyes, and he wore his graying hair in a queue, the old-fashioned way. He was naturally dark but not weathered. Dink supposed him to be the sort of man who ran a shipping company from a cluttered office somewhere but was out on the trail a great deal, taking a personal hand in things.

"What would they do if they caught Vanishing Jack?" he asked.

"Oh, they'd celebrate. Lock him in a room. Bully him, try to get him drunk, maybe give him a Mickey, try to bribe him, threaten to kill him. Torture the secret out of him.

But if they kill him, they lose it, so mostly they just want to beat him until he cries uncle, and then steal his mine."

"Who?"

"Oh, every bartender, bullyboy, saloon man, gambler, bunco steerer, constable, judge, whore, dime-a-dance girl, opium peddler, confidence man in town, for starters. But that's just the sporting class. There's another batch, the mining engineers, foremen, mining men, accountants, clerks, vice presidents, and geologists, who itch all the harder. They've seen the quartz. They've assayed it. The sporting types are simply greedy; the mining company brass lust."

The tall fellow laughed heartily.

"What about the Yellow Rose?" asked Dink.

"I wish I knew," the boss said. "She doesn't like it when anyone's got something she wants."

"That's the commotion I heard?" Dink asked.

"I just lost two teamsters, saddled up any mule they could lay a hand on and took off. Vanishing Jack drives 'em crazy. They'll be back, and I'll dock their pay."

"You own the company?"

"Yes, John Starr, Starr and Son Express, through service to Salt Lake City."

"Me, I'm Dink Drago. I nail rats, when I have the chance. Last night I needed a place to stop."

"We need a dozen rat catchers here. What's the original first name?"

"Tom. But my Uncle Ernest began calling me Dink. He would sit in my father's house and say, 'Look at that little dink running around.' The name stuck. Mind if I wash up in the horse trough?"

Starr looked him over. "Why don't you stay here? I'll trade you some rat catching over in my grain bins for whatever you and your nag need."

"I'll clean out your rats fast. In a week you'll be free of them."

"Damned rats eat five dollars of grain a week, I think. You're on."

"Tell me more about this Vanishing Jack. Does he ever say anything? Give any clues?"

"Oh, I don't know much. Mostly he laughs. He won't enter a saloon. He never touches a drop of booze. He knows he'd get a Mickey. This town has dropped more Mickeys into drinks than any other place on earth, including the Barbary Coast. It's the local sport. So they can't get him that way. Once some roughs jumped him, but he shrugged them off. Actually, he left them sprawled in the dirt. This prospector, he knew a few things, including some back-alley warfare. Might have been in the Army. Might even have been an officer. He has that bearing. Proud, stands right up."

"What does he want? What's the point of keeping a gold ledge undeveloped?"

Starr shrugged. "Feeds himself, I imagine. But there's one thing. He always takes a good look around town. Often he's cased the whole burg before anyone catches on to him. Just walking, like any other pedestrian. Since he's always in different garb, it's not easy to peg him."

"There must be a purpose in it, a plan in it," Dink said. "You got any idea what?"

Starr shook his head slowly and Dink knew intuitively that Starr wasn't letting on what he thought.

"How far out is this ledge?" Dink asked.

"That's a matter of controversy," Starr said. "Best guess is that it's a day's haul into Skeleton Gulch. No one finds campsites where Vanishing Jack spent a night or built a fire."

"What about winter? Tracks in the snow?"

"Old Jack's pretty wily, waits for the right moment, but he comes into Skeleton Gulch most any time. In winter, he comes right down the road, mixing up his tracks with everyone else's. By the time they look for him, fifty freighters with ox teams have run over his tracks."

"What does he look like?"

"Like someone different each time. He's tall; everyone's agreed about that. But fat, skinny, bearded, shaven, long-haired, short-haired, brown-haired, white-haired. You hear all of that, and it never agrees. Get two men talking and they'll give two different descriptions."

"Who spreads the alarm?"

"Oh, most often it's the millmen. They're on the take. Fifty men in this town want a hot tip and it's worth five dollars to them. So Jack rides in there, wants to trade out his ore, and next thing, the millmen are tipping everyone off, half the town hears about it."

"Where did he go this time?"

"Straight up, past the Victor Mine, over the shelf, and along that slope toward the glacier. And then he was gone. No one saw him after that. There's still people scouring around up there."

"He sounds like a man I'd like to know."

"I'd like to know him too," Starr said. "He's the only man in the territory that's got Skeleton Gulch licked."

Chapter 11

Dink Drago stood in the alley behind the saloons and dives along Yellow Rose Street, absorbing the stink of urine and the miasma of murder. The morning sun was blurred by a yellow smoke lowering over town, driven by a trick of the wind. The smoke drifted between the buildings, billowing as the down-wind caught it, choking the citizens of this mining camp.

Skeleton Gulch, which lay in a verdant notch of the towering blue mountains, might have been a small paradise in another time and another circumstance. Now it was a death trap that snared unwary miners and people passing through, and butchered them. Dink walked slowly over the littered ground, seeing countless runways, holes in foundations, burrows, thickets of brush, each harboring a city of rats. Thousands of rats. So many they turned murder into a shadow of itself, for who could say what a pile of bones might mean? Or whose they were?

He coughed as a sulphurous blast of the smoke caught him as he inhaled. This was mostly stamp-mill smoke, the product of a thousand logs, generating steam to run the stamps that pulverized some of the richest quartz gold ore in the world. Add to that the boilers of the mines, building up steam to run the lifts and pump air into the cramped, dark, hot holes where tough, daring, laughing men shattered and mucked rock ten hours each shift for their four dollars.

They were virtual slaves, as was most everyone except a predatory class that feasted on them. The whole town was designed to keep these humble men in debt and prevent them from escaping it, or their alleged creditors. And all the threads led back to the coarse woman who lived up the hill in a mansion built of mortared mine rubble, fireproof, bullet-proof, weatherproof, but not disease-proof.

Dink knew so little about her, and most of that was guesswork. He had no proof; David Cook had no proof, just a letter or two asking for help. Dink had come here on a mass of rumor, shadowy accusation, and now he stood in the most deadly alley in the world and thought that he knew little more than when he arrived. But it was the alley where he had almost perished, and he intended to do something about it.

Another cloud of yellow smoke boiled through town, abrading lungs. Mining camps were not healthy places. One could wander through the graveyards of most camps and discover short, brutal lives chiseled into the tombstones.

He headed for the bakery and changed out two traps loaded with rats, and sealed off another hole they had gnawed in the night. At Doc Cutler's he found no rats in the attic trap, but cleaned two box traps loaded with them out of the crawl space under the floor. He put them in his wagon while Doc watched.

"Doc, sealing that foundation won't help much. They'll bore under it," he told Cutler.

The doctor eyed the two boxes, loaded with restless, alarmed rats, and shrugged. "How many, twenty? Every day, remove twenty rats from Skeleton Gulch and something will be achieved."

"They're breeding faster than that, Doc."

"Today I treated half-a-dozen cases of rat-bite fever, and another several I'm not sure of. That's answer enough."

Dink headed upslope, having to snap his whip over his dray horse to get it to tackle the grade to the mines. He knew the mines were full of rats. He knew the rats lowered the productivity of the mines by causing sickness. Maybe the managers would hire him.

On top, the smoke cleared off and he could see into the quiet forested slopes of the mountains. Here was the mighty Victor Mine, its timbered headframe stabbing the blue sky. Next to it was the Alice, and beyond, the Belle. And on the other side, the famed Queen, and last and smaller, the Lucky Cuss. Between them they employed over five hundred miners, plus countless woodcutters, teamsters, mechanics, shopmen, drill-bit sharpeners, powdermen, and clerks. Here, the very earth had been torn; heaps of yellow rubble had avalanched down gulches, and rickety rails on trestles took the rock from the bowels of the earth and dumped it.

Dink let the nag rest; it had swallowed too much yellow smoke, and now its sides heaved. Then he headed for the offices of the Victor. Someone in there might purchase his services for all the mines. Unlike the buildings in town, the offices showed some sign of manicuring. They had been whitewashed and their windows shone. A gilded sign announced the Victor Mining Company. There was even a hitch rail.

He entered an office complex with a few clerks in sleeve protectors toiling over ledgers.

No receptionist received him. He hunted for someone, anyone, in command, but found only empty offices. These were neither austere nor elegant, but the occupants of these offices worked in great comfort. Mines come and go; the company that built lavish headquarters merely wasted its capital.

But then, as he was about to give up, he spotted a suited gent in a corner at a trestle table, eating a lunch out of a paper bag.

Dink approached him, mostly because the man wore a cravat than for any other reason.

"May I interrupt your lunch, sir?"

The gent, who wore his jet hair in bushy sideburns, nodded, and continued to masticate a cold beef sandwich.

"I'm Dink Drago. I hear you have a rat problem in the mines. I'm a rat catcher. That's my profession. I can clean out the mines. Your workers will be healthier and happier and you'll get more work from them if they're not sick. Rat bites can cut into your profits."

"Don't I know it," the man said, never pausing in his demolition of the sandwich.

"I'll clean the rats out of all five mines, a hundred a month, results guaranteed."

"All right," the man said.

Astonished, Dink wondered if his bulk price was too low.

"What's your name?" he asked.

"Creek," the man replied.

"All right, Mr. Creek. I'll set traps in the bottom of the shafts, at every vestibule, and in any lunch or rest area."

"Every one of these mines is so full of rats that dead ones show up in most of the ore cars reaching grass," Creek said, tackling an apple. "The lifts kill them, knock them into the shafts. They go down in the cages, in empty ore cars. Once down there, they raid lunch buckets, eat anything, including dead bugs in the timber that goes down there, and bite the hell out of anyone taking a break. You clean out the rats and I'll give you a bonus. They're costing me money. When a good man gets bit and gets sick, I have to hire a sub, and that sub can't do the work. And next I know, production drops."

"You're the head man for all the mines?"

"President of Victor, yes. I'll send word to the mine managers."

"You own the mines?"

"Hell, no. The holding company owns them. I'm salaried, but I get bonuses for pushing production up. I've been thinking about a rat catcher for months, Drago. Never got to it. I'll have to get permission, but it makes sense and I think I can get it."

"Permission?"

"From the owners," Creek said with finality.

"How do you want to do this?"

"I'll give you a blanket pass. It will open any mine. Take your traps down, tell the foremen to leave them alone, and you can clean out the damned rats. You can't do it fast enough to suit me. Show me the result. I want to see dead rats. If I see dead rats, I'll pay you cash on the first of each month. Where are you staying?"

"The Starr wagon yard until I can find someplace."

Creek wiped out the apple, core and all, and tossed his paper bag into a wastebasket. "All right, come with me, Drago, and we'll get this rolling. I hate rats. I'll personally strangle every damned rat you bring out of those holes."

"Lots of rats in town too. Some of your men must be getting sick in their cabins."

Creek stared at the plank wall a moment. "Don't know of any," he said.

Dink pushed it. "I'm new here. But all I see in Skeleton Gulch is rat holes, rat nests, rat runways. I think I'm about to get rich. I charge two cents a rat, and here's ten thousand rats. I see people on the street, they got bit. A rat bite is something I know all about, and I see bit people. I've talked to the doc, and he says there's a rat problem here. . . . So where do I start? Who do I talk to? Who owns the land?"

Creek rose abruptly. "Not my business. I'll write you a pass for all the mines, and instructions you show the foremen, and we'll get started."

"I'll want twenty dollars in advance as a surety."

Creek stared and nodded. He unlocked a drawer and extracted a double eagle. "This was stamped in Denver with Victor gold," he said. "Right from here."

It was a handsome new-minted gold coin without a scratch. Dink pocketed it.

"I'll start in. I have bait and traps outside. Where do I see the layouts of the mines? The mine maps? Who'll tell me where the rats are worst?"

"Mine plans are right here; ask for them. The foremen will tell you what's what down there. You been in a pit before?"

"Many times. I've cleaned rats out of Golden, Leadville, Central City, and Telluride, among twenty places I've worked."

"What do you do with the rats?"

"Drown them inside the box traps."

"Serves 'em right. All right, we'll try this. Drago, one word of advice. Don't ask a lot of questions in Skeleton Gulch. Like, who owns what. Just do your job."

Dink saw his chance. "Who owns the Traveler's Rest Saloon? I saw a lot of rat dens back of there. Regular rat city."

Creek smiled blandly. "You clean out the mines. That's going to make the shareholders happy."

"Who are the shareholders?"

"Closely held, Drago, closely held."

"But not always. These mines used to be independent. Who bought them all up?"

Creek smiled. "Victor Mining did."

"How? By trading stock with the owners of other mines?"

Creek ignored the question and penned the pass and instructions, dipping his nib pen into the bottle on his desk and scratching out his orders.

"Drago, here's a pass," he said. "Now I'll excuse myself. I've a dozen matters pending."

Dink thought it was a start. He studied the mine maps in the bull pen and headed out. The five mines were linked on the third level by crosscuts that served to ventilate all the mines. They were also the probable rat boulevards for the whole mining complex. He thought he would start at the top; wherever air was pumped into the mines, so would the rats be.

Chapter 12

With the help of the topmen at the Victor Mine, Dink loaded his baited box traps into an empty one-ton ore car, donned a felt cap, grabbed a carbide lamp, and took the cage to the lowest level, three hundred feet under the surface.

That's where the miners were at work gouging quartz from a thick seam. The cage dropped through pitch darkness, endlessly descending through hotter and hotter air, and finally jarred to a halt and swung lazily on its woven steel cable. A miner opened the gate and Dink pushed the ore car into the vestibule. Several men peered restlessly into it.

"Rat traps," Dink said.

"Well, the damned rats are all over here," one man replied.

A foreman barged up. "What are you doing here?"

Dink produced his pass from Creek, which the foreman ignored.

"I don't want you around here," he said, his voice laden with threat.

"I won't be long. Your front office wants the rats out of the mines and these traps will do the job. You're losing too many men to sickness."

"Take 'em somewhere else," the foreman said.

The man was twice Dink's size. Dink opted for a way out that often worked. He ignored the foreman and began unloading the big box traps, which he had baited with rotting meat topside. He began hunting for likely rat warrens and found them everywhere, especially in the timbering around the sandbox latrines, and wherever miners stored their lunch pails. The foreman glared darkly and then vanished.

Dink didn't like the smell down there. In a mine where air is a scarce commodity and every odor is magnified, Dink was smelling a lot of things—rats, rotted food, sweat, urine, waste, and something else: death.

He ran a dozen traps along the drifts in both directions from the main shaft, and then peered down the shaft, which extended ten or twelve feet below this bottom level of the mine. He held his carbide lamp over the shaft and saw oily black water below, some stained timbering in the corners, and more. The water, several inches deep, only partly covered bones. Lots of bones, human bones, skulls, femurs, rib cages, hands, pelvises. And in every niche in the sides of the shaft was movement. This was a rat restaurant. Even as he watched, the stink of meat in his traps just above was stirring interest in those black creatures, but it was too dark to make out what was happening down there. The cage dropped suddenly, and he pulled his head back and waited for it to unload an empty ore car and three miners. Then, out of the darkness, someone shoved a new rock-laden one-ton car into the lift, pulled a cord twice, and the lift bounced once and shot upward with more wealth in it to line the pockets of the owners.

Dink peered over the lip of the shaft once again, holding the carbide lamp out where he could see down to the bottom. The hole was seething with rats. They were crawling over the timbering and lagging and had gnawed holes and nests in the wood. He thought about poisoning them, but decided mine shafts were not the places to do that. He studied the bones again, realizing that there was not the slightest clue as to who had died, how they had ended up in the pit, or why they had died. Accident? Murder? Some wild brawl? A foreman's way of disciplining his men?

Did the miners hard at work to either side of him have any idea what lay down there? He doubted it.

Something struck him in the back. A giant fist that pitched him over the lip of the shaft, and he found himself falling, and then splashing into the foul water at the base of the shaft. The water had broken his eight-or-ten-foot drop. He stood at once, up to his knees in water. Noxious gases choked him, and he knew he could not breathe that for more than seconds or he would end up another pile of bones.

Someone had murdered him, or tried to.

He had only seconds. Now the rats were stirring. They would swim if they had to, little torpedoes ready to bite him to death. He leapt upward, trying to suck cleaner air, but inhaled air so foul and acrid that his lungs hurt and he immediately felt dizzy. Whatever gas was in that pocket of foul air, it would kill him.

He hunted a way up. But then the cage dropped, down, down, right over him, and he had to crouch to escape being knocked flat. Now it was pitch dark, the floor of the cage blocking whatever light filtered there from the vestibule. He felt upward, found the bottom of the cage with his hands, found some beams, a pipe, and at last, a place to hang on. He heard the clatter of an ore car rolling onto the cage and felt it sag on its cable. He would have about a half a second to do it right—or die.

If he hung on, he would be lifted at high speeds, higher and higher, right past various vestibules, until three hundred feet of air separated him from the floor of the shaft.

And any bounce would shake him loose. Then he would feed the rats.

He heard the clang of the signal, felt the cage jerk upward, jammed his feet against the wall of the shaft, and pushed hard as the vestibule hove into view. He landed in a heap, scraping flesh off his arm, bloodying his hand, but on solid rock. He was alone. His heart pounded wildly. He was alive. He kicked away two or three rats and sat up, his pants and boots dripping slime.

He studied the dark drift, hearing the sounds of toil in the distance. Mines were noisy places, often deafening. Off a ways came the familiar sound of jackhammers pounding drill bits deep into the quartz vein. Later, those holes in the face would be cleaned out and stuffed with powder. Fuses of various lengths would be attached and if everything went as planned, a series of explosions would blow rock out of the middle of the face first. Then the upper and finally the lower portions of the face would blow. Once the air cleared, muckers would begin reducing and shoveling the ore into cars. Hard, sweaty, cruel, noisy, bone-crushing toil. Dink could think of better ways to make a living.

He pulled the signal bell, unsure how many tugs it took to get the hoist operator to respond to his call. But the cage did slip down and Dink entered it, tugged the bell twice, and rode up, with two other stops. He stank so much that three other miners who boarded on the fourth level stared at him. He didn't care; he was alive.

He reached grass, as miners called the earth topside, and stepped into sunlight. That was a fine feeling, stepping into sunlight. The last of the slime dripped from his moccasins. His wagon stood where he had left it, the dray horse yawning and masticating not much of anything. He returned the felt hat to the topmen.

"Lost my lamp in the shaft," he said.

"You'll have to pay for it."

"All right, I'll talk to the bosses."

The topmen let him go.

He picked up the lines and hawed the horse away. The sun felt good. He sucked clean air into his lungs, sensing that the toxic gases in that shaft had hurt him, maybe worse than he knew.

Who pushed him and why?

It was deliberate. Two rough hands behind him, a shove, his body sailing down into the mess at the bottom.

He was looking at bones when he was shoved. Human bones, murder maybe, or the bones of a concealed accident, or the bones of some careless miners who had fallen in. Three skulls, the rest a pile of bones. At least three.

The foreman? He had the most reason. He was the boss down there, the man who cracked the whip. He was the man who dealt with rebels and rowdies. He was big enough to handle any miner. He was absolute lord of his kingdom down there, and it didn't matter to him what anyone topside said or sent down there. That was his kingdom.

And Dink had casually defied the man, ignored his harsh command. Probably the foreman. Who else would shove him?

Dink paused at the office, hoping his fouled moccasins and pants didn't stink too much.

He dropped the carriage weight and headed inside, looking for the nearest clerk.

"What's the name of the foreman in the bottom level of the Victor?" Dink asked.

"Bull Brown," the clerk replied without pause. "Actually, he's the manager of the Victor."

"Who's his boss?"

The clerk smiled and shook his head.

"Creek?"

The clerk shrugged. It was plain Dink would get no more out of him about that.

Everything in Skeleton Gulch was a secret.

"Say, is there is record of the accidents or deaths in the Victor?"

The clerk hesitated. "What do you want to know for?"

"I'm the rat catcher. I need to know."

"There's a sickness report."

"I'd like to see that."

The clerk dug through some files for a few minutes and returned with an employment ledger, scratched out in blurred ink, and much blotted. One glance told Dink that was what he wanted. It listed each miner, date of employment, weekly earnings, shift, leave for sickness, accidents, and termination.

"Yeah, I'll just take a look. I want to know who's been sick and how long," he said.

"Don't leave here with it," the clerk said. "Say, you mind opening the door?"

Dink's fouled moccasins were smelling up the place.

The records were incomplete. Most entries recorded beginning of employment, weekly pay, sick leave, and in some cases, departure. But there were several that showed the pay stopping, and no departure listed.

"You mind telling me what happened to Igor Finn?" Dink asked.

The clerk glanced at the ledger. "Someone forgot to make an entry. Finn quit, I think."

"Where is he now?"

"How should I know?"

"Did he leave a widow?"

The clerk eyed him unhappily, snapped the gray ledger closed, and tucked it away on a shelf.

Dink thought better than to ask about some other missing entries. He would see whether Finn left a widow. He thought there were a lot of widows in Skeleton Gulch.

Chapter 13

Dink awakened to a June day so sweet that he could think of nothing but a hike in the mountains. Zephyrs cleared the yellow smoke from town and toyed with every leaf. In every direction, snowcapped blue ridges vaulted into an azure sky.

It was Sunday. Not that anyone in Skeleton Gulch observed the Sabbath. The gin mills and bordellos and dives ran nonstop. The mines and the stamp mill never quit. It was too costly and slow to fire up cold boilers, so Sunday was like any other day, two ten-hour shifts at each mine and the stamp mill.

If there was a church in Skeleton Gulch, Dink hadn't seen it or heard of it, and if people worshiped any god but money, they did so privately. If they even paused to marvel at the glorious day or let their hearts reach out to the mountains, they kept it to themselves. Skeleton Gulch was not a sentimental town.

He dressed in fresh-washed clothes he had gotten from the Chinamen, and contemplated the day. He decided on a picnic. Maybe a special picnic if he could persuade someone to join him. He wandered into the sleepy town, avoiding Yellow Rose Street, as he called it, because the

steerers at the door of each dive were likely to drag him
into a saloon. On Middle Street he found a general store
open, as well as the bakery, and loaded up on pastries and
bread and cheeses and a jug of wine at the saloon. At the
livery barn he hired a black buggy with a hood that piv-
oted up in case of bad weather, and he demanded a
strong mountain horse rather than the trotter the hostler
tried to fob off on him.

The sturdy horse proved to be a good one, and pulled
him easily up the sharp grade to the rectangular establishment of the Yellow Rose, snoozing silently in the
morning sun.

He parked and entered. A yawning and aged nymph
greeted him.

"The Yellow Rose, please," he said.

She shook her head. "Not up yet."

"It's eleven. She's up. I'd like to give her a treat."

"A treat? You want to give the Yellow Rose a treat?" She
eyed him and snickered.

But she vanished into the dark bowels of the building
and in short order the madam herself appeared, once
again in the handsome silk wrapper with embroidered
roses over it.

"Rat catcher, why did you wake me?" she said.

"You were up, I think. It's a great day for a picnic. I have
a rig outside and a picnic lunch for the two of us."

The Yellow Rose's stare would have frosted a steam
boiler, but Dink endured it.

"I'm Drago, Dink Drago, waiting to take you into the
high country. The wildflowers are out. I reckon my rig can
take us up the logging roads."

She laughed. "Rat catcher, why would I want to do
that?"

"Because you'd enjoy the trip."

"I should have run you out of town."

"I'll be waiting in the buggy."

The sound of her scorn echoed through the hall as the door closed behind him. He climbed into the buggy, which creaked gently under him, and waited. She would be in no hurry, just to teach him who was who in Skeleton Gulch. He watched the botflies swarming under the nag's tail, and knew they were laying eggs where it was moist and warm. The horse switched its tail furiously, annoyed.

Dink waited.

In a while the Yellow Rose emerged from the house of ill repute, dressed handsomely in a sky-blue velvet suit, with a great straw hat framing her hawkish, harsh face.

At the door, her houseman, Igor, studied Dink, looking for any good reason to hammer on Dink or his rig.

The lady stepped into the buggy and settled beside Dink, who slapped reins across the rump of the horse, starting it.

"One hour," she said.

"It's the Sabbath. A day of rest."

"I have absolutely no religion except money, and if you are going to talk about that, stop the rig."

Dink nodded, and headed along a woodcutter's trail that had intrigued him. Like most mining camps, Skeleton Gulch devoured firewood and lumber. The first few miles around the camp were denuded of live trees, and one could find little but stumps. But beyond, within sight, lay sweet green valleys.

"Why are you doing this?"

"This is the most perfect June day I've ever known," Dink said. "I thought to share it."

"You should be hunting rats. The mines are full of them. They cut into my profits."

He gazed at her. She was not looking at him, but at the sky, as if she had never seen it before.

The horse tackled a sharp slope uphill and Dink thought

to conserve its energy, so he let the dray horse pick its way along a rising two-rut road favored by woodcutters.

She pulled a small five-shot lady's revolver from somewhere within her commodious bosom. "Maybe you deserve to be shot," she said.

He noted the weapon, a shining, well-made British revolver, perhaps thirty-two-caliber. She sat with it in her lap, one hand holding it loosely.

"I think you'll like the scenery," he said. "When we get past the cutover area it'll be a virgin world."

"What I want is every tree on this mountain shoved into my boilers," she said.

Dink smiled.

A breeze caught a strand of her hair and it slipped across her face. She restored it angrily, jamming it under a comb. Then she stared straight ahead, presenting him with a hawkish profile. They climbed higher, reached a plateau that bordered a broad valley, and found themselves alongside a cheerful runnel that was laughing its way out of the high country. Ahead loomed the wall of the giant blue glacier.

"What did you bring for the picnic?" she asked.

"Bread, pastries, cheese, wine."

"You have pedestrian tastes."

"You have a lot of money."

"You could have brought caviar, champagne, smoked salmon, truffles, a hundred things. You think you can buy me so cheaply? You want to lay the madam in a mountain meadow, and you bring bread? You better add a hundred dollars to it."

"Rat catchers can use most anything for bait," he replied. "Bread works very well."

She stared at him, suddenly amused. "I think you're an idiot, Drago," she said.

"The cheaper the bait, the higher my profit," he said.

"Rotten meat salvaged from a butcher works excellently. The riper the better. Rats aren't particular."

"How the hell did you get to be a rat catcher?"

"I ask myself the same question. My stock answer is that I am small enough to crawl into dark places."

"Small enough to crawl into my dark place," she retorted.

Dink smiled and pointed. An eagle was riding a thermal off to the left. She watched it and sighed.

They passed the last of the denuded stump-fields and into a half-timbered area where woodcutters were currently dropping fir and pine to feed the boilers of Skeleton Gulch. The two-rut road began to fade, and Dink had to steer the horse around thickets.

"Turn this damned thing around," she said.

"Why?"

"Because I said so."

"No place to do it here." He eyed her. "You want to try?"

She conceded. Trees and stumps and brush crowded the narrow trail they followed. She lifted her revolver, aimed at a red squirrel that was chattering on a limb, and pulled the trigger. The revolver barked. The squirrel vanished, and began whirling through brush and limbs.

They pushed into a thicket barely adequate for passage of the buggy, with fragrant pine limbs lashing the rig and themselves, and then emerged into bright sunlight, a vast mountain meadow, and breathtaking prospects. The meadow lay at the foot of the glacier.

Before them was a paradise carpeted with a riot of blue lupine, yellow buttercups and primrose, purple penstemon, yellow and white asters, purple monkshood and Jacob's ladder, some of them perfuming the air along with the pungence of pine and fir and spruce. A cheery rill tumbled along, dividing the meadow. Beyond, dark forest blanketed steep slopes that vaulted upward and upward into gray rock and snowfields that dazzled the eye.

He steered his way slowly forward, not turning around, though he easily could.

"Oh," she said.

He drove another hundred yards, past blue fields of lupine, and finally came to a small aspen grove beside the creek. He stopped.

"Why are you stopping?"

"Picnic."

"I'm not hungry."

He ignored her and dropped the carriage weight. The dray horse would not be lacking a meal. Rich timothy grass sprouted between the wildflowers.

"This'll cost you a hundred dollars," she said. "I don't come cheap."

"I thought you'd enjoy the flowers."

She stepped down, ignored him, and wandered through the field, pausing here and there to admire a lush bloom, or a rich color. She lifted her skirts to negotiate around brush or rock, looking more and more like a girl instead of the woman Dink knew. She plucked a buttercup and stuck it into her hatband.

She drifted a long time, and he caught glimpses of her meandering through the meadow. She had removed the hat and let her imprisoned brown hair respond to the breeze in perfect liberty.

When she returned, he had a lunch laid out on a faded blanket.

She settled beside him and ate the bread and cheese, saying nothing.

"We found a virgin place, sweet and untouched," he said.

"I should kill you," she replied. She drew her little revolver and tried to drop a distant hawk. The bark startled the Sabbath.

Chapter 14

The Yellow Rose nibbled on Swiss cheese and then settled into the blanket, her sharp features softened with contentment. A bee hummed and vanished. Clouds hung on distant peaks.

They were only three or four miles from Skeleton Gulch, but utterly alone, and in an Eden. Dink had never seen an alpine meadow so rich in color. They were surrounded by blossoms, as if the world itself had become their bouquet. He was content to sit quietly.

"All right," she said, "where's your hundred? That's what it costs for the madam."

"I didn't come for that."

She began undoing the buttons of her fitted blue velvet suitcoat, revealing a silky yellow chemise. "What do you mean you didn't come for that? You brought me out here and didn't intend to pay me? You want it for free?"

"I want to get to know you. This is a picnic. You interest me."

"Damn you, Drago, I'll show you what I do with little pricks."

She jammed her revolver into his crotch and pulled the trigger before he could react. He jumped, felt sparks from the black powder singe his britches, but knew she had not shot off his privates. She had blown the shot between his legs. Smoke curled from his pants, charred by black powder.

"You missed," he said, slapping sparks burrowing into the cloth.

She laughed malevolently. "Pay or die."

"What's your name? I'd like to call you by your birth name," he said.

"Rat catchers don't interest me socially."

"How'd you get rich?"

She sat up, astonished, and waved that mean little revolver around. He was pretty sure she had fired all five rounds, and wished he had counted.

"It was the mines, wasn't it? You got hold of all the mines in Skeleton Gulch and the town lots and waterworks and everything else."

She smiled dangerously, and Dink thought he had better be careful. She was big, almost two feet taller. But he persisted. This was the one time he might learn something from her own lips.

"Yellow Rose, here's the big question. You got rich first and then became a madam. You didn't need to become a madam. Why is that?"

"You don't want to know, because if you knew, it would be fatal, rat catcher," she said.

"All right, tell me. I'll die with an answer in my mind."

"Damn you, Drago. I've never met anyone like you and I'll make sure we never meet again."

"Those portraits in your office? Those are your parents?"

"Yes," she said.

"Do you have siblings?"

"They're dead."

"Brothers, sisters?"

"Brother."

She was answering him. He had pierced one of her veils.

"What happened to him?"

She stared into the sky. The sun sharpened her features. He thought she looked better in shade, where shadow couldn't highlight that hawkish face. For once she was reluctant. She had flaunted her wickedness, but now she retreated into herself. She wasn't going to answer, so he changed the subject.

"You wanted to charge me a hundred dollars. Why not charge two hundred?"

"Let's go, Drago. You've asked too many questions."

"I don't even know your name, Yellow Rose. When you tell me your name, the names of your parents, the name of your brother, where you're from, what they did or do, then we'll go."

She erupted to her feet, lowered the little revolver at his head, and pulled the trigger. It clicked on empty. She pulled and pulled. Then she laughed.

Dink's heart gradually slowed down.

"You want to drive the rig?" he asked.

She shook her head and buttoned up her fitted suit-coat. "You're a sucker," she said. "You could have had me."

"Would I have enjoyed it?"

A shadow flitted across those stony features.

He held her hand as she boarded the buggy and settled into the quilted leather seat. He walked around behind, lifted the carriage weight, clambered in beside her, and took the lines.

"It's the prettiest place I've ever seen," she said.

"I'll bring you back."

"No, you won't. You won't ever bring me here again."

He didn't haw the dray horse, but sat watching a cloud-shadow drift across the green foothills and dot the great glacier.

"Go back, damn you," she snapped.

He turned the wagon slowly, hating to crush the wild-flowers beneath the iron-rimmed buggy wheels. Behind him, two-wheel traces through the lush flowers profaned the virginity of the land.

"No rats here," she said.

He thought maybe there were.

They traversed the meadow, following the rill, and then plunged into dark woods, the passage so narrow that branches brushed them. Gradually they reached areas where the woodcutters had been butchering forest, and sunlight began to filter through. They finally emerged into a place denuded of forest and marked by stumps.

"I won't stop it," she said, leaving him to guess at her meaning.

He concentrated on driving.

Then: "You can't stop me with a pretty scene. I rape scenery and enjoy it."

She was trying to be bad. That interested Dink. The Yellow Rose never stopped being as bad as she knew how to be, as if in some horrible moment some sweetness or kindness might bubble up within her and give the game away, as it had up in the meadow. If the picnic had achieved anything at all, it was his newfound knowledge that she worked at evil, embraced it, flaunted it, as if her life depended on it; as if the ghost at her table was a loving and innocent girl she had disowned.

Maybe that would explain things.

"You resemble your father more than your mother," he said.

She yanked the revolver around, pressed it to his head, and pulled. The click of hammer on empty rang loud in his ear.

Half an hour later they rounded a bend and the head-frames of the mines hove into view, along with pillars of yellow smoke. The thump of the stamp mill caught Dink's ears.

"What did you pay for the Victor Mine?" he asked.

"I stole it."

"From whom?"

"From my parents."

"How much was it worth?"

"I stole the other half from my brother."

"What's his name?"

"He's dead. Damn you, Drago, shut up."

"How did you get the other mines? There's two or three million dollars of mines right there in front of us."

"There's more than that, and if you think you can screw me out of it, just forget it, Drago."

"I'm just a rat catcher. . . . What did you say your name is?"

Her fist slammed him so hard in the shoulder he almost toppled out of the buggy.

He righted himself and tried to ignore the ache flaming through his arm. He moved the lines from his numb right hand to his left.

They reached the rough road connecting the mine heads. The world had changed. What was Eden was now Hades. Dirty rock lay in heaps, choking every gulch. Eventually they reached a point that overlooked the shabby town.

"What do you own?" he asked.

"It's not what I own, it's what's left to own. Ninety percent, and I want the other ten."

He turned the nag down a steep grade, worn smooth by the brogans of miners who traversed this stretch thousands of times. The buggy hurried the livery nag along, and Dink let it.

"I'm going to call you Carlotta," he said. "You look like a Carlotta. Maybe half-Spanish, or French. Maybe half-Scots. Who knows?"

He braced himself for another shot to the arm, but she didn't respond.

"This Carlotta, she's different. She and the Yellow Rose share quarters in the same handsome body."

"Drago, when we get to the livery, you pack up and get out of town."

"I'm catching rats in the mines. I've got some traps in the Victor. The more rats I get, the safer the mines. The miners don't get so sick. The more profit you make. Rat-bite fever can cut your profits, same as accidents. Same as too many men quitting on you. You want profit or not?"

"The only thing that interests me, Drago, is myself."

"Is Carlotta a good guess?"

"I'm the Yellow Rose, Drago, and that's the only name I own."

"It's the one you disown that interests me."

The look she gave him would turn steam into snow. He steered through the grim town, row after row of weather-stained, unpainted shacks that housed miners and their families, then up Yellow Rose Street, where the big grabbers at doorways waited for their chance to shove them both into a saloon, and on up the grade to her place, softened by late afternoon light.

"Drago, don't come calling."

She stepped out of the buggy, and it shifted under him. But she didn't go in.

"You're the third agent General Cook sent," she said. "The others croaked."

Chapter 15

So she knew. Or was she guessing? A shot in the dark? Whatever the case, Dink knew she had powerful sources of intelligence, the best her fortune could buy. Someone had ratted on him.

He had sat there a moment, while she grinned at him. "I don't know what that's about," he had said.

She laughed, that mean laugh full of razor edges, and headed inside. He hawed the horse down the grade to the Howdy Livery Barn, and turned in the buggy and dray horse to the sullen hostler who studied the buggy for damage. Then Dink collected his own wagon, harnessed his nag, and headed out to Starr's wagon yard below town.

How and what did she know? She obviously knew the Rocky Mountain Detective Agency was looking into her affairs. She had obviously identified some of the ones General Cook had sent, and may have tortured plenty of information out of them before murdering them.

Who told her? Did she have paid snitches around town? No doubt of it. Was Doc Cutler one? Dink doubted it, but kept the question open. It would not do to trust anyone just then. Someone else seems to have been in contact with General Cook, someone Dink didn't know.

One thing was plain: If she had wanted to kill Dink, she'd had plenty of opportunity. She was toying with him the way a cat does with a half-dead mouse, cruelly enjoying slow death. The warning was valuable. Dink now knew that she could and would kill him any time she chose; she had the means of knowing everything there was to know about him and his purposes; she had not killed him for reasons unknown.

He had few defenses, but still there were some. He dug into his wagon for a watertight canister with a screw-down lid, and opened it. Within were numerous waxed packets of *Dichapetalum toxicarium,* West African rat's-bane seed, one of the most toxic seeds known, which grew on a West African shrub. He could spread a few seeds and kill a few rats. He could spread piles of the seed and kill piles of rats. It had cost him weeks of work to afford this ultimate rat-killer, so he used it sparingly, and only in desperate circumstances. He stuffed half-a-dozen packets into his pockets, thinking that the deadly seed might come in handy, and might escape notice if he were suddenly imprisoned—and thrown into a hole.

He had work to do. The Yellow Rose had tacitly agreed to ridding the mines of rats and he would proceed, making sure he was watching his back this time. There were traps to empty in the Victor, and also at the bakery and Doc Cutler's offices.

As he dug into his bedroll in the wagon, he thought it had not been a bad day. The picnic had revealed more information about the veiled woman than he could have gotten from months of poking around Skeleton Gulch. He had gotten not only a family portrait, but an absorbing glimpse into her character. Why would any woman, especially one of means and family, work so hard at being bad? What drove her? Why had she softened in the meadow, plucked blossoms, let herself for a few moments be the person she was trying so hard not to be?

Guilt?

It was hard to say.

The next morning he headed for the Victor Mine, showed his pass, and descended once again with a one-ton ore car loaded with empty traps. On the bottom level he found his traps loaded with rats, exchanged the full ones for the newly baited ones, and brought over three hundred rats up the shaft and into daylight.

"Ain't that something?" said an amazed topman.

"Lots more down there. You'll all be healthier when I've cleaned them out."

"Fuller, you mean. Them rats could get into closed-tight lunch buckets. One made off with my pasty once, and I sorrowed on an empty belly all the rest of that shift. How come they get in there?"

"Rats follow humans. They feed off of us."

"Well, there's more of them than they is of us, I wager. Leastwise in Skeleton Gulch."

"I'm hoping to change that."

"Quit your gabbing, Hjortsberg," yelled a straw boss.

Dink loaded the rat traps into his wagon. These miserable things were half-dead, having fought among themselves. The creek would finish the job and clean the refuse. When he didn't have a creek at hand he fed them a little rat's-bane, and that did it. These were all Mediterranean rats, dark brown or full black, smaller and meaner than the Norwegian rats, more likely to survive in holes. Dink halfway liked the Norway rats; but these mean little devils that hopped ships and sailed the world he hated.

He stopped at Doc Cutler's chambers next and cleaned three box traps of rats out of the crawl space. But they totaled only fourteen. He was making progress. Rats intuitively knew when a place was dangerous to them when their numbers were fewer. They knew enough to watch out for poisons too. Let a few of them die from eating some bait, and the rest would steer clear. They had uncanny understandings.

He waited until Doc was done with a patient, who was suffering from an abscess on his left buttock, according to the talk that drifted to Dink from behind that curtain. When the miner left, Doc scribbled in his journal, and then pulled his spectacles free of his bony face.

"Only fourteen this time, Doc. But that foundation's porous. There'll be more. Do you have cats?"

"Only thing cats are good for is cat soup."

"I'm thinking of putting some chemical rat's-bane down there. That's arsenic trioxide mixed with bait. There's a herbal rat's-bane seed too. But not if you have pets, or if you see any way it'd affect your patients."

"Better not," Doc said. "Make people sicker than they are now, no. Just the traps."

"I'm cleaning out the Victor Mine."

"How the devil did you get into that?"

"I talked to Creek, the manager, and I talked to the Yellow Rose. She didn't seem to mind."

"There's nothing she doesn't mind."

"You know her real name?"

"I haven't the faintest idea. The gossip's only gossip. Why do you want to know?"

"Just curious."

Doc's face crinkled to life. "Just curious. Just almighty curious."

"You know any reason someone would not want me poking around the Victor Mine? Or catching rats down there?"

"Why? What happened?"

"Oh, I'm just watching my backside."

"No, you're doing more than that. What happened?"

"I was pushed down the shaft."

Doc turned silent. "Obviously, you get out. What did you find down there?"

"Skeletons and rats and slimy water. Any miner come in here after quitting? Someone sick who was quitting his job?"

"I don't keep track of all that. I just patch and pour and ship them out."

"They let me look at the employment ledger. There's one or two where the pay just stopped, no other entry. No firing, nothing. Dead, I think. Or disappeared, maybe the bones down there."

Doc Cutler pursed his lips. "Some rat catcher you are, Drago." He dug into his desk drawer. "Here's a half eagle. You owe me more rats."

Dink took the small gold piece. "I'll look around your chambers, Doc, and make sure we've got them sealed."

"You do that."

Dink patrolled the walls and floors, found no evidence of rat entry, and left.

At the bakery he collected both attic and ground rats, found evidence of new break-ins, sealed the bakery, and hustled the rat traps out to his wagon.

"Wait now," said Gerta. She handed him two dollars and a bag of fresh-wrapped pastries.

"More than you bargained for, but I'll accept gladly," Dink said. "You want a receipt?"

"Yust getting rat droppings out of my kitchen is receipt," she said.

Dink drove the wagon to a point below town near the cemetery, lifted the loaded traps, settled them into the stream, and waited a few minutes. The rats died in anguish. He emptied the traps and left. Scavengers would swiftly clean up the remains.

He cleaned the traps and loaded them back into his

wagon, staring at the dour city above him, a cancer upon the virgin slopes beyond. How does one clean up a whole city? It wasn't just the Yellow Rose and her loyal praetorian guard who needed to be rooted out. The city was rife with murderous saloon keepers, crooked gamblers, rapacious bawds and pimps, opium peddlers, all of them predators devouring those who worked and produced, who mined and sewed and cooked and delivered and served.

He decided what he would do, and wondered whether he had lost his sanity. He drove to the lumber yard, purchased some boards and nails, then bought some black paint, and spent the rest of the day manufacturing street signs. He was no great hand at lettering, but with patience he created legible signs. By the time the sun was sinking below the western mountains, he had created signs for every major street and cross street: Middle Street, Yellow Rose Street, Victor Street, and so on, and the lettered cross streets, A, B, C. . . . He invented names. A street of cribs he called Clapp Street. A sorry street lined with miners' cabins he called Lung Lane.

They dried swiftly in the arid air, and by dusk he thought he could install them that very evening. He collected his hammer and some nails, and set out, anchoring the signs to buildings wherever he could, sometimes smudging his hands on the tacky paint. No one halted him. One merchant, whose building he borrowed to support a sign, even nodded his approval when he headed out the door to discover the source of the hammering. Sometimes Dink had to stand on his wagon to raise a sign high enough. But by full dark, which came late to Montana Territory in June, Skeleton Gulch had street names, and Dink knew that by the very act of naming the streets he would make them less hospitable to crime, and Skeleton Gulch would begin to lift itself out of its misery. It had become a place on a map.

Chapter 16

There was one more thing to do that June night, something that required the cloak of darkness. In his wagon, he baited half-a-dozen box traps, this time with barley seed soaked in arsenic trioxide, and then drove slowly toward Yellow Rose Street. He parked well below the sporting district and quietly carried two baited box traps up the alley behind the saloons and bawdy houses, watching rats scurry away as he drifted along.

This was one of the silent nights. Sometimes raucous noise barged out of the joints, a piano, a fiddle, stomping, rowdy laughter. That's when the inmates and the suckers who wandered in were all pretending to have fun. Other times the tenderloin was so silent it radiated a haunting sorrow. This was such a night. The pain emanating from the saloons became almost a miasma lowering over the area like the toxic yellow smoke from the boilers above.

Dink drifted along, wanting not to be noticed. He intended to plant a few wire box traps here and there along that murderous alley and see what would happen to them. If they disappeared or were smashed or emptied, he would resort to other means. If he could fill them up and they were unmolested, he would expand his operation there in the heart of the saddest quarter of Skeleton Gulch.

He found good locales for the first two, wedged between two buildings. A little debris on top would conceal them well. No sooner did he retreat than he saw rats pushing toward the traps, wary but lustful, slowly overcoming their reluctance. He didn't wait to see; he had witnessed such sights a thousand times. Instead, he returned to his wagon for two more box traps and set these in a urine-soaked hollow and behind a midden of rubbish. No sooner did he retreat than the ground seemed alive, and he saw the rats edge toward the traps.

Good.

He collected two more and headed into the next block, where the alley ran behind the cribs and bawdy houses. And there he stopped. In the dim light was a seething swarm of rats, a whirling mountain of them, furiously crawling over something . . . which was a body. A woman's body, her pink wrapper largely devoured, her face gone, only her long dark hair announcing her gender. She hadn't been there long, but already she was beyond identification. So intent were the rats at their supper that they didn't even leave as he slipped close, but rose on their legs and defied him to do anything about it. Some jerked toward him, ready to drive him off, or maybe eat him too. Rats in packs became hunters; he could end up the hunted. Slowly, he backed away.

Another murder, another victim who became nameless, anonymous, a pile of bones. By morning, not even the hair would be around, much less any remnant of a skirt or, in this case, Dink thought, a wrapper. She had worn nothing else when she had been pitched into the alley, and was probably drunk, drugged, sick, or already dead. It wasn't suicide. No one wants to die of rat bite.

He debated what to do. Get the constables? He was

already in trouble with them, and they were likely to knock him in the head and let him suffer the fate of the woman. Get Happy Kilgore, the undertaker?

He heard a door. A shadowy figure loomed in the dark. Dink froze, glad he was wearing dark clothing. He heard the sound of pissing. The figure wrestled with his britches and vanished.

A rage flooded through Dink, rage and disgust, rage and fear, dread of this evil hole, this snakepit, this ghastly alley where life was cheap. That woman was probably young. There were no old people in Skeleton Gulch, no old whores, no old men. No one lived to forty. Dink took his traps back with him this time, leaving the four in the other block, and returned to his wagon. He rode quietly down the slope, steering toward Kilgore's parlors.

He tugged rein, slid down, and rapped on the dark door.

It took a while, but Kilgore finally opened, a lamp in one hand.

"There's a woman's body in the alley," Dink said.

Kilgore yawned. "You could have waited to morning. It ain't gonna help her any now."

"The dead deserve whatever we can give them. They've run their race," Dink replied.

"You telling me my business?"

"Respect," Dink said. "You're in the business of offering respect."

"Drago, you try to change things in this town, and you're going to pay the price."

Kilgore slammed the door.

Dink didn't like the sound of that. He settled in his wagon and rode softly downslope toward the wagon yard, pondering the life and death of that woman in the alley. She was someone's daughter. Maybe someone's wife. She had lived a hard life. Maybe she had been abandoned. Those who rescued her weren't her friends. She had been used, worn out, torn up, drugged, and finally killed. Some life, he thought. Some life.

He was as melancholic as he ever got by the time he reached Starr's yard. Somehow, a woman in that alley made it worse. He thought of mothers and daughters with creamy skin and sleek hair and hands that comforted and fed and nursed and sewed and loved. He thought of missing wives, orphaned children, desperate girls.

He slid into his bedroll charged with purpose. He would clean up Skeleton Gulch. He had little more than a small body and lots of rat poison, but he would do it. By the time he was finished, there would be no more rats, and Skeleton Gulch would become a cheerful little camp, relishing its life and health and wealth.

That poor woman could have been someone's kid sister.

Starr was in the wagon yard the next morning. Dink found his way to the company mess and caught a cup of java while Starr and his teamsters harnessed one sixteen-mule team and slipped oxbows over a twenty-ox-team outfit. They were going to do some heavy freighting, he thought.

"Drago, how goes it?" Starr yelled as he slid a collar over a big black mule.

Dink set down his coffee and helped. There was harness to buckle and a bridle to slide into the mule's mouth and lines to straighten out.

"Lot of rats, Mr. Starr."

"John. I'm John. If you say Mr. Starr, I'll think you're talking to my father."

"I'm cleaning them out of a few places. There are plenty of others that don't want the rats touched. They have a sort of vested interest in rats. You know why?"

"I can guess."

"I'm cleaning out the Victor, and when I'm done I'll work on the other mines."

Starr paused. "How'd you get in there? Getting into the Victor is harder than getting into Fort Knox. If they don't know you, or don't approve, you'll get knocked on the head."

"I told 'em the rats were slowing down production, making miners sick."

"They bought that?"

"The man in charge, Creek, wrote me a pass."

Starr finished up with the black mule and dragged a collar over the neck of a gray. Dink helped harness that one too.

"You talk to the owner?" Starr asked.

"The Yellow Rose? Is she the owner?"

Starr nodded.

"I talked to her. She doesn't much care whether the mines earn anything or not."

"That's about right," Starr said.

"You know her?"

"Yes."

"What's she like?"

But Starr was staring into space, almost a vacant look in his hawkish face. "Better be careful, Drago," he said.

"Would you explain that?"

"I've had dealings with the Yellow Rose. That's all you need to know."

"I need to know more. What does she own? Who runs everything for her? Who is she? You have a name for her? I'd like a name. Funny, this town is owned and ruled by a woman whose name appears to be some deep dark secret."

Starr ran a harness strap through a buckle and tightened down the belly band. "Yes, I know her name. Lots of people know her name, even if no one will say it. Her name's Consuela Estrella-Cooper."

"Spanish?"

"Spanish and Scots."

"Where is she from?"

"Galveston, Texas."

"Is that her family, those oil portraits?"

"Those were her parents."

"What did they do?"

"Her father Dagobert was a privateer."

"I'm a landlubber, Mr. Starr."

"A privateer is the owner of an armed vessel employed by some government to wage war against its enemies. A licensed pirate, Drago."

"That was her father? She inherited the blood."

Starr laughed easily.

"How do you know all this?" Drago asked.

"It's common knowledge even if no one dares to talk about it. Anyone known to say anything about it is rat bait."

"But you're talking."

"I am." Starr broke into a bland smile, baring even white teeth, and began tightening a cinch.

"Who's the son in your company. Starr and Son, Freighting."

It caught Starr by surprise. He finished harnessing the gray mule and turned to Dink.

"He's dead, Drago. He didn't live long. His life was stopped cold before he was twenty-one."

Dink waited quietly; this wasn't over. Starr took his time, selected another collar, and headed for another mule.

"He was murdered," Starr said, and turned away.

Chapter 17

The sight of that woman's body, what little was left of it, haunted Dink all morning. He fashioned two more street signs, Rat Alley and Death Alley, which he intended to post on the alleys to either side of Yellow Rose Street. Let them serve notice. When the paint was more or less dry, he rode over there in his wagon and found suitable places to nail each.

No one stopped him. It was early afternoon, a time when the hellholes were at their lowest ebb. He banged away with his hammer, posting each street sign. The alley to the north became Rat Alley; to the south, Dead Alley. No one but a yawning barman bothered to see what the hammering was about.

Now there were names. He believed in the power of names. Death Alley was a name that would be remembered. That was the alley where the girl, or woman, or bawd, or stranger, had died hours before, but now there was no hint of that heap of gnawed flesh and bone. Happy Kilgore had cleaned up. He always cleaned up. For a price, no doubt. Hap got along with everybody.

The alleys slept in the midday sun, which pummeled the urine smell out of the earth and sent it wafting away on the breezes. Dink checked the traps, found them full of dead rats and unmolested. He quietly emptied the dead ones and set fresh traps in place. He thought he was being observed from various dark and grimy windows, but he couldn't be sure.

These alleys would need more than four traps to control several thousand rats in each block. He headed for his wagon and withdrew a bag of arsenic-soaked barley, put on some gloves, and then quietly scattered the barley everywhere he spotted rat dens or runways. Maybe, maybe, maybe someone thrown unconscious into that alley would have a fighting chance to live. Maybe someone who was the victim of a Mickey Finn might walk away. Maybe someone who survived the alley would supply evidence against the scores of bartenders, pugs, bouncers, steerers, toughs, gamblers, pimps, and bums whose business was pillage.

Even as Dink spread the poisoned bait in broad daylight, aggressive rats, normally nocturnal animals, ducked out, nipped at the seed, and retreated. There were so many, and they were so famished for food, that not even bright sunlight deterred them.

Dink was pleased. By this evening there would be no poisoned bait left. There might be five hundred fewer rats. Maybe this very evening some poor soul would live rather than perish. Maybe some poor woman who wasn't earning enough to please her masters would survive and walk away.

It would be a start at any rate. He knew he would have to apply the poisoned bait over and over, and switch because rats had uncanny ways of avoiding poisons they caught on to. A month of this would not clean all of them out.

He was preparing to leave when he found himself surrounded. Big, mean brutes rose out of nowhere, some in once-white aprons. One snagged the bridle of his nag; another easily pinned the wagon wheel in his fist.

"Whatcha up to?" asked one with wattles under his jaw, maybe the very barkeep who delivered the Finn to him in the first hours after he arrived in Skeleton Gulch.

"Hanging street signs. This is now Dead Alley, across the way is Rat Alley. That's Yellow Rose Street. I'm sorry I'm not more handy with the paintbrush but I got all the names right anyway. I think it'll do the job."

"Who are you, pal?"

"It says on my wagon."

"You tell me."

The man couldn't read. "Dink Drago, Rat Catcher. You've got rats around here, all right."

"Git down off that wagon, you little turd."

Dink saw he was about ten seconds from a beating that might well kill him.

"Have you checked with the Yellow Rose?" he asked. "You'd better."

"Who's dat? Never heard of her," said another brute, whose ham fists were slowly clenching and unclenching.

"Hop in, come with me, we'll drive up the hill and have a visit with her," Dink said. "She'll take good care of you. She takes good care of me."

He waited boldly while the wheels turned in the brute's slow-moving brain.

"All right, I will," he said, and climbed up beside Dink.

The wagon creaked under the man, who probably approached eighteen stone. A fetid odor leaked from his every pore.

"Let go, Boxhead," said a skinny one with cadaverous black pits under his eyes. He was a walking funeral parlor.

Boxhead instantly obeyed.

The skinny one turned to Dink. "I'll see about it. Maybe you're rat bait."

"Take my business card," Dink replied. "She and I go on picnics."

"Picnics? You say picnics?"

"Picnics. Ask her," Dink said. "She likes picnics."

One of the four brutes nudged another. The third leered. He let go of the bridle. The pug stepped out of the wagon, which creaked again.

"Picnics," muttered the wattled barkeep. "Picnics."

Dink nodded and hawed his nag away from there. It had been close. They stood behind him in their soiled bar aprons, their gazes hooded.

That afternoon he cleaned another load of rats out of the Victor Mine and left baited traps. No one stopped him. Apparently Yellow Rose's approval sufficed to keep him safe—for the moment.

Consuela Estrella-Cooper. What a name. Daughter of Dagobert Cooper, privateer. What a name and profession. Handsome, hawkish man, judging from that oil portrait. Dink wondered if some contradiction of the blood made the union of Scots and Spanish crazy. It had to be something like that. Mate a Spaniard to a Scot and all hell broke loose.

He rode on down the slope to Kilgore's Funeral Emporium, and parked there, using his carriage weight. He opened, triggering a cowbell, and Hap Kilgore emerged from the curtained door.

"It's you," he said. "Wake a man up for no reason."

"You identified her?"

"Who?"

"The woman in the alley."

"What woman in what alley?"

Dink sighed. This town swallowed up human beings and stamped on their memory.

"You holding a service?" he asked.

The undertaker shrugged. "You want, you go down there and say a few choice words."

"Where is she?"

"Buried in a barrel, where else, Drago?"

"What did you charge the city?"

"I never charge Skeleton Gulch for anything. It's a public service."

"You do it for free."

"I didn't say that."

"What was her name? Age? Cause of death?"

"Just a worn-out slut."

Dink was getting nowhere fast. "You need some rat poison around here," he said.

Kilgore smiled.

Dink boarded his wagon and drove slowly down the slope until he was well below Skeleton Gulch, and then turned right onto a two-rut trail. When he reached the cemetery he kept on, pushing through brush, until he reached what he was calling the barrel corner. There was a fresh pile of earth there. He slipped off the wagon and walked over to the miserable grave.

"I wish I knew your name," he said. "Then I could grieve better. Things don't seem real if they don't have names, and that's the whole trouble with Skeleton Gulch. No one has a name. But I know you had a bad life, and I'm hoping now you'll have a better one. We don't mean to fall into hard lives; it just happens. Sometimes it's our own weaknesses; sometimes bad things happen and no one can stop them. Like consumption, like being orphaned. But anyway, whoever you are, whatever you did, I'm here to say good-bye and wish your spirit well. Maybe that won't mean anything. Maybe I'm doing it for me, not you. I don't know. But I know I care, and I am grieving, and I am trying to end the sort of world that devoured you and spat you out.

"I guess I'll give you a name as long as no one has one for you. I'll call you Lorena. I like that name. Now that you're Lorena, you're more real to me. You're a person with a voice and a smile and a dream. I never knew a

Lorena, but I do now. Rest in peace, Lorena," he said, and stood quietly there, alone in the weed-choked corner of the world.

He drove slowly over to the wagon yard, found a piece of pine plank, and carefully lettered a new name on it. Soon Skeleton Gulch would have a Lorena Street. He thought of a good place for it, a side street over near the cribs. Maybe every girl there was Lorena, one way or another.

Near the wagon yard at the bottom of town, he had discovered a wild rose bush, and now he knew what he would do. He extracted a spade from his wagon, found an old bushel basket, and headed for the wild rose, which had not yet bloomed. It would be a bad time to transplant it, but he intended to anyway.

He dug carefully, working far away from the roots, and in time was able to lift the wild rose into the bushel basket. Then he filled a pail with water, harnessed his horse, and rode slowly into Skeleton Gulch. He veered into Yellow Rose Street, which was coming alive as evening neared, and then into Dead Alley, where he drove through the stink of urine, the smell of rats, and the sourness of stale beer and booze. He found the place where Lorena had perished. Across the alley, as far away as he could get from the dives, he scraped away trash, shattered glass, ancient pieces of wood, a rat's nest, some manure, and began a hole. The soil was soft. Several bawds, sitting at the windows, watched, and he was glad they did. He finished the hole, lifted the wild rose into it, tamped down the soil, and poured the bucket of water over it.

Then he stood there, hat off, before his rose in Dead Alley.

"Hey, banty, come visit me," said one bawd. "I'll give you a fine old time."

Chapter 18

Dink didn't much care for the body he inhabited. If he had grown into a man of normal size, he would have enjoyed a different life. Men dismissed him. With one arm they could lift him by the scruff of the neck. Women usually ignored him, especially those looking for a mate. Not even his words seemed to carry any weight. But for his height, he might have entered a profession. He might have a circle of friends. He might have been a professor or schoolmaster.

He was a loner now, not that he wanted to be. When you live in a world where you're staring uphill at everyone you meet, you begin to see Alps where others see level ground. It had been hard to make friends.

Rat catcher. It was an opening for a small man. An opening for someone who could crawl under floors, through attics, down drainages, and kill small creatures. He wasn't a midget by any means, just a wisp of a man no one noticed. His compliments, when he offered them, meant nothing to others. His esteem was not sought. Neither was he feared or respected. Little fellow like that, why worry? Friends? What friends? Who wanted him for a friend?

A few did, one or two girls he had loved, an old Civil War

vet missing an arm and an eye, a stern but affectionate spinster teacher he had known, a poet, a journalist who scribbled for the *New York Herald*. It had not been easy for them to befriend him. He was not easy to know. He understood that and treasured them all the more for it. His friends were few, but the friendships ran deep and held no secrets. He sometimes thought that he was better able to be a friend than most. But so many of his days slid by without a friendly nod.

Still, he performed a service. Because of him, some people lived, others escaped sickness, foul hellholes were sanitized. And now he had a twin profession, cleaning up bad places. This was the worst he had ever encountered, maybe the worst in the world for all he knew. And General Cook had entrusted him with a task where others had failed.

He had turned into himself, never accustomed to being alone, but making the best of the cards that life had dealt him. There were a few assets too. If he was not a threat, no one troubled him, at least no one in other places. In Skeleton Gulch, there were hulking men who considered everyone a threat. He probably owed his life to his smallness. Had he been average size, the Yellow Rose would long since have blown his lights out.

He couldn't say he was happy, but there was little he could do about it, so he made as much of a life as he could and let it go at that.

He scrubbed himself as best he could at the horse trough; working in rat warrens left him covered with filth, and he was always out of fresh clothing, even when he employed the Chinamen to wash up his duds. He had nothing fresh to wear this night, so he scraped as much stain and filth as he could from his shirt and britches and headed for Yellow Rose's parlor house.

The powerful class of men who patronized her place

and were mostly her mining employees wouldn't notice him, or if they did, would instantly label him as a trades-man who should not have come in the front door. Maybe the Yellow Rose would boot him out, but he doubted it. He knew he intrigued her, like a pet Chihuahua, which is why she toyed with him.

He hiked through town, avoiding the bullies on Yellow Rose Street, and knocked at the great carved door of the parlor house on the hill. It opened. A liveried bouncer eyed him dubiously.

"I'm a friend of the Yellow Rose," he said, pushing past the man, who was gotten up in military tan. The doorman let him pass. Maybe that was another virtue of being small.

From the foyer one could turn left into the hand-somely furnished saloon, or right, into a red-wallpapered anteroom where nymphs du monde would swiftly appear, all ersatz smiles. They would all imagine they were about to embrace a boy. He smiled. He might be small, but not all of him was small and nothing of him was a boy.

He headed into the saloon and approached the brass rail. A suspicious female barkeep waited, her expression dubious. Her breasts almost but not quite overwhelmed her white blouse.

"Bourbon and branch," he said.

She delivered the drink and took his last dollar. She offered no change.

He turned to observe. The night was young and these gents were not yet boisterous or uninhibited. He saw no sign of the Yellow Rose, Consuela. Some serving girls circu-lated among the several men, a few of whom were roughly dressed in mining clothing, foremen and bosses perhaps. But most wore acres of black broadcloth, bowties, and high-top laced boots polished to a spit shine. Everything was for sale. Probably even the barkeep, had he asked.

The serving girls interested him. They circulated through

the male crowds, their faces masked, their expressions numb, their thoughts buried deep in the back of their heads, invisible to these customers, who were more interested in the flash of thigh in their split skirts and what lay under gauzy blouses. Men casually fondled them as they served, a hand here and there, as if the fondlers were bestowing favors. Dink never saw a serving girl object, nor did he see any favor a customer with a smile. Were they doped? On one he saw corrugated flesh on both arms and hands, scarred and bitten flesh that had been stripped away by merciless rats. She was a rebel perhaps, or had merely been punished for some infraction of laws known only to the Yellow Rose. This place, like all the others in Skeleton Gulch, policed itself with rats.

The bourbon proved to be rotgut only days old. Not even in her classy parlor house was the Yellow Rose going to do anything but cheat her customers out of all she could get. But it was still the safest place in town. For the customers. Not for the girls.

He sipped one small dribble of booze, felt the rotgut sear down his throat, and sipped again. He waited to see whether a Mickey had been dropped into this drink, but felt no ill effect. If he fell to the floor in here, no mortal would ever see him again. He eyed his neighbors at the brass rail, all of them a foot or more taller and talking with each other or just staring into space. There was no privacy here; buy a drink, go select a girl, head into the curtained rear chambers, and the whole town knew it. That no doubt worked in favor of the Yellow Rose.

He mostly wanted to listen. These men, the bosses and supervisors, the enforcers and bullies, talked freely here, thinking they were among their own, so Dink sipped and listened. That's all he planned to do, catch fragments of telling conversations, learn how Skeleton Gulch was put together, what he must do to clean it up, if one small mortal could achieve such a thing with little or no help from the Territory.

He noted names, memorized faces, seemed to be gazing raptly at the nudes on the wall, while all the while he was blotting up useful information, the sort of things General Cook and his detective agency needed to know.

A barmaid slipped to the rail next to him and ordered drinks.

"You're the rat catcher," she said, not looking at him. Plainly, she didn't want this conversation noticed.

"Yes."

"Help us. We're desperate. We can't escape. If we try, we disappear. . . ."

He glanced sideways toward her. She stared ahead, watching the barkeep pour drinks, her face a mask.

"Into a rat hole?"

"I've been in it. One minute is an eternity. God has no mercy; he doesn't hear us."

"And about three minutes is death, am I right?"

The barkeep slapped two drinks onto the serving woman's tray and the woman set off for an alcove Dink hadn't noticed. Men sat within, half-curtained by red drapes. The serving woman looked bent and old, but she was probably young. He could see corrugated flesh along the woman's arms and it was not from age. It was scar tissue.

He sipped, eyed the males sipping in the alcove, discovered Creek, the manager of the whole mining complex, among them. It took another ten minutes before the serving girl appeared, once again to get drinks.

"Bourbon and branch, rye and branch," she said.

"Listen," he said, staring straight ahead, "here's a packet of seed. It's called West African rat's-bane. It is lethal to rats. Use it to save your life in the rat hole. More whenever you need it."

He slid the packet her way, but she shook her head slightly.

He saw that someone was staring, so he gradually slid a hand over the packet and retrieved it.

She never approached him again. But he knew that if he came back and she was serving drinks, she would.

She wanted her freedom if she could get it. But right now she wanted to escape rats and the punishments doled out to her and her sisters. He thought about those girls across the foyer, told to make men happy and smile a lot, told if they failed they would be lowered into the rat hole and no one would hear their screams.

He wondered about that rat hole. Where was it? To keep rats around, you had to feed them. Garbage probably, in between tastes of human flesh. How many rat holes were there in Skeleton Gulch? And who used them?

What sort of cruel woman was the Yellow Rose?

"You want another drink?" asked the barkeep. "Or something else, sweetheart?"

She leaned forward, a pasted-on smile covering her pale face.

"Can't afford it," he said. "You took my last dime."

"We don't allow vagrants," she replied.

"I'm leaving. Next time I have an eagle, I'll spend it here."

"If they let you in," she said.

He headed for the door, only to find the Yellow Rose herself blocking it.

Chapter 19

There was no way around her. All six feet of the Yellow Rose blocked the door, and just in case Dink might wiggle free, two of her silent bullyboys stood at a discreet distance.

"Rat catcher, come into my web so I may sting you," she said.

"No, thanks."

"Ah, but you will. No one turns down my hospitality. It is famous."

"Then I will turn it down. Your fame precedes you."

"I would be very vexed with you if you were to refuse me."

"How vexed?"

"We both like picnics. Only you'd be the picnic."

Dink stared. She was talking murder.

She beckoned him to follow, and led the way through silent rooms to her study. It was as magnificent as he remembered it, dominated by the grand oils of her parents. The painter had that skill that made their eyes seem to follow him as he entered the room.

He surveyed the room for escapes and found very little. A grilled window would let in daylight, but now the room was lit by an oil-lamp chandelier of cut glass.

"Well?" she said, and there was that edged quality in her voice again. Knives and razors and blades in everything uttered.

"Your parents are handsome."

"You're snooping, Drago. General Cook should send more experienced detectives."

"You'd better explain," he said.

She laughed, a throaty, sarcastic laugh he rather enjoyed, to the extent that he was able to enjoy anything. It was as if they shared a secret.

"You're poking around, trying to rescue my inmates," she said, her voice suddenly dulcet.

"I came for a drink."

"The ladies know you're a rat catcher."

"So?"

"They don't like rats. No, that's too mild. They live in terror of rats."

"No, they live in terror of you or your bullies feeding them to the rats."

She laughed. "You have a way about you. Bantam rooster."

"Is this interview over?"

"Drago, it's barely begun. I want you to pity those poor women. I'm a white slaver and they are innocents. It amuses me that not a one of them voluntarily entered the profession. There's not a slut in the bunch. They're mostly the widows of miners. We lose miners regularly, Drago, as fast as I can arrange it, and just before the widows leave town I kidnap them. They are never seen again, at least in open society. I have several who weep constantly. One came to me, clutched my feet, and begged to be freed. I told her that her virtue would reward her in heaven, but as long as she's in here, she's my slave. She stumbled away, weeping. Some turn hard. They grow less and less useful, because they take to the life and the men are disappointed. I always throw them away."

"It is something you seem to enjoy."

"No, much worse than that. It is because I am cruel. It is my cruelty that I enjoy. I think of them, grieving, their man dead or vanished, packing up, and suddenly they are here in this sink of iniquity, and I tell them to pleasure every man who buys them, to learn the arts and skills, and if they don't do it, or object, they will face certain music, the sound of a thousand rats eating them."

"Why?" he asked.

"Because, Drago, I am depraved."

"No, you don't look depraved."

"A depraved person knows exactly what virtue is, what good is, what morals and ethics are, and does evil anyway. That is to say, a depraved person is unregenerate. That's me. I know exactly what evil is. I am keeping innocent women in a state of degradation and terror. I've occasionally arranged for mining accidents to destroy a husband because I took a fancy to the wife, and thought she would make a good slave. I am doing it even though I pity them and you pity them. My customers pity them. It's no good, you see, if we don't pity them. If we're too hard. My customers enjoy sporting with women who aren't professionals. What is more exciting than ravishing a virtuous woman? They tip well. You see? It's all for money. I make fortunes degrading innocent women."

"You already had a fortune, Consuela."

Her eyes lit dangerously. She circled around him, again and again.

"Who told you that?" she asked.

"It appears to be common knowledge, from what I've heard."

"Answer my question."

"You're the daughter of Dagobert Cooper; your

mother's name was Estrella. He was a privateer operating out of Galveston. She was an unhappy woman."

"Unhappy, yes, poor dear. That is because he was very bad in bed. Helpless, that is the word. Dagobert couldn't make love to a knothole. My mother sighed and turned bitter. He was a pirate and took what he wanted, but he could not take my mother. She grew weary of him. See how her mouth is turned down in the portrait. That is the mouth of starvation. See how the lips give her away. A thousand Spanish women would recognize that look instantly. That's because he was such a poor lover. It is a miracle I was born. She told me it was only because he had his mind on a recent conquest of ten thousand troy ounces of gold bullion. I resolved not to have his faults."

He gazed up at her. "Spanish and Scots leads to all sorts of trouble. A bad mixture of bloods. It is lucky you aren't mad."

"You make jokes at my expense, Drago, but I will have the last laugh."

"I don't think you're anywhere near as evil as you pretend. There is some other reason for it. What is it?"

She loomed over him, all six feet, rage in her face this time. "Drago, you are already my slave. You will never leave Skeleton Gulch. When I am through with you, I will dispose of you."

"The question was, why are you trying to be bad?"

She lifted him easily by his shirt until he was standing on his toes, and then shoved. He landed on an Oriental carpet. He wasn't hurt. Obviously he had touched on a sore point. This composed lady had become, in a flash, volcanic.

"I'll come back when I have some money," he said. "You charge too much for red-eye."

He wondered whether he would escape, or escape unscathed, but she was oddly quiescent for the moment. She oscillated between extremes, one moment almost civil, the next violent.

"Who is Vanishing Jack?" he asked.

The question astonished her. He was good at that, slipping in the unexpected.

"Vanishing Jack is going to vanish for good next time he comes to town," she said. "It doesn't matter that he has a ledge somewhere and chips out some quartz. Next time, we'll catch him and knock his head in. He's the only thing in Skeleton Gulch beyond my control, and I'll soon fix that."

"You are candid. I wonder if you'd actually do it."

"Wait and see, Drago, wait and see."

"So you can prove to me what? That you're as bad as you say?"

"Out," she said, the knives back in her voice.

He walked out. Still alive. Free.

She puzzled him. Her conduct was as strange as anything he had ever encountered. He wondered whether even to believe her threats. As near as he could fix it in his mind, she was going to prove to him how depraved she was and then kill him.

A puzzle indeed, and one to report to the detective agency. The general expected him to take risks and do the job if he could, but also to be prudent and get help if the odds were stacked against him. There was a code to be employed. Dink debated whether to send the message, and decided to wait a few more days. He didn't yet know enough to break the case or clean up the town.

Somehow, he wasn't as frightened as he should have been when he was temporarily snared by the Yellow Rose, and maybe that was a mistake. A woman who threatens death ought to be taken with all due gravity. Still, purely on intuitive grounds, he knew nothing serious would befall him that night. But the mystery had certainly deepened. He slipped into his bedroll more puzzled than ever.

In the morning he found John Starr in his cubicle of an office, the safe open, filling brown manila pay envelopes for his teamsters. A revolver lay on his desk inches from his hands.

"Oh, it's you, Drago. Sit there and don't distract me while I count. But first tell me your business," Starr said, his hands never stopping as they shoved greenbacks into envelopes. "Most of my teamsters get ten a week; some roustabouts and herders get seven. My foremen and captains get thirty and deserve it."

Dink watched him a moment. As Starr filled each envelope, he checked off something on his gray ledger book.

"I want to know more about the Yellow Rose and any ideas you have about her conduct," Dink began. "I was there last night and I wondered whether I would walk out that door. She spent a lot of time and energy telling me how bad she is, depraved was the word. What do you know of her that would explain that?

"She also revealed something of interest. The next time Vanishing Jack shows up, he's going to be knocked in the head. She said the ledge doesn't matter to her; what matters is snuffing anything she can't control in Skeleton Gulch."

Starr did pause at that, smiled, and then continued his counting.

"Tell me why a rich woman who owns five mines and most of the businesses in Skeleton Gulch would open a house of ill repute, conduct herself as badly as her imagination permits her, and grow angry at me when I suggested she was not as bad as she made out."

"I'd say the bloody bitch is her father's daughter," Starr said. "Or, to refine that a bit, she wants to think she is but knows she isn't."

"How would you know, Starr?"

"I listen to the gossip," Starr replied.

Chapter 20

Drago was intrigued by the tall freighting man, who seemed to be the only person in Skeleton Gulch with any answers.

"You got time to talk a little more, John?" he asked.

"We're deadheading wagons to Corinne this morning; got to get busy."

"Deadheading? Doesn't this town export anything?"

"It sucks everything into itself, Drago, and ships nothing. All my freight business is one-way."

"You know more than anyone else around here, and I'm curious about things."

Starr eyed him quietly. "I'm sure you are."

"Like the gold from the mine. Here are five mines up on that ridge, and a stamp mill, and I've heard they're producing over a million in gold each year. I see no armed couriers, no Wells Fargo gold shipments leaving here, and I don't see you carrying the bullion out. How does it leave here?"

Starr gazed levelly at Dink. "That sort of question could get a man into big trouble."

"I'm asking it anyway."

"It probably doesn't leave here."

"Where does it go?"

"I hear it goes into the vaults of the Yellow Rose, right up there on the hill. It's piling up in the best vault money can buy."

"Why?"

"Ask her."

"But she needs to pay her miners, pay her woodcutters, pay for her bosses, for rail and lifts and cables and ore cars. For a stamp mill, for mine timbers, for accountants."

Starr smiled. "It's a mystery, Drago. But I can answer one part of it. She doesn't import currency. There's not a bank in Skeleton Gulch. Ever wonder about that? She pays the miners with company scrip. It buys anything in town. Miners get four dollars of scrip a day, a dollar more than the going wage. That's why they accept it."

"Who turns that into cash and where does the cash come from? Those gamblers in the Golden Hind, they don't take scrip. It's cash or you don't play. There's some cash around here."

"Beats me, Drago," Starr said. "I'll tell you this: No one's seen any sizable shipment of gold ever leave Skeleton Gulch. Maybe it's spirited out. Maybe there's three or four tons of it in her vault."

"Creek gave me a double eagle he said was Victor Mine gold, so some must leave here."

Starr shrugged. "It's easy to ship a few hundred pounds now and then without being seen."

"How does she pay her bills?"

"She's rich, Drago, remember? She probably has cash by the bucket stashed away. Enough to buy anything she needs to keep the mines humming."

"She ever approach you about shipping gold out under guard?"

"She doesn't know I exist, Drago."

"Well what about the Wells Fargo coaches?"

Starr paused a moment. "One of the oddities here is that there is no highway robbery. Not like Virginia City a few years ago, when highwaymen robbed everyone entering or leaving the mining district. You won't find road agents preying on the coaches. That's because there's nothing much in any of them. The coaches leave Skeleton Gulch with nothing of value."

"Who handles her money? Someone must."

Starr rose. "You got me. Now I've got to get this train off. Corinne's a long way."

Corinne, Utah, far to the south, was an entrepot on the Union Pacific. It supplied most of the goods reaching western Montana Territory; Fort Benton, at the head of navigation of the Missouri River, supplied the rest. In a year or two the Northern Pacific, steadily building west, would offer a more direct and cheaper route.

"Sure, and thanks," Dink said.

The more he probed into Skeleton Gulch, the more of a mystery it became. All the gold from the mines still here? He couldn't imagine why.

Starr's teamsters had harnessed four freight wagons to mule teams. Starr personally examined every harness, every animal, every wagon wheel, and nodded. With a burst of profane encouragement and the lash of a few tasseled whips, the teamsters stirred the train into action. They were a colorful lot, most of them bushy-bearded, all in slouch hats, none of them familiar with the inside of a church.

"What are they carrying?" Dink asked.

"Not a damned thing," Starr replied. "Skeleton Gulch doesn't export anything but filled coffins."

The mules lowered into their collars and began tugging the steep-sided freighters down the hill, toward the level valleys that would take them south to Utah.

Starr was reluctant to talk anymore, headed for his office and closed the door.

Dink rearranged the traps in his wagon, cleaned house, and harnessed his old dray nag. He headed directly for the alleys flanking Yellow Rose Street, curious about his results. He drove into Death Alley and was smacked by the stink of rot and urine. He collected his traps, which were loaded with dead rats, emptied them, and stuck the traps into his wagon. A little farther up, he came to the rose bush he had planted where a wretched woman had died. The bush was curling up and all but dead. He dropped off the wagon and walked to it. The stench of urine told him what had happened. This town was pissing the rose bush to death. Damn this town, which couldn't let one sweet and clean thing live.

From the grimy windows of the whorehouses pale faces gazed at him. Maybe it was the girls who did the pissing. But he was not done. He put on his gloves, pulled a bag of arsenic-laced barley from a sheet-metal chest, and once again dropped grain around rats' nests, runways, building foundations, until he was sure he would harvest another large bunch. The day he found uneaten and rotting garbage in the alley, he would know he had eliminated most of the fierce little devils.

He drove over to Rat Alley on the other side, collected his traps, and spread more poisoned barley. It would take weeks to finish a job like this.

No one interrupted him in the bright morning sunlight when the joints dozed and one surly barkeep kept each place open, and the second shift from the mines had tumbled into the wooden bunks in their cabins.

He watched a golden eagle soar. It was hunting food. He hoped it wouldn't come feasting on dead rats full of arsenic. The bird glided majestically, but in the foothills south from town. Once it caught a thermal and rose without flapping a wing, circling higher and higher until it vanished over a distant blue ridge.

"Stay away," Dink muttered. "Good and far and damned well miles away."

The dead rats could be hard on dogs, cats, birds, skunks, anything else that ate flesh. But most of them would die in their dens, far from light and air. Still, he felt a certain remorse, for some innocent animals minding their own instincts would perish.

That done, he stopped at the bakery and checked the traps under the floor. Full of black rats, as usual.

Gerta peered through the trapdoor.

"Always more rats, Drago, eh?"

"Black rats. You mind if I use some poisoned barley down here?"

Gerta rubbed her blue eyes, trying to make the wetness of tears vanish. Dink ignored her as best he could.

"So much killing," she said. "I thought maybe two, three, five rats. Not like this."

"I'd like to use some poisoned bait, Gerta. The traps don't do much."

She stared a long time, and then nodded.

He spread a cup of the bait under the bakery, backed out, and closed the slanted trapdoors at the rear of the building.

"Keep pets and children out of there. I've looked upstairs. There's no more Norway rats," Dink said. "Your attic's clear and there's tin over the holes. You should have a pretty clean bakery by now."

She brightened. "Yah, good riddance," she said. "You come."

Within, where the fragrance of fresh-baked bread smacked him and set his stomach growling, he waited while she wrapped two loaves in newspaper.

Dink accepted his payment, knowing he would have to scrub hard before he touched any of the rich pastries. He drove over to Doc Cutler's, discovered Doc had a patient behind the velvet curtain, and headed for the crawl space. The smell that greeted him was pure rat. He wasn't making much progress. He crawled in, collected some full traps of live rats, and wormed out into daylight with them. They were all black rats. He thought about it. The foundation was so loose that rats would keep coming in. He didn't want to use poison bait, not here, where some of Doc's patients might sicken.

He thought of the West African rat's-bane seeds he carried in waxed packets. They would work nicely. He pulled a packet out of his shirt and began spreading seed around, right on runways and entry areas, a few seeds here and there. It wasn't easy. He had to crawl into dark corners, lit only by the distant trapdoor. Above, the muffled voices of Doc and his patient drifted his way, but he couldn't make out what was being said. Not that he wanted to. He didn't much care to learn about someone's piles or clap.

Then the patient's voice caught his ear.

"She's getting impatient with that little turd, and the word's out. Get him."

"Why'd she wait so long?"

That was Doc's voice.

"He amused her for a while. Feisty. But he's stirring up her girls. How'd you figure him out, Doc?"

"Easy. I told him I wrote Denver and he suddenly lit up. I can read people well enough."

Laughter. "Here, take this. She says you earned it."

"Godalmighty, she's getting generous in her old age."

Laughter. Footsteps. Door closing.

Dink sighed. He liked Doc Cutler, or did. So Doc was the Judas who ratted on him.

And he was warned.

Chapter 21

Drago quietly loaded the rat traps, washed his hands employing a jug he kept for the purpose, headed around to the front of Doc Cutler's chambers, and entered. He just wanted to look at Doc, see the man who had betrayed him.

Cutler met him at once.

"Well, Drago, come in and let me look at those bites."

Dink followed the doctor into the examination room and unlaced his moccasins. Cutler studied the bite on the nostril and then the ones on the toes.

"Healing up," he said. "Nothing more to do. Keep those toe wounds protected."

"Well, we're even," Dink said, staring at Doc. "Nothing more I can do about your rats. The black rats under here, they'll be a problem until the whole city's cleaned up. You'll need to apply some mortar to the foundation if you want to keep them out of there. At least they're not getting into your quarters anymore."

"Foundation? Not much point in it. This building isn't built to last. About the time I fix the foundation, the mining company will be saying the ore's running out. Mining towns dry up and blow away."

"Along with the rats," Dink said. "When people go, so

do the rats. I'm done. I pulled my traps from under there and spread some West African rat's-bane. It's a seed, a natural rat-killer. It's safe for you. The stuff's imported from Africa, so it's not cheap. But you'll be satisfied."

Cutler thought about that for a moment, a frown building on his sallow forehead. "Oh. When did you do that?"

"Just now. You had a patient."

"I see. . . ." He smiled suddenly. "Well, good luck with the rats." He began fussing with his bottles.

Dink wasn't going to make it easy for Doc. "You've patched up the bites. But you've done more for me, Doc. You've helped me get started here. The town needs cleaning up. I've been working the alleys behind Yellow Rose Street where the rats are dangerous. Too many rats there. Maybe I'll save a few lives. And you've helped."

"Aw, hell, Drago."

"We can make the world a better place or not, Doc. We can help the sick, like you do, or help control filth, prevent disease and death, like me. I'm making this town a better place to live, a place where a child can play without getting bit. A place where you can buy bakery bread that doesn't have rat turds in it. That's what I'm here for. I'm sure you can feel proud of yourself, being a physician and sticking to it night and day, here where folks need you, for almost no money because your patients don't have any. A little scrip from the mines to buy necessaries, and that's it."

"Dammit, Drago."

"So maybe you have something to be proud of, Doc. You can walk away from Skeleton Gulch some day standing tall. Like you say, these towns don't last, but you can go to some good place with roots, maybe California, and look back and think you left the world a better place. You're lucky. You can like yourself. Not everyone can."

"Yeah, well I'm busy, Drago." Some angry heat rose up

in the man, reddening his face. Doc stabbed his finger toward the door.

Dink nodded and left. A backward glance revealed a crumpled Doc Cutler, staring at the sunlight, pouring through the doorway.

Dink hawed his good old horse up the steep grade to the mines. The constant lowering smoke and toxic air had cleaned every last blade of grass from the shelf where the headframes poked the azure sky. Behind the shelf, a naked brown slope, gullied by storms, lifted for half a mile into distant green foothills. Far away, faint in the great cup of heaven, he saw the eagle again, patiently circling. Beyond, an infinity away, the dark, forested slopes basked in bright summer sun.

"Stay away, eagle," he muttered.

He thought about Doc, slumped there, running a bony hand through his graying hair. It was dangerous to tamper with a man's conscience. Some men had one, some didn't. Doc did, and Dink's pointed soliloquy had shot darts into Doc's soul. Some men, confronted by their own conscience, shrank into themselves and tried to blank the trouble out of their thoughts. Others turned as deadly as vipers, ballooned up with hatred and an itch to destroy what tormented them. Doc probably wouldn't. He was a man on the take, that's all, and Skeleton Gulch was a good place to take a lot. Somewhere along the way, Doc had gotten tired of his own ideals.

Still, Dink had had warning enough, and would need to be careful. He was disappointed. Doc was a good man gone astray. Dink was angry too. Doc had betrayed him for his thirty pieces of silver. He wished he knew who had been talking to Doc; who had delivered cash. The Yellow Rose had a shadowy army.

He parked his wagon at the headframe of the Victor Mine, found a topman, and said he needed an empty ore car to bring his traps up. The man recognized him, pointed to an empty, got Dink a freshly filled carbide lamp, lit it, and told Dink to shove the one-ton car into the cage next time it came.

Dink waited for the cage, and when it came, he jammed the ore car in. Two miners joined him, silently studying Dink, who was half their size. The cage dropped sickeningly, plunged into total dark, slid to a halt at level two, where the miners got out, and then dropped hard and fast through midnight, suddenly bouncing to a halt at level three, where Dink wanted to go. He yanked the door, dropped his lamp into the ore car, slowly heaved it out of the cage, and pulled the cord. He was alone on level three, with only the friendly light of his lamp to guide him.

It took a moment to adjust, to get used to the dank air, the foul vapors rising from the pit of the shaft next to him, that place of bones and slime. Some places in mines are unbearably noisy; this place was silent, like the interior of a coffin six feet under.

He found his box traps, all loaded with rats and most of them dead. He carried them two at a time back to the ore car parked at the vestibule, and settled each burdened trap into the bottom of the car. They jumped him just as he dropped the last two traps into the car.

Six of them, big men, meaty faces, grime-and-sweat-stained, reeking of rock and powder and smoke. Two grabbed his arms, two his legs, one wrapped a thick arm around his neck, and for a moment Dink thought he would be choked to death. They lifted him easily—for miners he was nothing but a feather—and walked smoothly to the vestibule. No one said a word. Then they swung him in unison, and pitched him once again into the black void of the pit. He plummeted down into inky dark, landed again on the bones and slime, and felt the foul liquids flood over his body, defiling every pore. Far above, he heard a soft laugh and muffled words, and then blackness overtook him.

The Yellow Rose's word had gotten around.

He knew the rats in there would be on him in an instant. Before, when there was a bit of light, he had seen the rocky walls and lagging come alive with them. This time he stood straight up, standing knee-high in foul water, his feet resting on human bones.

This crew didn't know that someone else had tried this.

He remembered there was some ladder-work on one side, a way for maintenance men to get down there. It was in the timbering of the shaft. All he had to do was find it in the dark.

He felt his way carefully toward the side that opened on the vestibule above, which he could feel but not see. A rat landed on his shoulder and bit. In a rage, Dink shook it off. He felt others swimming around, nipping his canvas pants, clawing their way onto him, sudden vicious weight.

Out of nowhere one bit his left hand. He shook it spastically, throwing the little rodent off. He waded until he bumped suddenly into the side of the shaft, felt around for wood, felt only rats moving under his hand, and then wood, a horizontal board. But not a ladder.

He floundered around, feeling wildly, and then the cage dropped down, and he ducked, flattening himself, his head just above that slime. He heard the scrape of the gates, saw flashes of light, felt an ore car rumble into the cage, and heard voices. Then the cage yanked upward and it was black again.

Frantically, he felt his way around the pit, scorning rats, until at last his hands closed on wooden crossbars, the crude rungs of a ladder. He clambered up, higher, until they quit suddenly, and he found nothing but smooth lagging. He could stand there and hope the cage would clear him next time it dropped past him. If it didn't, it would scrape him off, break his bones, and cast him back into that slime. If it did clear, he had a chance, a slim chance, of making it to daylight on top of the cage. For once, he was grateful to be small.

He heard the cage fall, the cable humming. It stopped at the level above and he saw flashes of lamplight. Then it plunged again, whining down. Dink jammed himself against the lagging, turned his head sideways until his ear flattened against the wood, pressed tight as if that rotten old wood was his lover.

The cage pushed air before it, slapping air into Dink, and then rocketed past, scraping him, clawing at him, a relentless force yanking him into its maw. And then, suddenly, it was below him, halting, swinging on its woven cable. When light appeared, he found himself looking down on its tin roof. Some lifts had no roof, but this one did. There was little time. He heard ore cars sliding in and out. He lowered himself, rung by rung, until he could step onto the cold, wet sheet metal. The cage yanked upward, spilling him, and he clung to the cable anchor for all he was worth. The cage rocketed upward as fast as it had dropped, but now Dink had a floor under him. He only hoped, once he reached the headframe, that there would be room enough between the floor that supported him and the whirling pulleys above to give him breathing room—and an exit.

Chapter 22

The cage burst from the earth into blinding light. Dink blinked. It jarred to a halt, bounced, and quieted, its roof a few feet below the giant pulley that suspended the woven cable. Below him the gate clanged open, the rattle of ore cars filled the air, along with voices.

He had seconds. There was no convenient ledge, but a few feet up was a massive cross beam. He clambered onto it just as the cage plummeted downward. The cable hummed by him and the pulley whirred. Ten feet below, topmen were pushing the ore car toward the tailings dump. In the distance, basking in June sun, was his wagon and dozing nag. He spotted an access ladder on the far side of the headframe, and slowly made his way to earth while no one was watching. His legs buckled under him.

He was dripping slime. He saw no sign of the filled traps he had been putting into an ore car below when the thugs had jumped him. He had ten traps down there, probably lost for good.

He caught his breath and walked slowly toward the Victor Mine offices, a whitewashed board-and-batten structure, fifty yards distant. He was not a pretty sight, dripping the foulest-smelling slime he had ever known, muck blackening his canvas jeans and covering his moccasins and smeared over his face.

He entered, shocking the fat pale clerk, who recoiled at the sight of Dink.

"I'll see Creek," Dink said.

"Mr. Creek is in a meeting," the clerk replied. "And I don't think you would want . . ."

"In there?"

The clerk rose. "You can't go in there."

Dink ignored him, walked past the clerk, occasioning stares from the rest of the clerks, and faced the massive door. He opened it.

The room, brilliant in midday sunlight, contained a dozen black suits, penguins in boiled white shirts, silk paisley cravats, acres of broadcloth, and shoes that gleamed in the white light.

He recognized only Creek, perched behind his desk.

Creek rose suddenly, as if confronted by Banquo's ghost.

"You," he said.

"I want to be paid. Now. And you can pay me for the ten traps still down there."

"But Drago, we've no cash here and I wouldn't pay you anyway. You're not done."

"I'm done. Open that drawer, right there, where you keep the double eagles, and pay me."

Creek didn't hesitate. He rounded the desk, giving wide berth to the reeking Drago, and headed for the door.

"Throw this man out of here," he yelled.

Clerks gathered, but recoiled at the sight of Drago, dripping slime over the red Oriental carpet. Finally a larger one closed in on Drago, who refused to move.

"Hands off," Drago said. "When I'm paid, I'll leave. Until then, I'll smell up the place. You know what this is, Creek? It's slime from the bottom of the shaft, when I was knee-deep in the stuff, and standing on human bones. That's where half-a-dozen of your thugs threw me. That's where I didn't catch any rats because you didn't want me to. Now fork over and I'm out of here."

The clerk, a six-footer, grabbed Dink from behind and wrestled him out. Several others assisted, having decided it would pay off to win the approval of a dozen bosses.

Dink could scarcely resist and didn't try hard. Instead, he was memorizing faces, men he'd never seen, the top echelon of the Yellow Rose's empire, every one well paid and ruthless. Trimmed moustaches, sideburns, clipped gray hair, coifed black hair, liquid brown eyes, pursed and disapproving lips, clean manicured fingernails, close-shaven jowls, bold blue eyes, slate-gray eyes, one Vandyke beard, starched collars, flicking avaricious tongues, old school colors, woven gold watch fobs. By the time the door slammed, he knew them all. They were stamped in his brain. Every damned one. The clerks hauled him outside, threw him into the barren clay, and retreated, daintily wiping slime from themselves.

In the distance, the topmen watched the fray.

Drago picked himself up, climbed aboard his wagon, and hawed his sturdy nag away. It had been a hard day. And he was dead broke.

But there was this: He now knew the faces of those who ran Yellow Rose's empire. No names yet, but faces he could identify anywhere. That wasn't a bad day's work at that. And what he had overheard at Doc Cutler's was true: His life wasn't worth a plugged nickel.

He rattled down the grade and into Skeleton Gulch, headed for Dead Alley, drew on his work gloves, spread a bait of poisoned barley once again, repeated his task at Rat Alley, and drove off. Again, no one stayed him. A few more gallons of poisoned barley and the deadly rat population in the sporting district would diminish. He was hungry, filthy, angry, and exultant. He was closing in.

The only place where he might find help was the Starr Freight Company wagon yard, so he rattled downslope to that friendly quarter.

Starr himself was in the yard.

"Drago, you look like you crawled out of a grave."

"I did. Mind if I use your horse trough?"

"Go ahead. Empty it afterward and fill it. I'll be in my office. I want to talk to you, but not when I have to stand twenty feet away."

Drago nodded. The sunbaked yard stood empty and silent. He stripped, lowered himself into the icy water, gasped, scrubbed the muck out of his hair, and felt the sting of cold cleanliness. He was used to mucking around in crawl spaces, used to rat-crap filth, but he hoped he would never find himself in the sort of mess he had escaped. What was it about Skeleton Gulch that made it so filthy?

He emerged after getting chilled, discovered his spare clothes were still at the Chinamen's and he couldn't pay for them anyway. So he plucked the waxed packets of African rat's-bane from the pockets and plunged everything he owned into that horse trough. Then he emptied the trough by tipping it, hand-pumped another load of water to rinse with, and finally wrung his duds by hand and scraped them onto himself. Getting into soaking clothing is not easy.

He collected the wax packets, deciding to wait until he was wearing something dry, left them in his wagon, and headed for Starr's humble office.

Starr looked him over, grinned, waved toward a wooden seat. "Tell me," he said.

Dink decided to leave Doc Cutler out of it. There was a faint chance that the muffled talk Dink heard was perfectly innocent. But he described the rest in detail.

"She's after you," Starr said, leaning into his swivel chair. "She seems to have it in for you. Any reason why?"

"That sort of question could get you killed around here," Dink retorted.

Starr grinned, then turned serious. "They didn't pay you."

"No. Creek had some clerks manhandle me out of the office."

"And they won't pay you." It was a statement.

"I wasn't really done. There are rats down there. They have an excuse."

"You got something safe to use around here? No poisoned barley. It'd sicken my stock."

"West African rat's-bane, a natural rat-killer. The seed is lethal to rodents. But it costs."

"I imagine. How about selling me some? Ten dollars of it?"

"That would only buy a pound."

"Then a pound of it will be fine."

Starr's gaze held Dink, and Dink nodded. What was there about Starr that seemed so familiar? Why had Starr discerned that Dink was in trouble and needed cash?

"I'll get it," Dink said. He headed out to his wagon, feeling the sun pound his wet duds while the breeze chilled him. He extracted eight two-ounce waxed packets and returned.

"This'll take care of a lot of rats," he said. "But keep it away from your livestock."

Starr examined the waxy packets, put one in his shirt pocket, and the rest into a desk drawer.

"Why are you a rat catcher?" he asked. "Is this something you like doing?"

"Not at first. It was an accident. People needed someone my size to crawl into holes and bait traps. No, I didn't grow up wanting that."

"How did you grow up?"

"Reading and running. We were poor. My pa was a widower. I ran errands to help him. I was a delivery boy for an apothecary shop, a nickel a delivery. Sometimes I made forty or fifty cents when I ran both ways and the apothecary had a lot of compounding to do. There weren't libraries, not like now, with Carnegie building them from one end of the country to the other. But there were professors and they had books, and when I'd take some powders to one of them, they'd show me their books, and pretty soon they let me read some. I thought maybe I'd be a professor someday, but there was no money for college, and by the time I was fourteen I was on my own, and Pa was in his grave." He eyed his interrogator. "How'd you grow up? Were you always going to be a teamster?"

Starr smiled. "I grew up at sea. My pa was a captain. I worked as a cabin boy as soon as I was old enough, and all the while my pa shoved books at me. I got through the ABCs and some arithmetic, enough to keep a ledger. I hardly know the front end of a mule from its rear, but I learned how to hire men who do. I'm not a teamster, I'm a captain, like my pa. He knew the command of men, and it was something I picked up without really knowing it."

"You an only child?" Dink asked.

"No, there were others, but I was the only one sleeping in a fo'castle hammock. Here, Drago, go rescue your clean clothes from the Chinaman."

He dropped an eagle into Dink's hands. It glowed in the late light.

"And be careful, Drago," Starr added.

Chapter 23

It had been a brutal day, one that had almost destroyed him. Dink waited until ten-thirty for the shield of darkness to protect him, and hiked into town in his soggy duds, turned left, and headed for Lorena Street, that sordid corner of Skeleton Gulch where all vice was silent. There were cheap cribs, opium parlors, and burlesque there featuring nude tableaux.

There was also Hop Sing's laundry, open day and night. Dink slipped through the darkness, wary of footpads out to fleece anyone they could grab. In the Third Street block he found the laundry, lit by a single delicate lantern, and entered. A bell jangled. A woman appeared at once. Dink had never seen a woman there; only short yellow men wearing long queues, which he discovered had religious meaning to these people.

Dink realized suddenly that his laundry ticket was gone, a sodden bit of paper washed away. But he remembered the number, 207, and seeing a pencil, wrote it. The woman stared. She had a fine clear skin, a flared nose, and lovely silken hair. He wished he could see her almond eyes, but she averted her gaze. She returned in a moment, bearing a neat packet wrapped in white butcher paper, and a laundry list: trousers, drawers, shirts, stockings, linens. There were various check marks before each category. She added up the figures and said something Dink could not grasp.

She smiled suddenly and carefully wrote 78. The laundering would cost seventy-eight cents. Dink handed her the eagle. She frowned, examined both sides, and retreated into the shadowed rear of this plain and utilitarian structure, which bore not the slightest evidence of Oriental design or decor apart from the paper lantern. She returned with four dollars, a heap of Victor Mine scrip that totaled five dollars, and a two-bit piece. Seventy-five cents then. He accepted the scrip, not really wanting it. At least it was valid in town.

He gestured toward a curtained booth and she nodded. He pulled the curtain, broke open the parcel, and was struck by the acrid smell of fresh clothing. In moments he changed, enjoying the soft fabric over his body, left his wet duds with her, and carried the rest of his clothing into the night. A rat catcher needed a lot of clean clothing.

She waited for him to leave and then vanished into the dark confines of her home.

He walked quietly past an open door half a block away. The strange sweet scent of narcotic smoke wafted past him. He paused, wondering who was in there resting on some shelf, staring into space, lost in some furtive paradise that always betrayed the fugitive wandering there. There were so many ways to die, some of them pleasant, and that was one.

He walked back to the wagon yard, dark now, and left his clothing in his wagon. The lamp in Starr's cubicle was extinguished. It had been a hard day but Dink didn't feel like sleeping. Not yet. He filled his pockets with the waxen packets of African rat's-bane, and headed into the night, mostly to see whether his poisoned barley had cut into the rat population in the alleys.

If what he had overheard while under Doc Cutler's office was true, he was a wanted man. The Yellow Rose wished to be shut of him. He would be careful. That's where his smallness helped. He was good at slipping through darkness unobserved. He was utterly alone now; the hope of cultivating friends and allies had vanished this day. He probably would trust Starr, but no one else in all of Skeleton Gulch.

His narrow escape that morning had stirred something in him. He must get the goods, act fast. The clock was ticking. Every minute he remained in Skeleton Gulch, he was in mortal peril. There were new questions. This morning he had confronted a dozen men in black suits and silk cravats. These were the Yellow Rose's trusted managers. Where did they live? He had not seen a single house suitable for these sorts in all of Skeleton Gulch, a place of jerry-built stores and mining shacks and a few original log buildings, all of them small and nondescript. He would try to find the rich men's quarter this moonless night, and on the way home, check Death Alley.

He enjoyed the walk, dressed now in comfortable clothing, and intuitively headed up the slope toward the Yellow Rose's parlor house. But he didn't stop there. Beyond was the mouth of a foothills valley not visible from the heart of Skeleton Gulch, and when he softly approached that mouth, he grew aware of a wooden fence across it, and what might be a guardhouse. He slowly filtered upslope, off the road, until he could get a better view into the gulch, and there, as he expected, were seven or eight substantial houses, mostly clapboard, one or two board-and-batten, all of them with plenty of gingerbread and broad verandas. A guarded area for the elite. For the bosses, if they could be called that. Given the amount of casual murder and rapine of strangers, it might be called a criminal enclave. So Skeleton Gulch wasn't just a hodge-podge of mining shacks.

Lamps lit a few windows up there, but most of the homes bulked dark and silent. He slowly retreated, sticking to deep shadow, and headed into town. In sunlight, he would climb some slopes nearby with field glasses and study who and what lived in the gulch behind the Yellow Rose's parlor house.

He drifted back into town. On the bench above, the clatter of the mines never ceased, and occasionally choking yellow smoke from the stamp mill boiled over him, making him hold his breath as long as he could. Skeleton Gulch had various ways of killing its inhabitants and the smoke was not the least of them.

He thought about the managers living their sequestered lives back there in a guarded gulch, carefully separated from the hurly-burly mining town. Was it because they were afraid of the mobs below? Was it because they wished to be invisible? Skeleton Gulch was a town loaded with nameless people, nameless streets, everything unmapped and unknown. There was safety in that if one was engaged in dark deeds. The virtuous could live in sunlight. The very nature of that hidden enclave said everything.

He drifted toward Dead Alley, the one behind Traveler's Rest and other saloons. It was late and a chill breeze out of the peaks was cutting the warmth out of him as he slipped along, listening to the sounds of fiddles, and hoarse laughter, and was it the sound of sobbing from a window?

He was not conscious of rats, though it was too dark to say for sure, and their odor permeated every square inch of soil, every foundation, every half-dead bush, every rock. He froze, watched a drunk urinate, lamplight silhouetting him, and then the alley was bleak again. He reached the rear of the Golden Hind, one of the fancier joints, if anything in Skeleton Gulch could be called fancy.

A gambling parlor mostly, where tubercular tinhorns dealt off the bottom of grimy decks of marked cards. A place of pretense, with cut-glass chandeliers supporting six smoking coal-oil lamps.

Then he saw the lump before him, someone alive and thrashing slowly, great oaths spewing from his lips. Drunk maybe, or another victim of a Mickey Finn. There were rats, some kept at bay by the thrashing arms, some darting in for a bite of the man's cheeks or ears.

"Damn you, damn you," the man rumbled, wallowing in the alley filth.

There weren't very many rats; not like the hundreds, thousands, that had devoured anything edible in days gone by. Dink peered about sharply, looking for footpads who might jump him and make a pile of two bodies out of the evening. A dim glow from the Golden Hind's sole small window facing rear cast lurid yellow light over the scene.

Dink trotted forward, found the man cussing softly, knocking rats right and left. A big man, bigger than Dink could carry.

And familiar.

"Doc. Get up fast. Right now."

"Wha . . ."

"I'll help you. Now make yourself get up."

But Doc Cutler couldn't manage. He rolled, tried to rise, tumbled into the filth.

"Doc, crawl. Follow me. Keep on moving. I'll chase the rats off."

Cutler stared, dazed. Slowly his energies focused.

"You," he said.

Doc rolled over onto his belly, managed to get up onto all fours, and crabbed along until he was out of lamplight and in deep dark, and then collapsed.

Dink could see rats gathering. Not many. His poisoned barley had scythed through their numbers. But enough to make Doc deadly ill, even if he survived the bloodletting.

Dink saw a patch of yard away from the gambling joints.

"Crawl there, Doc. I'll help."

Dink half-dragged, half-lifted Doc through the muck and manure and broken glass in the alley, his small frame straining at the task of moving a large man. He was winded in a minute. But at last Doc was tucked away from the alley, in a barren patch of yard.

"Doc, this is Drago. I'm getting my wagon. I'm going to get you out of here. I'm going to give you a stick, and you swing it at anything that moves. There's still rats. Enough to kill you."

Doc grunted. Dink found a piece of fence and handed it to Doc. "Keep on breathing deep, Doc. They gave you a Mickey and tossed you out."

Doc was breathing heavily, drained of the last of his energy but alert. Several rat bites bled freely.

"I'll be back in ten minutes. Have to harness."

"Drago," Cutler said, but then shut up.

"Be very quiet. Don't open your mouth. Don't give yourself away. You're half-hidden."

Doc grunted.

Dink trotted toward the wagon yard, almost as filthy now as when he was pulling himself out of the mine shaft. What sort of town was Skeleton Gulch to make such filth faster than nature could wash it away?

He reached the wagon yard, threw harness over his dray horse, hooked it to his wagon, and started back. It had taken twenty minutes, not ten. He parked at the cross street, Fifth, and scouted before driving in. But it was late now, quiet, and the night sky had vanished under a massive layer of cloud.

Doc was sitting up, swinging the stick softly at a seething

congregation of rats, cursing them in language largely unemployed by the medical profession. Dink managed to get Doc up to the seat beside him, and headed for Doc's house. Dink knew that this time, he would play the doctor.

Chapter 24

Doc was raving. Ahead, trouble loomed. Some hooligans emerged from the black shadows, ready to grab the harness. Dink snapped the whip across the nag's croup, the wagon lurched forward, and Dink lashed at the lowlifes as they tried to stop the wagon.

The whip cracked over one's neck, evoking a howl. Another began trotting alongside the wagon, leering, trying to pull Doc off.

Doc roared, and shoved, and the hooligan tumbled behind. Then suddenly the wagon was free and Dink steered it out of the alley and across Yellow Rose Street, running recklessly into deep dark silence.

"Bloody bastards," Cutler yelled. He was still waving his arms, half demented from the Mickey Finn.

Blood dripped from a patchwork of rat bites, and he cursed softly.

"Take me home, Drago, you sonofabitch."

Drago did, trotting recklessly through dark streets unlit by any lamp. He pulled up beside Doc's chambers, set the brake, and helped Doc out. The man tried to walk on rubbery legs and tumbled to the earth. Dink tried to lift him.

"Leave me be, dammit," Doc roared, and then gasped for breath.

Dink saw him crawling toward the door, so he opened it, let Doc in, and finally helped him up on the examination table.

"Light that lamp. Get the bottle of whiskey over there," Doc ordered.

Dink fumbled around, found a lucifer in a capped porcelain jar, and lit the lamp. Doc lay there, bleeding in a dozen places, especially around the face. His eyes had the wild look of the demented and he was puffing.

"Hurry, dammit. I should horsewhip you. Clean the rat bites with whiskey. Hard. Rub it in."

Dink found the bottle of red-eye and a cloth while Doc fumbled with his shirt buttons, and finally, violently, yanked the shirt off himself with almost superhuman strength.

Dink poured whiskey into a cloth and approached. "This'll sting, Doc."

"No more than a rat bite, and hurry up, you little turd."

Dink washed each wound with whiskey while Doc roared and howled. There were plenty of wounds around the neck.

"Pour it on, Drago, rub it in, scrub, scrub! Soak every bite."

Dink did, by the small yellow light of the coal-oil lamp, soaking every wound while Doc grunted and growled, spasmed and jerked.

"You get bit in the pants, Doc?"

"How should I know?"

"Better drop your trousers."

"Give me the bottle, Drago."

Dink handed him the brown bottle of red-eye, and

Doc pulled his belt forward and poured whiskey down his belly, patting the booze into every crevice.

"What about your legs?"

"Well, what about 'em?"

Doc growled, and lowered his pants, revealing long white drawers. There were only a couple of bites, both on calves, and Dink washed them with booze.

"What does the whiskey do?" Dink asked.

"It sanitizes. Maybe it'll stop rat-bite fever. I'm a follower of Pasteur. There's microbes too small to be seen with the eye that cause fevers. Lister's had success with carbolic spray. He can operate without a patient getting infected. Clean everything! Clean it with alcohol."

Dink washed Doc's legs and smelly feet with the whiskey on general principles. There were, all told, nineteen or twenty bites.

"How long were you there in the alley, Doc?"

"How the hell should I know?"

"When did you go into the Golden Hind?" Dink wanted to ask why, but didn't.

"How should I know. Early. I intended to get drunk. That's because of you, Drago. Getting drunk was the only thing left after what you did to me."

"What did I do?"

"Just shut up."

Dink didn't. Doc lay there on the table, breathing hard, still woozy from the Mickey, his face red, his rage brimming and boiling.

"I put a lot of rat poison in that alley, Doc. A few nights ago you would have bled to death in an hour, been eaten alive in the space of five or six hours. A pile of bones. You've got, let's see, nineteen bites. Not ten thousand."

"What am I supposed to do, thank you?"

"No, I'll thank myself. Someone thrown into that alley

has a chance now," Dink said. "What happened in the saloon? Did anyone know you?"

"Not a soul. I never go there. I ordered a double of Kentucky and got served up and that's when the light went out."

"So you were another stranger to roll. And a few drops of chloral hydrate did the job. You lose money?"

"Dammit, how should I know?"

Dink dug through the fouled clothing, finding nothing.

"Nothing here. How much were you carrying?"

"None of your damned business, Drago."

"Enough for a good drunk."

"Go to hell, Drago. And wipe down those bites again. I'm feeling hot."

Doc looked fevered. Dink put a hand to his forehead and found it burning. Maybe Doc was in grave trouble after all. Dink began dabbing at those bites again. Most had quit bleeding and crusted over.

"Drago, I'm damned sick. And it's all your fault. I should be dead. A pile of bones."

Doc wallowed off the table, stumbled toward a corner where a bucket rested under a counter, hunched over it, and threw up with huge, rolling spasms that rose out of his gut. Dink gagged, quieted his own stomach, and helped Doc wobble to his feet.

"There," Doc said, aiming toward a darkened room at the rear of the chambers. Doc headed through darkness and tumbled into his bed.

Dink got the lamp so he could see, and helped Doc pull a sheet over himself.

"You want cold compresses, Doc?"

"Just stay here. Damn you six ways to Sunday, Drago, you almost killed me, and maybe you did."

Baffled, Dink didn't reply.

"The Golden Hind, that's one of her places, full of tinhorns and green tables. I shouldn't have gone in."

"Why did you?"

"Because of you, Drago, because of what you said, that I'm a good self-sacrificing doctor. It wasn't true, damn you. I'm no damned good. I thought I had it figured out. Make a pile and get out of this godforsaken place. All figured out. I've got seven thousand banked. Blood money. Make a deal with her, feed her anything she needed to know, get paid for it."

"Like?"

"Like who the Denver detective agency was sending here. I told her it was you, Drago. I told her, I ratted on you, and it was worth a thousand to tell her. I pretend not to know what happened to those poor bastards. And then you went and reminded me of what a swine I am. You didn't say it. You just said I was some sort of saint, helping people around here with little reward. So all I could do was get drunk, and that's how you killed me maybe."

Doc was crying. Big tears welled in his eyes. Dink headed for the water bucket, found a clean towel, brought the bucket and the towel into the dimly lit room, and began applying cold compresses to Doc's forehead.

"I mean to get you past the fever, Doc."

"Goddamned rat catcher."

"You weren't in touch with General Cook? You didn't ask for an agent?"

"Hell, no. Someone else around here is. I said that about writing him myself to lure you out."

Dink dipped the compress into cold water and applied it to Doc again. "Who's in touch with the Rocky Mountain Detective Agency?"

"Damned if I know. I could get two thousand from her for the answer to that."

"But you won't."

"Goddamn it, if I spend the rest of my life giving free medicine to poor people, I won't make it up."

"Doc, you already made a big start."

"I'm done for."

"No, you're going to do fine. You won't be at war with yourself."

Doc was swiftly settling into sleep.

"Drago," he mumbled. "Thank you."

"You're welcome."

"And damn you to hell and back."

Dink changed the compress once more as Doc slipped into silence. Then again. Then weariness overwhelmed him too. He turned down the wick until the flame blued out, made sure the front door was locked, slipped out the back door and into a chill starry night.

The horse whickered.

Dink clambered on board, pulled the brake lever, and hawed the horse. The clop of hooves in the wee hours of the morning had an oddly pleasant sound, as if the night air turned noise into the music of castanets. Dink reached the Starr Freight Company yards in pitch darkness, and only the instinct of the horse saved him from missing the turn. He pulled harness off the nag and shooed it into a pen with a water trough, and then crawled into the back of his wagon.

Never was a bedroll so welcome. This day he had almost died when he was thrown down a shaft into a cesspool. This day he had escaped doom, burst into an office filled with the enforcers and bosses and cohorts of the Yellow Rose, memorized their faces, and found the enclave where they lived apart from the tawdry flats of Skeleton Gulch. This day he had befriended John Starr, a man he liked and trusted. And this day he had, in the morning, said something to Doc that stung his conscience, and this night he had rescued Doc from death, doctored him, and listened to the painful confession of a repentant man.

It was a day's work, all right.

Chapter 25

In the morning, Doc Cutler's face was so swollen that Dink barely recognized him. Doc lay abed, suffering from a score of rat bites around his neck and ears and cheeks.

Dink pressed a hand to Doc's forehead and found fever there.

"I'll put on some compresses," he said.

"Water, Drago."

Dink found the bucket empty and headed for the backyard, where he jacked a pump and filled a pail of fresh cold water. He carried it to the kitchen, drew some water with a dipper, and filled a glass.

"Here, Doc, can you sit up?"

Doc struggled to sit abed, and slowly sipped the cold water.

"I never knew water to be so good," he said.

"Food?"

"Not hungry."

Doc sipped again. "Drago, why are you here? Why bother with me?"

"For the same reason you bothered with a few hundred people who needed you."

"They could pay, some company scrip, a spare chicken, something like that. I can't pay you. Not ever."

"You already have paid me."

"Damn you, Drago."

Dink removed the compress, rinsed it in cold water, and laid it gently over Doc's forehead.

"You'll be all right in a day or two, Doc."

"I'll never be all right again."

Someone rattled the locked front door.

"Don't answer," Doc said. "I'm not open for business."

Dink checked. Whoever had wanted Doc's attention had drifted away.

"Not much use to anyone today."

Dink sensed that Doc wanted to talk. "Do you treat those women in Yellow Rose's parlor house?" he asked.

"She doesn't believe in doctors. Especially for those women. But I've been summoned a few times anyway."

"There are some rat holes around town, and one of them is in there. She boasts about it. If a girl complains, she gets thrown into the hole and eaten alive."

Doc sighed. "That's the Yellow Rose, the woman I took money from."

"There's a way you can help, Doc. Next time you get called up there, I want you to slip a few packets of seed to them. It's West African rat's-bane, and it's lethal to rats. I want them to toss the seed into that rat hole, not once, but often."

"Count on me."

"I'll leave a few packets. It's expensive and hard to get, so don't waste it. The girls in the cribs in town get the same treatment from her bullies. There's a rat hole or two down on Yellow Rose Street. Maybe you can slip them some of the rat's-bane too."

"They never see a doctor, Drago."

"Well, find a way to treat them if you can."

Doc stared at him through slits of eyes. "You can't tackle her alone and win."

"I'll have an ally now, Doc."

"An ally." Doc wheezed unhappily. "Some ally."

"You're what I need, Doc."

"Do you know what you're up against? She has dozens of lieutenants who will instantly do whatever she asks. If she wants someone dead, that person dies. If she wants a merchant shut down, that merchant vanishes. If she wants territory officials or tax collectors out, they disappear. If she wants to hurt someone, she calls on someone who can break bones, cut flesh, knock in heads, crush toes, bust knees, and of course feed anyone to the rats. Feed you, Drago, to the rats. Let them eat you alive, bite by bite by bite."

"We'll change that, Doc."

"And feed me to the rats too, Drago. I'm joining the losing side now. I was on the winning side. I'll end up one more pile of bones for Kilgore to jam into a barrel."

"You up to answering some questions for me?"

"I'm not up to anything."

"Well, I'll ask them anyway. Why does the Yellow Rose try so hard to be bad, to glory in it, to flaunt it? She wants the whole world to know she's the worst human being ever born, and she tries to live up to it. Maybe she is, Doc. But why?"

Doc didn't reply, but Dink sensed that behind those slit eyes and that puffed-up face, wheels and cogs were turning.

"Guilt," he said. "Something a woman schooled in a convent would do."

"Convent? Are you sure?"

"Not necessarily a convent, Drago, but there's a famous one in New Orleans, one where lots of young ladies were schooled. And she's from New Orleans."

"Shreveport, I think, from the accent. But guilt?"

"Well, dammit, you asked me and I told you," Doc snarled.

Dink backed off. "I'll just listen," he muttered.

"Well, I'm not talking. You just get the hell out and leave me alone."

Doc closed his eyes and shut Dink out. Dink waited for a while, saw that Doc Cutler was not going to budge, and then Dink quietly backed off, straightened up the kitchen, and went out the rear door. The yellow smoke from the mill lowered over Skeleton Gulch this morning, blotting the sun, bleaching the blue sky, fouling the lungs of everyone there.

He stood in the hazy street, knowing he had come to a crossroads. He could report what he found to General Cook and let the agency take over. He knew the name of the spider at the center of the web, could identify some of her lieutenants, knew where the bodies were buried, knew there had been multiple murders, white slavery, thuggery, brutal treatment of strangers, and much more.

He knew that the Territory of Montana had somehow been kept at bay, and the criminals ran Skeleton Gulch without hindrance. He knew that the previous agents sent by the Rocky Mountain Detective Agency had been discovered and murdered. He knew that those who joined the racketeering outfit as privates and corporals and sergeants were paid well for their services, while those who resisted vanished. He knew the gold from the mines probably didn't leave Skeleton Gulch, at least most of it, but was locked in a vault. He knew that his own life was in peril; that word was out to pick him up and kill him.

He could turn his wagon around and ride out of town. He could head down the road and be safe. He could drive to Helena and send a coded wire that would result in swift action by the detective agency, with maybe federal marshals and other figures in on it.

Or he could stay, try to find out more, and take risks. He thought about it and chose risk. There were plenty of things about all this that he didn't know; things that only the Yellow Rose could answer.

It was not yet nine in the morning, an hour when hard-living Skeleton Gulch was at its lowest ebb. It might be a good hour to find out some things up at the parlor house. He poked around the rear of his wagon, stuffed some packets of West African rat's-bane seed into his pockets, and then drove the coughing horse slowly up the grade to the parlor house, which was enveloped in yellow smoke, lowering down from the mill on the shelf above.

He parked before the silent building, aware that the poor inmates were snatching whatever sleep they could before their mistress forced them into more darkness. He set the brake, eyed the unhappy horse, which had tears in its eyes from the acrid smoke, and decided not to stay long. He was banking on something: The Yellow Rose would be asleep.

He walked in, triggering a small tinkling bell, and moments later a sleepy nymph appeared silently, forced a painful smile, beckoned. Her eyes were black pits.

"Sweetheart, I'll fetch all the girls if you want, or you can find your delights right here."

He eyed her. She looked forty but was probably half that age, and the smile was something painted over her sadness. She showed no sign of rat bite, and probably had tried hard to please the impossible madam. But her fate would be to die soon, just as most of the others had vanished. And she would know what it meant to be dinner to a voracious rodent.

"Bar open?"

"Noon, sweetheart, but I can pour you anything you want."

"I guess it's not a good hour."

"Oh, we're always open, and always happy to see you."

There was something singsong in this rote expression of hospitality.

"You get any sleep?"

"I never need sleep, sweetheart. Now how about letting me show you a good time. A very good time."

"Who's the madam here?"

The slightest pause. "She's asleep. But I can get one of her assistants, Jake Noise."

"Pour me some whiskey, okay?"

"Glad to, hon." She steered her way toward the saloon. Her gauzy robe let morning sunlight through, highlighting the almost visible flesh beneath it. She knew it, and paused in the light of the sole window. Then, coquettishly, she smiled.

She lifted a brown bottle.

"I rather like fresh whiskey from a new bottle," he said.

"Whatever you want, hon," she said. She dug under the bar, and pulled out a corked bottle and showed it to him. The red-eye had no label at all. He didn't trust it, but a small sip or two should tell him what he needed to know.

She smiled and poured a generous dollop of it.

"You want branch, hon?"

He nodded. She added water, employing a dipper.

"Ah, a dollar, hon."

That was a lot of money for a ten-cent shot. He dug that much scrip out of his britches. She smiled. Sunlight from the sole window caught her gauzy gown and pierced it, revealing the shadows of heavy breasts. She caught him looking and smiled.

"Ever make love in daylight, hon?"

"I'll enjoy the booze while I think about it."

"How about right on top of the bar? I'd squeal, I think."

Dink laughed. He sipped tentatively and felt no sudden response. He sipped again. The booze was safe.

What a hell of a thing it was to have to check your booze for chloral hydrate every time.

"You been here long?"

"Not long enough, hon. I'm just so happy."

"Six months?"

She eyed him now, assessing. She had soft eyes, innocent eyes, of a color he couldn't determine. "Not that long," she said.

"I'll buy you a drink," he said.

"Oh, aren't you sweet." She reached for another bottle and poured some tea-colored liquid into a glass.

He slid another scrip dollar to her.

The place was eerily quiet. He wondered how long he might have before the place awakened from its slumbers.

"Here's to you, sweetheart. What's your name?"

"Cherry."

"I mean your real name."

"Drink up," she said. "I'll always be Cherry."

"Were you married?"

She eyed him uneasily. "No questions."

"You in it for laughs?"

"I'm in it to make you happy," she said.

That's when Bruno, or Hugo, or whatever the name, suddenly emerged from the shadows.

Chapter 26

The pug bellied up to the bar.

Dink noticed the man's massive hands. They weren't smooth. They had been lacerated, the finger flesh was chevroned and knobbed. The fingers and wrists were checkered, dull fish-belly white and red. Could it be rat bites?

"Hey, Jake, this here's a customer," Cherry said, sipping her tea-filled whiskey glass.

"Actually, Jake, I'm a drummer. I represent the Acme Rat Trap Company, and I've come to sell you a product that you need worse'n anything else in the world. Yes, sir, you've got big trouble right here in Skeleton Gulch, and I've got just the item on my wagon to solve your problems."

"See?" she said, eyeing Jake.

The pug smiled slowly, anticipation building. It was no match. Never in Dink's life was he given an even match. This pug was two feet taller and weighed twice as much and had more muscles than he needed to lift a carriage by the axle.

"Yes, sir, it's me, and I've come to sell you rat traps. Do you know, sir, that you have rats in this fine edifice? That rats cause disease? Do you know, sir, that rats bring the black plague, and the plague kills whatever it touches, and the plague might kill you? Do you know, sir, that the Acme Rat Trap is the solution, that a few of these babies, properly baited, can guarantee, I say *guarantee*, the health of your lovely ladies, and your own? Do you know, sir, that the bite of a stray rat may be fatal? That just by living in an unprotected building like this, you are risking your very life every moment of every hour of every day?"

"You," he said. "The rat man."

"Friend, have you rats under your bed? Rats in your attic? Rats biting you at night? You need the Acme, the dandiest, sweetest little rat catcher in the Far West. Just think: You can sleep all night without sweat, without thinking about rats. That's what the Acme does."

"Zat so?"

"Now, the Acme trap is a bargain, at nine ninety-nine, that's less than ten dollars, one little eagle, and for that you receive a guarantee that it'll keep you free of rats. You have a bed somewhere? You bait this trap, you set it up near where you seek repose, and you will discover that the next morning there will be rats in the Acme Trap, rats that didn't bite you. Now just as a special, this time only, I'm willing to sell you the genuine Acme Rat Trap for seven and a half dollars, that's one-fourth off, just seven and a half dollars, along with clear instructions in plain English, and for that you'll be assured of a long life and an escape from plague. For only seven and a half dollars, friend, you can sleep easy even while the plague sweeps through this building, cleans out every room. Yes, sir, I can smell rats. You've got trouble in the house of the Yellow Rose, right here in Skeleton Gulch."

The big galoot studied Drago.

"What do I bait it with, runt?"

"Anything you want, friend. That's the beauty of the Acme. If it smells a little rank, all the better. Put one in your room, and feel the difference. It's like the fountain of youth. With an Acme in your bedroom, all women love you. They'll be knocking at your door."

Drago watched those thick, wounded fingers drub the battered top of the bar, over and over, and then they stopped.

"Get me one," said Jake.

Dink nodded, slid off his bar stool, headed into the sunlight, pulled a trap from his wagon bed, and returned.

"Here you are, Jake. This one can hold ten, twelve rats. You open the top here, with these wing nuts, and put some bait in that metal dish there, and next morning there's some rats for you to get rid of. You'll sleep better."

The goon pulled an eagle from his pants. Pure gold.

"Spend it on me, hon," said Cherry. "I'm worth it."

"Next time, Cherry," said Dink. "I'll spend it all. You're the cherry of my life. You're the queen of the Yellow Rose."

She pouted a little, eyed the trap sadly, and sipped her tepid tea.

Jake picked up the trap, eyed it suspiciously, and saw how it worked. It was a wire box with a one-way chute into it. Once the rat dropped off the end of the chute to get at the bait, he was caught.

"This been used," Jake said.

"That's right, my friend. Every Acme Rat Trap has been tested to make sure that it catches rats. I will guarantee that none escape. Why, I can guarantee that every Acme Trap catches rats if used properly and according to directions. Now, friend, let me buy you a whiskey and branch just to let you know that a good drummer makes a friend out of each customer."

Jake stared at Dink, grunted, and vanished into the nether regions of the Yellow Rose's parlor house, a subversive box in his hand.

"Cherry," Dink said. "You got rats, so you just very quietlike spread a little of this seed around and keep it quiet. You take a few of these packets, and where there's lots of rats, you toss some seed. It's rat's-bane, an African seed, and it'll do the trick."

"You aren't going to have some fun with me?"

She was trying very hard, afraid of what might befall her if she didn't try hard.

"Not at nine or ten in the morning, sweetheart." He smiled. "But I'll ask for you next time."

She started to say something with an edge to it and then shut up. Dink pressed three of the seed packets into her hand. She eyed them suspiciously, her lips pressed tight.

"They kill just rats?" she asked.

Dink instantly regretted giving her any. "They're lethal for rats," he said, "but they can sicken livestock a bit. Might be hard on a dog or a cat maybe. So be careful not to feed the cat."

And hard on any living animal that ate the seeds.

Cherry stared darkly, through eyes set in black holes in her face, accepted the waxen packets, and nodded.

"You want more seed, you ask for Dink, the rat catcher," he said.

Cherry was rubbing her thighs, fooling with her gauzy nightgown, licking her lips. He pitied her; he pitied every inmate imprisoned in this grim place.

Dink thought he'd better get out while he could. If the Yellow Rose showed up, he'd probably end up in the rat hole himself.

"Next time, Cherry," he said.

She pouted. He slid out the door into sunlight. The yellow smoke was pouring over the house, the town, the valley, a grim opaque haze shrouding Skeleton Gulch and obscuring the blue sky.

He steered his wheezing nag down the grade and into the gloomy town, depressed by the whole place. Skeleton Gulch exploited every chink in human armor, wormed every cent out of everyone with cash, snuffed life out of everyone who wandered into town, kept its heaped-up gold in a vault, buried its victims in barrels, silently, softly, with never a hurrah. That was the mark of this place: Everything was hidden and quiet. It was not a wild town. There were no crowds of miners or cowboys hurrahing Skeleton Gulch. There were no shots in the night, the local jail wasn't filled up with drunk and disorderly miners, there were no church bells. Its sin was secret and sullen, the opium-eaters on their dark shelves, the saloons as quiet as cemeteries, the whores as furtive and desperate as their clients. And over the town rested a yellow smoke that choked the life out of everyone in it.

Dink had never been in a town like this one. Nothing resembled Skeleton Gulch. Most mining camps were wild, happy places, with the sounds of pianos and fiddles cascading into the lanes, with good humor ricocheting along the bars, laughter, an occasional fistfight for spice, and the rattle of roulette wheels spinning. But not Skeleton Gulch. Rowdiness is noisy, but evil is silent. Real evil is shadowed and dark and furtive. Dink knew that Skeleton Gulch was the most evil place he had ever been to, maybe the most evil place on earth.

Dink drove slowly down Middle Street, letting the nag pick its way through the choking smoke. Then he heard shouts, saw men running, a whole posse of them racing down the slope toward the lower edge of town.

One beefy citizen wheezed past him.

"What's the trouble?" Dink asked.

"Vanishing Jack!" the man replied.

"Where is he?"

"Around here somewhere. He brought two loads of ore to the mill. They paid him with company scrip. Now everyone's after him. Say, can I get a ride?"

"Sure," Dink said. The red-faced gent clambered onto the seat, and Dink hawed the coughing nag.

"Gotta get to the livery barn."

"You going after him?"

"There's a reward this time. Yellow Rose wants him."

"How much?"

"Five hundred."

"You figure you can tail him?"

"Sometime he's gonna make a mistake. Someone's gonna find out where that mine is. This time they paid for his ore with company scrip, so he's gotta spend it here."

"You figure you can catch up with a seasoned prospector?"

"It's worth a try, pal."

"How often does Vanishing Jack show up?"

"Who the hell knows?"

There were few saddle horses in Skeleton Gulch. This was a mining camp, not a cow town. Men rode in and out by wagon or stage.

Men flocked down the street, headed for the barn where they hoped to rent a nag.

"They're going to chase after Vanishing Jack without getting a kit together? Food? Bedroll? Slicker?"

"Lissen, friend, these that are after Vanishing Jack, they grew up in Hell's Kitchen, places like that. They'll keep on going until they get him."

Dink knew he was talking to a pug utterly innocent of wilderness skills. Most of them would return in a day, half-frozen, soaked, exhausted, and starved. Not a few would end up injured. Others would wreck their horses and owe the livery barn some cash.

"What do you do?" Dink asked.

"A barkeep is what I am, at the Traveler's Rest."

Dink stared at the man. The pug's straight jet hair was parted in the center. A web of veins added a redness to the man's pallor. He was still puffing from his trot to the livery stable. If this was the sort of hound pursuing Vanishing Jack, the prospector would have little trouble. But Dink guessed there were far better men renting saddle horses, gathering kits and arms, collecting some chow, and heading upslope to the mill to try to pick up the trail of two mules and a saddle horse.

Dink slowed the nag when he reached the barn and the pug jumped off without a thank-you. A swarm of men inside the yard were saddling, shouting, dickering, coughing. A vagrant mountain wind whipped away the yellow smoke and Dink caught the sight of a solitary man above the rocky shelf where the headframes rose, riding away into the vast wilderness, two unburdened mules behind him. There was not a pursuer in sight.

Chapter 27

Smoke obscured the lone prospector for a while, but an eddying mountain wind blew a window in the sky, and Dink watched Vanishing Jack climb higher and higher and then vanish behind a ridge. No one followed. Not yet anyway. There would be clear tracks up there and in a while a mob would be riding hell for leather.

It was all a mystery. Who was he, and why did he bring his fabulous ore to a notorious town? Dink ached to see the man once again, but the whirling yellow smoke from the mill boiler obscured the high country and he couldn't see whether a mob had saddled up and followed.

This was a mining camp. Dink had scarcely seen a saddle horse since he arrived. He had seen plenty of dray horses and ox teams and trotters harnessed to buggies and long strings of mules hitched to high-walled freight wagons, but not any saddlers. There weren't even hitch rails in front of the saloons and stores. A mining camp couldn't get up a posse in moments the way a cow town might. Maybe Vanishing Jack was counting on that.

Dink thought he might try John Starr again. The freighting company operator seemed to know more about Skeleton Gulch than anyone else, and he wasn't telling all he knew. But first things first. Dink turned his coughing nag toward the steep grade leading up to the mines and the mill and let it pick its weary way upslope through the acrid yellow haze. He hated to burden the nag, but there were questions that cried for answers. He watched sweat foam around the nag's withers as it tackled the grade, and knew he was pushing his old plug too hard. He and his plug went back a long way to a time when both were young.

He reached the small flat where the mill stood, feeling the ground shake beneath him as the twenty huge stamps thundered up and down, crushing quartz to powder. The roar and thump of the mill pervaded the whole town, and one came to believe that the quartz mill was like a heart. When it stopped beating, so would Skeleton Gulch.

He found a few fox-faced men milling about, trying to separate the hoofprints of Vanishing Jack's stock from the thousands that dimpled the dust there. They wouldn't have much luck, Dink thought. The pursuers were mostly pasty-fleshed saloon men, some with grimy white shirts, black sleeve garters, and green eyeshades, a slimy green cigar stub jammed between thick lips. They were the least likely bunch of manhunters Dink had ever imagined. But there they were, lusting to capture Vanishing Jack, lusting for the chase, lusting for . . . the five hundred dollars promised by the Yellow Rose.

Their indifferent gazes dismissed Dink with a glance, which was fine. He steered his weary nag to the office door, set the wagon brake, and slipped to the ground.

The spartan mill office reeked of acrid chemicals that offended Dink's throat. Some bored clerks hunched over ledgers.

He waited patiently until it became plain that no one among these clerks wished to be bothered and they were all making a point of it. He chose the biggest and most slack-jawed of the lot, pushed through a spindle gate, and headed for the man's warren on the far edge of the bull pen, where he hunched over a rolltop.

"I'm Drago. You probably know me," Dink said, guessing the man didn't. "I'll ask a few questions. I want good smart answers. Be sure to get it right. Every detail counts."

The clerk set down a stubby pencil, surveyed Drago, and grunted. "Who are you?"

"I'm asking the questions here and I want good answers and they'd better be true." He stared unblinking at the jowly accountant with the dark stubble covering his jaws. "What does Vanishing Jack look like?"

"Vanishing Jack? I dunno, hard to say."

"What does he do when he comes here?"

"Why should I tell you? I don't know you."

"You're about to. I'm Drago. Does that mean anything or not? It'd better mean something. Understand? I always get answers for my clients. Do you know who my clients are? You'd better."

The porky clerk eyed Drago from under hooded eyelids. Something seemed to click in his mind and he sagged slightly. "Oh, him. The prospector. He arrives any hour of any day. His ore's in canvas bags. He always has four bags, two on a mule. We weigh the bags and give him a receipt."

"For what?"

"For so many pounds of ore."

"Then what?"

"We mill the ore. Man, Drago, that's good ore. Maybe yields five hundred worth of gold. We deduct our percent and pay him."

"While he waits?"

"No, he never waits. It takes a day to custom-mill. We pay him for his previous load."

"Who pays him?"

"I do. He hands me the receipt; I look up the last

transaction. So much gold at eighteen an ounce, minus our milling charge."

"How do you pay him?"

"Gold coin or bills. This last time with company scrip, because I was told to. He didn't like it."

"So he has scrip to spend here?"

The man shrugged. "Nowhere else to spend it. It ain't worth beans in Helena."

"He's tall, they say. How tall?"

"Lot taller than you or me."

"Hair color?"

"Now that's a strange thing. One time I thought he was fair; next time black-haired. Once I swear he was red-haired."

"Beard?"

"No, but some gray stubble, like he scrapes his chin once every two weeks. He's weathered like old leather. His hide, it's seen the sun and wind, all right. His hands, they've swung a pick and lifted rock."

"How often does he come?"

The doughy clerk thought and shrugged. "Not regular. That's how he gets away. He don't come on a schedule so no one's waiting for him to show up. Sometimes it's one or two days apart, sometimes it's months."

"Did he ever say anything to you?"

"He ain't a talker, that's for sure."

"You sure it's the same man each time?"

"Now there's the question. I'm not sure. Seems like Vanishing Jack's about three men."

"That ore of his, it's pretty rich?"

The clerk looked annoyed. "It's so rich it beats anything anyone's seen around here, beats anything anyone's heard of even. That gold practically falls out of the quartz, beads, wires, flakes. He's sitting on a fortune. He could hand me a chunk of that quartz, like one fistful, and I'd be five dollars richer. There's people here who'd kill to get it."

Dink pondered it. "Why does he come here, bringing four bags at a time?"

"Drago, if I knew that, I'd be rich myself."

"Where does he mine it? Did he ever say?"

"I asked him and he just smiles. But he does hint a little. He says it's not far away."

"Is he always in a hurry?"

"He takes his sweet time, I figure. He's not worried about anyone nabbing him far as I can see. And even if anyone did, he's not about to tell them where his mine is. He's got all the aces. But he does do his shopping beforehand and hides it around here somewhere. And after that he brings in his ore to the mill."

"Unrecognized."

"Drago, there's only a few millmen and me ever got a good look at him. Down in the gulch, no one's ever laid eyes on him, at least to figure out who he is. Maybe he's someone everyone knows."

"What'll you do next time he comes?"

"Word is, and this comes from right up the ladder, Drago. You get me? Word is, I should delay paying him, make excuses, let the superintendent know. Then we can grab him. We'll jump him, six or seven of us."

"You expect him to hang around through all that? If you start making excuses, will he sit down and wait?"

"Well, what other idea have you?" The clerk stared belligerently. "Now are you done? I got work to do. Payroll."

That was enough for the moment. Dink had a good idea how the transactions went. The bookkeeper had talked readily enough.

"What's your name? I didn't catch it," Dink said.

"Just call me John, but not Vanishing. John O'Tweedy." The man smiled, so Dink smiled too.

He headed outside into the smoke and felt his eyes ooze tears. The flat had emptied. If there were saloon pugs and hooligans and pimps chasing after Vanishing Jack, they were gone now. Dink smiled. Townies wouldn't have much luck against a savvy old sourdough like Jack.

Dink waited for the wind to shift, and then glimpsed a knot of trackers toiling up the distant slope, heading for timber far away. No wonder Vanishing Jack vanished every time.

This prospector was a puzzle. Dink wondered whether he was being sidetracked, trying to find out what he could about a lonely old prospector who dropped into Skeleton Gulch now and then to do a little business. But Dink couldn't help feel that these visits were somehow linked to the whole trouble here. That if he knew what Vanishing Jack was really up to, he might have the key he needed.

He hawed his coughing dray horse, intending to drive as far away from the lowering mill smoke as he could before his own lungs, as well as the dray horse's, were shot. Tears were leaking from the big brown eyes of the nag, forming black streaks across its sorrel hair, and it lowered its head. Dink eased slowly down the grade, letting the wagon press into the horse's harness for a brake, and found his way to Starr's wagon yard, where the air was better. He freed the weeping plug, wiped it down, penned it, and headed for Starr's office. But the teamster wasn't there.

"He's freighting a load of potbellied stoves and two-roller wringers from Corinne, Utah," said his yard man, Jesse Boggs. "Back in two weeks or so if a mud slide or washout don't stall him."

That disappointed Dink. Starr was the only man in the gulch who seemed to know anything about the Yellow Rose's past, but he was gone for a few days. Dink had come to another impasse.

He headed for his wagon feeling blue. Skeleton Gulch

was getting to him. There was something about this godforsaken place that drained every ounce of joy out of life. What kind of town was it that would try to hunt down an old prospector who had a little luck? The rats, the murders, the enslavement of widows, the torture, the brutality toward newcomers and strangers, the plagues and sorrows hung heavily on Dink's heart. That and the choking smoke, the littered alleys, the blooming rose bush that had been pissed on until it died, the mucky streets without so much as a boardwalk, the sweaty fear in the face of everyone he talked to.

All that was bad enough, but what worsened his mood was the impregnability of the combine that was running the town and the mines. He had hunted for a crack, a weak point, a way to throw some sunshine into this mountain aerie, but all he had done was collect a few bits of information and risk his life. He was getting nowhere and wasting the money of those who employed him. Maybe he should wire General Cook with the bad news. Maybe he wasn't big enough for the job.

Chapter 28

Dink's melancholia deepened through a restless night. It wasn't just that he was caught in the most predatory hellhole on the continent, but that he had failed. He was no closer to cleaning up Skeleton Gulch than when he started. Maybe General Cook would turn over the task to someone better.

He tossed in his bedroll and found no comfort in the stars. For the moment at least, the mill smoke was rising away, into the night sky, and not choking Skeleton Gulch.

Dink Drago, Rat Catcher. He wished he had chosen another vocation. There was something strange about catching rats for a living; something that makes people turn away, glance askance at him, as if he brought with him a reminder of the foulness he fought. It didn't matter that he performed a service no one else cared to do; that he gave them health and a cleaner world. None of that mattered. He could have been anything else, doctor, lawyer, baker, teamster, clerk, jeweler, clock maker, tinsmith, carpenter, and he would have been honored for his skills. But what rat catcher was ever honored for anything? Even for catching rats better than anyone else? Of all the world's callings, his was the loneliest.

What women ever paid him the slightest heed? What men bothered to listen to his views? Why the hell was he alive? He couldn't answer any of those things. He couldn't sleep, and finally got up. He didn't know the hour, but knew it was not far to dawn and he faced yet another day in the worst little town in America.

He stepped down from his wagon and sucked in sweet clean air. He found Polaris and the Big Dipper, reminding him that some things were eternal. For the moment, Skeleton Gulch could breathe sweetly, and the men and women and children residing there would not cough their way into perdition.

He thought of Cherry, up there in the Yellow Rose's sinister parlor house. Cherry, the prisoner, desperately trying to stay alive. He liked Cherry. There was something tender in Cherry's eyes, something alive and warm and sweet that not even the brutality of the Yellow Rose had crushed, though Dink supposed it would only be a matter of time before every last bit of gladness would be wrung from the girl.

He was lonely. He had been lonely many times. It came with his job. But this time his loneliness was a ravening hunger that flooded his whole being. In a place like this there was no one to trust, no one to befriend, no one to relax with. In Skeleton Gulch there were no friends.

He slipped into clean clothing gotten from the Chinamen, and padded quietly into the chill night. It was perhaps ten uphill blocks from the wagon yard to the parlor house. Maybe a drink with Cherry, if she was the one left on duty while the inmates slept, would hearten him. Nothing else seemed to.

He hiked up Middle Street, wary of footpads, but at this hour not even the muggers prowled because there was no one to prey upon. The storefronts loomed darkly. The sour smell of rats and stale beer and urine affronted him.

Except for the bakery, there wasn't a bright store facade in all of Skeleton Gulch, nothing to delight the eye, cheer the heart. And the deep darkness only made it all the more oppressive.

The thump of the stamp mill marred the peace. It was maddening, this steady hammering and pounding that shook the earth night and day, Sabbaths and dawns, twilights and noons. Down in the wagon yard he barely heard it. But as he approached the center of Skeleton Gulch, it intensified, as if the boom of a hundred kettle drums permeated the town. How could anyone sleep? How could anyone dream? People's heartbeats even adjusted to it, matched it, syncopated with it. All those poor immigrants who had arrived in town upon the promise of a fabulous four dollars a day mucking rock in the mines found only an implacable roar that, day by day, destroyed them.

Dink caught the scent of pines and rain on chill breezes eddying out of the high country, of clean wind and virgin meadows. And that only deepened the melancholia that crushed him. He stood at last before the massive rectangle built on the flat above town. No lamp lit its door. No light leaked from any window. He stood a moment, and thought he saw a crack of blue sky off to the east, the tentative birth of a new day.

Maybe Cherry wouldn't be there. Maybe there'd be some other girl. Maybe some pug would answer. Maybe no one would answer. He pulled the cord, jangling bells within. The muffled noise seemed loud, almost as loud as the obscene thudding of the stamp mill that pulverized quartz day and night.

Nothing happened. Then the door creaked open.

"We're closed," a female voice said.

"Cherry?"

There was a long silence.

"Cherry, how about a drink at least?"

"That you, the drummer? You looking for company? A good time? You can pay?"

"For a drink."

The door creaked the rest of the way open. A foul odor drifted out upon the night. Was there no open window airing that entire parlor house?

She was there in the gloom wrapped in a gauzy white wrapper.

"You can come in, hon. But you have to pay first."

"Cherry, I'll buy you a drink."

She sighed, a soft little meow. Then she closed the massive door behind him and headed for the bar in a darkness so deep he feared he would trip over something. A lucifer flared, and he watched her touch a wick of a coal-oil lamp and replace the chimney. The soft yellow light revealed a gauzy whiteness that failed to conceal her nakedness. Her lush figure stirred him, but the sadness of her eyes was what caught his attention.

"You are beautiful, Cherry," he said.

"Yeah, well, five dollars first. I should charge you five more for coming at four-thirty in the morning."

He gave her five, and two of company scrip. "Here's for you, and there's two for drinks."

She yawned, drawing the gossamer fabric tight over her curves, which only stirred him the more.

"I get stuck with this," she said. "I could be asleep."

But she uncorked a brown whiskey bottle and poured him a drink, adding water with a dipper. Then she poured one for herself from a different bottle with no label.

She shoved the drinks across the bar and smiled. It was the painted-on professional smile. The anything-for-a-buck smile.

She loosened the wrapper until it sagged openly. "Take your pick, sweetheart," she said. "I've got two."

"You're beautiful," Dink said. "It's in your eyes. You have

the softest, saddest eyes, and when I look at you I see something sweet."

She laughed uneasily.

"I think you'd like to be somewhere else," he said.

"Shhh. Don't talk like that. I love it here."

"Your eyes tell me you have dreams. What do you dream about, Cherry?"

She turned silent and sipped the fake whiskey in her glass. For a moment she seemed wistful, her mask awry.

"I hope you keep the dreams alive. Girl like you."

"We're not going to talk about me," she said, her gaze darting to curtained corners of the saloon. "You come upstairs, hon."

He lowered his voice. "Did the rat's-bane help?"

"The what?"

"The seed."

She slid into her own world. "I tried a little. This place is full of rats. They bite the girls."

"Just a little?"

She whispered. "I'm afraid. If I'm caught . . ."

"What would happen if you're caught."

"The hole!"

"What hole?"

"Under the kitchen floor. Where they dump the garbage."

"What's there, Cherry?"

She turned away, plainly not wanting him to see her face.

"Cherry, throw some of the rat's-bane seed in there."

She stared woodenly at him, her face masked with terror.

"I'll give you some. Throw it in there. A packet at a time. For a few days."

She smiled suddenly, her face carved into a grin. "Come on up, sweetheart."

"Cherry, you can escape."

"Shhh! Please!" Her hand thrust toward the sinister red drapery.

"Walk out the door with me."

"Oh, God, Drago, don't."

"We'll be out of here. You'll be hidden in a freight wagon. You'll be free."

"Don't Drago, don't."

Tears welled in her soft eyes. He wanted to lead her by the hand through that door into the dawn. A glance at the window revealed a grayness now. The night would not cloak them.

"Cherry, take these," he said, pushing half a dozen of the waxen packets of African rat's-bane seed. "Use it. Take it with you. Pour it into every corner."

"All I ever wanted was a cottage with a porch and a view of the green hills and purple lilacs growing beside it," she said. "All I ever wanted was my own babies and a man I could love. All I ever wanted was petunias. And someone to watch over me."

"How did you get here?"

"Don't, Drago."

"You can escape."

Fear blazed in those soft eyes. "Don't, please don't. You don't know. . . ."

"I'll find you a cottage with lilacs."

"I'm ruined, Drago. Forget it. I'm worse than anything you can imagine. There's nothing I haven't done, nothing I wouldn't do."

"That's because you have hope. If you didn't have hope, you wouldn't care. Cherry, I care about names. I don't know what your real name is. Maybe I should call you Laurie or Joanna or Sally or Diane."

"Don't, Drago. I'm Cherry. Don't ever call me anything else. If you call me any other name I won't let you see me."

Dink heard a thump and a stirring upstairs.

"Go," she whispered.

He didn't wait. He slipped through that massive front

door, into the gray dawn, even as she extinguished the lamp at the bar. The door creaked on its hinges and clicked behind him. He trotted off, but kept an eye on the windows above, and wasn't surprised to see a pale face peering from one.

Chapter 29

The smoke lowered again, hazing the town. Dink needed air. He hiked downslope, turned off Middle Street, walked a block, and knocked on Doc Cutler's door. No one answered. He rapped again, and met only silence.

He rounded the frame building and found the rear door unlocked. He opened it and yelled.

"Doc, it's Drago."

He heard some shuffling and then silence.

"Doc, I'm going to see how you're doing."

He pushed in, glad to escape the harsh smoke rolling down from the mill and mine boilers. There were times when Skeleton Gulch was all but unlivable. He closed the door tightly against the bad air outside.

Doc was up, wrapped in a shabby tartan robe and slumped in a stuffed horsehair chair, a grimy glass of booze in hand. His pale varicosed ankles rose out of ancient black slippers. He glanced at Dink without acknowledging a thing. The swelling in his face had subsided, but he looked poxed.

"You're up," Dink said.

"Go away."

"I want to see how you're doing. You look better. At least your eyes aren't swollen shut."

"Go away."

"Have you eaten?"

Doc glared.

"I'll find something," Drago said.

He headed for the kitchen, found the range stone cold, rummaged the shelves, and spotted some canned tomatoes. He shook the stove's ash grate, stuffed paper and kindling from the wood box into the stove's firebox, lit it, and watched the flame tentatively catch. It would take a while. He found an opener, clawed off the lid of the tomatoes, found a saucepan, and put the tomatoes on to heat.

"You haven't got much food in here," he said.

"Eat out. Hate to cook."

"I'm heating some tinned tomatoes. It'll take a few minutes."

"It won't do any good, Drago. Now, dammit, get out."

Dink didn't. He hovered around the kitchen waiting for the cold cast-iron stove to absorb some heat from the crackling kindling, smelling the wisps of smoke that eddied from stovepipe joints until the chimney draft began to work.

Doc was in a bad way. He had made Judas money snitching to the Yellow Rose about anything or anyone who threatened her. He might have caused the deaths of General Cook's agents. And now Doc was loathing himself for it, hating every bone in his body. As well he should, Dink thought coldly. And yet a man filled with remorse was a man worth caring about. And what the hell, he liked Doc even if Doc was a twisted old coot.

Doc was the sort who would drink himself to death, which was exactly what he was doing now. Dink spotted the half-empty bottle of Old Orchard on the counter and wondered if there were some empties too.

"I'm not going to eat," Doc said.

Dink waited until the stewed tomatoes were steaming and then served up a bowl, found a spoon, and handed the meal to Doc.

"Forget it," Doc said.

For a moment he thought Doc would throw the bowl on the floor, but then with a sigh Doc spooned the tomatoes into his mouth. He ended up eating the whole bowl and the rest of the tomatoes from the stew pot.

"Get me my bottle, Drago."

"All right," Dink said, but didn't get it.

"Now, dammit."

"So you feel bad. That makes two of us," Dink said.

"What do you know about it? How many people have you betrayed for thirty pieces of silver?"

"I need you, Doc. My employer, General Cook, told me to clean this place out. Just like that. Clean up Skeleton Gulch. I don't know how. Maybe you can tell me."

"How should I know how? She's got an army. She's got pugs and lieutenants and bosses. She's got bullies and killers and pickpockets and snitches like me. She's got whores that'd slit your throat. She'll kill you too when it pleases her. She's got rats by the thousand, an army of rats. Rats eat anything. Rats eat Dragos and Cutlers. Rats eat bartenders and General Cook's detectives. If you had any sense you'd get out."

"Why don't you get out?"

"It's easier to drink."

"I guess that's getting out your own way."

"I'm working on it," Doc said.

"Maybe I'll join you," Dink replied.

"By God, Drago, that's the first thing you've said that makes any sense."

Dink headed for the kitchen, found the bottle, and poured a half an inch. He had never before in his life started on booze before the sun was halfway up.

Doc eyed him cynically from his old chair. "Now fix me one," he said.

"Might as well," Dink said.

He fixed Doc a skimpy one, mostly cold well water, and handed it to Cutler.

Doc sipped. "Where's the booze, Drago? Dishwater, that's what this is. How the hell am I going to sterilize my innards with dishwater? I want ninety-proof blood in my veins."

Dink smiled and did not take the hint. "How are we going to bring civic virtue and democracy and charity to Skeleton Gulch, Cutler?"

"By blowing up the town, Drago."

"The woman owns the mines, the town lots, the saloons, the whorehouses, the buildings. She even owns the outhouses. She could go into the outhouse business. Everyone here works for her, one way or another. She lives in a fortress surrounded by her thugs. There are dozens of them. There are bosses at each mine and the mill. What should I do?"

"Kidnap her. Then the whole house of cards tumbles."

"Just like that. You sound like General Cook. Clean it up, he said. Clean up the town, Drago. One-hundred-pound man against a ton of gorillas. Kidnap the Yellow Rose. What do I do with her if I snatch her?"

"Kill her. Simple justice, wouldn't you say? Then kill yourself."

"I knew you'd be helpful, Doc. I'm feeling worse than you do, and you're not helping."

"I'm sorry. I'll see what I can do about making you feel still worse."

"Why does the Yellow Rose try so hard to be wicked?"

"Because she's a sweet girl at heart. Truly wicked people don't have to try. They don't even know how wicked they are. But she's always trying. Making herself look as evil as possible."

Dink pondered it, liking it. "Once I saw her walk through a field of alpine flowers bobbing in pine-scented breezes, walking through a paradise. It lasted a few minutes. Maybe it was a window. Maybe she gave me a brief look at what she once was, and then she turned nasty. Maybe you're right."

Doc jammed the glass at Dink. "Fill it up or leave."

Dink picked up the sticky tumbler and headed for the kitchen, where he dribbled some more booze into it and added a lot of cold water. He handed it to Doc, who downed half the glass and glowered at Dink.

"There, drink away, Cutler. Now tell me why she hates herself."

"Bad blood. She comes from a family of pirates."

"Privateers. There's a difference."

"Not if you're about to walk the plank. I'll tell you how it is, Drago. This woman stole the mines from her own family and then killed them. Or maybe it was the reverse."

"How do you know that?"

"The heavens opened up, a great shaft of blinding light shot down from above, it struck me dumb, and when I got up off the ground I had the secret of the Yellow Rose clawing my bosom."

Dink half-believed the doc.

"I couldn't relieve myself for two days," Cutler added.

"Be serious, Doc. I need help. I'm about to turn tail and get out of here. They'll need an army to clean up Skeleton Gulch."

Cutler sipped, and sipped, and when he finished, the tumbler of booze was empty.

"If all of Europe had stayed thoroughly drunk during the black plague, it wouldn't have killed but a few," Doc said. "Put enough spirits into the arteries, and nothing lives."

Dink thought for a moment that Doc was about to fall asleep. Doc nodded, pressed his fingers to his mottled temples, and then stared at Dink.

"Maybe the Yellow Rose wasn't happy with what she inherited. There was a brother, I'm told, who had the other half. The family had an interest in two or three of the five mines. Maybe her itch to have it all clawed at her bosom, ate at her until she couldn't stand it. Maybe she was obsessed with gold. She's keeping it here, you know. She won't let go of it. They say she's got it in a vault, except for what she needs to run the mines.

"Maybe her brother wouldn't sell out or wanted to ship gold out, or something. Who knows? Maybe she killed him. Maybe she couldn't live with herself after that, her own horror of her own conduct, the devil unloosed in her, filling her with despair. There could be no forgiveness.

"What do such people do? People who lose all hope of redeeming themselves? Make a pact with the devil. They wallow in their evil. They flaunt it, calculate what would shock the world the most. They tell themselves they came from bad stock, they're hopeless, and they set out to prove it. And in proving it, they turn into monsters. All because they cannot ever overcome that bit of conscience that lies in their hearts."

"You think that's the Yellow Rose."

"I didn't say that, Drago, damn you."

"That could apply to you, Doc. If you let it."

"Get out, Drago."

"What are you going to do with yourself the rest of your life, Doc?"

"You're already seeing it, Drago. Now, get the hell out."

Chapter 30

The shrill blast of a mine whistle awakened Dink. The gray light of predawn filtered through the canvas of his wagon. The nonstop howl echoed eerily down the valley, raising hair on Dink's neck. It was a wolf howl, mournful and urgent.

He had heard mine whistles ever since he arrived, announcing shift changes and emergencies. Short blasts indicated trouble, injury, cave-in. Even in a vicious town like Skeleton Gulch, death and injury in the mines evoked instant and generous assistance, the rush of rescuers, knots of anguished wives, and deep worry. There were decent things in town that not even the Yellow Rose could stamp out.

This whistle wailed into the predawn silence and then halted. He heard shouts from the teamsters in the wagon yard and heard a racing horseman on the road. It was not his concern but it evoked his curiosity. Trouble and sorrow haunted Skeleton Gulch more than any town he had ever been in.

He couldn't sleep, and finally threw off his bedroll and got up. The world was hushed and serene. He washed at the horse trough, lathered his face with a bar of orange

Naphtha soap, hung a small mirror on his wagon, and began scraping his stubble, tugging the straight-edge carefully along his cheek and jaw and neck. He had neglected his whiskers for several days and it felt good to clean them off. Some sweat-stained mules watched him from their pen, and yawned. Mules were curious about anything and everything, unlike most horses.

He would collect full rat traps this day, set out fresh ones, see Doc, and try to find some chink in the armor of the Victor Mining Company and its legion of black suits and thugs. He wondered what General Cook expected of him. How could one slight man collapse the most sinister organization in the West?

By the time he had completed his morning ablutions and headed into the yard, the teamsters had vanished and he was alone. That was fine. He had promised he would clean the rats out of John Starr's granaries and he was not yet done. And he was ready for a good cup of Java too, and maybe some flapjacks in the company kitchen. He stood, watching the sun illumine the distant slopes, painting them gold, dancing light off the snowy peaks. For the moment the mine and mill smoke drifted straight up and did not haze the town in choking gloom.

To his surprise he found Starr himself in the commissary, picking away at some flapjacks.

"You're back," Dink said.

"Fast trip this time, Drago. Have a seat."

Dink loaded up on the flapjacks, poured some syrup over them, and settled beside the freighting man. The flapjacks were spongy and tasteless, but at least they filled a man up.

"What was all that trouble an hour ago?" Dink asked.

Starr laughed, a blaze of delight across his face.

"Vanishing Jack. He showed up before dawn with some more of that great ore. Just two days after the last load,

I'm told. This time there was only a night clerk on duty, but he had his instructions. Victor Mining wants to jump Jack, and they've been lying in wait. Jack was armed this time. But the minute the company paid Jack off for the last load, the clerk hit the whistle. That was supposed to be the signal. But half the pugs in town are still wandering around in the woods trying to track Jack down from the last visit. And the other half were asleep. So Jack got away once again."

Starr relished the story and told it with wry good humor.

"They won't catch him unless they get very lucky," Dink said, "and they wouldn't know what to do with Jack if they do."

Starr chuckled softly. "There wasn't a single pursuer this time. He headed right down the road here. You may have heard him if you were up. Right through town, and not one of the Yellow Rose's pugs followed."

Dink pondered it. "He's lucky, John. Someday it won't be that easy."

Starr nodded.

"Where did you hear this?" Dink asked.

"I was up early."

For a man freshly back from captaining a freight outfit, he looked pretty chipper, freshly shaven and shorn.

"You must have got in last night."

"I don't sleep much, Drago."

"I'm going to change the traps in your granary," Dink said. "I haven't figured out yet how they're getting in. But I'll get you fixed up soon."

"Good. You getting much business in town?"

"Some shops. But I get no trade from anything owned by Victor Mining Company. There's a lot of rats, Starr. And I've taken to cleaning them out whether anyone wants me to."

"Really? Why?"

Dink pushed his empty plate aside and sipped some

coffee. "Because it's the right thing to do. I've spread some poisoned bait through the alleys behind the saloons. A certain man I know got rolled there the other night and pitched into the alley, and he survived. A few bites, nothing catastrophic. If he doesn't get the plague or a fever, he'll make it."

Starr stared at him. "Then you saved a life."

Dink thought of Doc, drinking himself to death. "I'm not sure he wants it saved," Dink said.

"I saw some street signs," Starr said. "Yours?"

"Yes. Give a town names, give it streets, and maybe it'll change."

Starr eyed Drago levelly. "You want change here?"

"I keep having the idea that Skeleton Gulch could be a good town, that mining men and their wives could make a good living and enjoy life, that shopkeepers could do a good business, that the sporting district could be tamed, that children could safely wander the streets. That a miner could order a beer with his friends in a corner saloon and count on going home for supper. That no woman would be held against her will in the hellish places. I guess I'd like to see people secure in their persons, able to walk the streets day and night without being kidnapped or mugged or worse."

"That won't happen until Victor Mining is brought to justice, Drago. Otherwise it's just wishful thinking."

"I am one four-and-a-half-foot, hundred-pound male," Drago said.

"Who was it, Archimedes, who said that if he had a long enough lever he could move the earth?"

"I don't have a lever."

"Yes, you do, Drago. Just ask yourself what would cause the whole rotten Victor Mining Company and all its rotten branches to collapse."

"Maybe you could tell me."

"It's no secret. The entire evil empire is owned by one person. Bring her before a magistrate, trace the deaths and theft and white slavery back to her, bring in the law, and it all comes tumbling down."

"Not if a hundred hooligans won't let it."

Starr smiled. "But you're a rat catcher. And rat catchers use bait, traps, and poisons."

Dink pondered it. He had a feeling that Starr was fencing with him, talking in metaphors; that Starr knew more than he was letting on. How, for example, had Starr gotten wind of what happened at the milling works only an hour or two before?

Dink downed his coffee and stood. "I'll look after the traps at your granary and then I'll see what business I can drum up," he said.

"You do that."

Dink left the freighting man to his Java, and headed into the yard to harness his nag. An evil yellow smoke from the mill boiler had settled over Skeleton Gulch and Dink dreaded driving into it. The old nag had been coughing and Dink wondered if the toxic smoke would be the death of the patient old beast.

He decided to walk. He hayed the horse, let it slurp up water from the trough, and returned it to its pen.

What the hell did Starr want anyway, asking questions like that? The man was always probing Dink, as if it mattered where Dink stood on all the issues.

He started up Middle Street, coughing his way up to Doc's house, unable to see a hundred yards because of the smoke. That was the trouble with Skeleton Gulch; you couldn't see half the time. He wondered why half the town hadn't choked to death.

And then he did see. Not the street and shops along his route, not the distant peaks, not blue skies, but *something else.* John Starr. Consuela Estrella-Cooper. John Estrella, John Starr. Vanishing Jack.

He stopped cold. What the hell was he thinking?

He remembered those handsome oil portraits in the Yellow Rose's office, oval portraits of her hawkish family. Dark, leonine, long-nosed men with hair drawn back and the look of eagles about them. John Starr, proprietor of Starr and Son, had the look of eagles about him, had the complexion, the long nose, the hollow cheeks, the look, the look, the look.

The family stamp of the Estrella or Cooper line.

They said Vanishing Jack was tall and lean and carved from sharp angles, that sometimes he had long hair. They had hinted that maybe Vanishing Jack was the brother of the Yellow Rose, or family anyway.

And Vanishing Jack, John Starr, and the Yellow Rose looked remarkably alike, as if some strong sire had stamped that look upon them all. Who was he?

There were some differences. The Yellow Rose was showing gray; John Starr could have been ten or fifteen years younger, maybe more.

But how could John Starr be Vanishing Jack?

Starr usually wasn't around, out on the road, when Vanishing Jack materialized at the mill. And where did the ore come from? And what was Jack's game? Why didn't he take the ore to some other mill in some other mining town?

Dink had no answers, but he knew something as surely as he knew he was breathing, and that was that Vanishing Jack was John Starr, and John Starr was somehow related to the Yellow Rose.

And something else: He knew who had written General Cook to enlist the services of the Rocky Mountain Detective Agency.

Chapter 31

Doc's house loomed out of a whirl of yellow smoke. Dink discovered a couple standing on the porch. The mother, who wore an old-world babushka over her head, held a swaddled infant.

"Oh, sir," the young man said. "Is the doctor in? The baby has the colic."

"The doctor's sick. But maybe he'll see you."

"We need help!"

The thin woman thrust the bundle at Dink, who saw a red-faced, coughing, gasping infant within. Its diapers reeked.

"Let me see," he said.

Dink wondered whether that infant would survive five minutes more in the smoke. He hurried around to the rear, let himself in, and hunted for Doc. The big man was slouched in the same chair, in the same manner, with the same gummy glass in his hand, as he was yesterday.

"Doc, there's people at the door. They need help."

"Go away, Drago."

"Help them. Their baby's sick."

"I heard it. Tell them I have leprosy."

"I'm going to let them in, Doc."

"Tell them I have the black plague."

Drago ignored him and headed through the gloomy house to the front offices, and there he unlatched the door.

The couple hurried in. The baby was choking. "Oh, sir, oh, sir . . ."

"I'll get Dr. Cutler. Here, put that baby there and wash its face."

Dink retreated to the gloomy parlor.

"They're ready for you, Doc."

"You treat them. You know more than I do, Drago. Feed the baby some of your African rat's-bane."

"I will offer what help I can, which is very little."

Dink pulled the curtain aside and entered the office. The couple was laving the baby.

"Doc Cutler's plenty sick. I don't know whether he can attend you or not. But let's see if the child has a fever and maybe we can cool it down."

"Oh, yes, please help us."

He found a towel and made a cold compress out of it.

Then Doc appeared in his ratty bathrobe and slippers. He smelled of whiskey. The couple stared at him doubtfully.

Doc Cutler eyed the couple and the desperate baby and somehow swung into action. The infant was dehydrated and feverish. Its diapers stank.

"How long has this been going on?" he asked the mother.

"Last night."

Doc worked swiftly and then reached for a small blue bottle. "This'll quiet his stomach," he said. "It's a baby-sized dose of opium. Good for gastroenteritis." He lifted the child, popped a tiny pill into its mouth, swiftly lifted a cup to its lips, and poured water. The baby coughed, twisted into a frightful spasm, and then writhed.

But the infant subsided, and soon Doc was able to feed it liquids without having them tossed up again. Dink and the mother laved the child with cold compresses. A slow, ticking fifteen minutes passed and the child settled into restless quiet. A half hour later the crisis had passed, at least for the moment.

Dink stuck his head out the door. A shift in the wind had lifted the smoke from Skeleton Gulch. Doc sat down, stared at the infant, and then at his empty glass.

"We owe you something, Dr. Cutler," the man said.

"A thousand dollars."

The wife gasped.

"We . . . can't . . ." the young man said.

Doc laughed harshly.

"Better make it two thousand, Doc," Dink said.

The couple stared at each of them, at the peaceful child, and at each other. "I have two dollars. I will try to earn the rest," the man said, faltering.

"Take this compound. If the baby's distemper returns, come back."

"But we can't pay."

"Of course not. I owe you the thousand," Doc said. "Maybe I should pay you two thousand."

The couple stared blankly, half-afraid, half-suspecting Doc was demented.

"We have two dollars," the young man said.

"Keep your money," Doc replied so gruffly that the couple slipped into silence.

Dink ushered them out. The infant had somehow purchased life and slept in its mother's arms. She stared at Doc with tears collecting beneath her eyes.

The door clicked shut, and Doc retreated to his shabby chair in the rear room.

"Two thousand dollars?" Dink asked.

"Get me a drink, Drago."

"You said you should pay them two thousand?"

"It evens out a little, Drago. Maybe I saved a life. Maybe I should spend the snitch money I got from the Yellow

Rose for ratting on you. Two thousand for the privilege of saving a life. Cheap for a skunk like me. If I save enough lives and pay enough of my blood money, maybe I'll balance the books."

Dink pondered Doc's accounting and thought he saw some daylight in it. If he didn't drink himself into oblivion, Doc might settle accounts in the ledger of his life.

He poured Doc a weak drink, mostly water, and handed it to the man. Doc sniffed, tasted, and splashed the booze into the braided rug.

"Dishwater. It won't help, Drago. Nothing will ever help."

"All right, sit there and feel sorry for yourself. I'm going to pull up the shades on your windows and unlock your front door. You can treat patients or not. But they'll be free to walk in," Dink said.

Doc glowered at him, but didn't object.

Dink headed for the waiting room, opened the front door, drew the curtains aside, let in sunlight.

"It's up to you now," Dink said.

"Drago, you have the fool notion that there is redemption. There's no such thing. I cannot redeem myself. Nothing you do will help me because I refuse to be helped."

"You and the Yellow Rose."

"Explain that, rat catcher."

"The Yellow Rose spends her life proving how bad she is, how far beyond redemption she is. The two of you suffer the same thing: You don't believe anything or anyone or any spirit or God can help you. You live in darkness, the place where there's no hope. For you, that means drinking yourself into oblivion, For her, it means proving it over and over."

"Go away."

"Tell me how to reform this town."

"Get me a drink."

Drago plucked up Doc's tumbler and headed for the

kitchen. If Doc wanted a drink, then Doc would get one. Dink poured a stiff one and handed it to Cutler, who slouched in his armchair.

"Ah," said Doc, after taking a sip. "You have not betrayed me this time."

Dink waited. Doc sipped.

"Let me get this straight, Drago. You are asking me how to reform Skeleton Gulch."

Dink nodded.

"The Victor Mining Company has a sole owner, as far as anyone knows. She is evil. She pursues evil. She hires an army to further her ends. She operates behind a wall of muscle and murder. She's so wounded someone unknown, here in the gulch, that this someone hires a detective agency. So the Denver detective agency sends you, a rat catcher, to clean up the joint. As if you possessed magical powers, Drago. Take on the mining company, ship the criminals off to jail, break its back. Are you a magician? A wizard? No, you're a man with a wagon full of traps and some bottles of rat poison. How does your boss expect you to perform this miracle?"

"He doesn't. He expects me to evaluate the situation and report back if one man can't handle it."

"Ah! Now we're getting somewhere. You are a vain man, Drago. You want to achieve the impossible. You want to be a Napoleon, cleaning up a town that would murder you if you try to do it. And that's because you are full of conceit. You want to report back to your Rocky Mountain Detective Agency that you did it all by yourself. You want a pat on the back from your boss. That's what you pine for. You don't want to be defeated. You don't want to wire the boss and tell him you can't do it alone. Send in the fools."

Dink didn't like the tenor of any of this. But Doc had

his own compelling way. Doc sipped, sighed, and grinned darkly.

"David against Goliath. All you need is the sling."

"That's right, Doc. I have no sling and no rock to toss."

"Conceit, Drago. It'll get you killed. Your boss isn't demanding that you clean up Skeleton Gulch. I take it he's not entirely lunatic. He's only asking you to come up with the evidence, the information."

It was true. No one had ever asked Dink to do the impossible.

"You're as bad as I am, Drago."

"I've got to leave here. I have some rats to catch."

Cutler stared dourly. "I won't see you again. You're bent on suicide."

Drago started to object, but Doc cut him off.

"Drago, there are three of us. The Yellow Rose is trying to destroy herself. I'm trying to destroy myself. And you are the third musketeer, busy destroying yourself."

"Go to hell, Doc."

Dink let himself out and into a bright day that, for the moment, was free of smoke. He stared upslope toward the mines and the mill. If those boiler stacks were fifteen or twenty feet higher, they probably would punch the smoke straight up and free the town of the misery of bad air. But they wouldn't rise one course of bricks higher as long as the Yellow Rose owned the company.

Doc's rebuke clawed at him. He should report to General Cook. He knew enough so that the agency could deal with it. But he was damned if he would do that. He was going to pull the Victor Mining Company down, send the legions of thugs and hoodlums packing, and put the Yellow Rose into the pen at Deer Lodge for the rest of her unnatural life.

Cutler had it right. He didn't know when to quit.

Chapter 32

One pint-sized rat catcher against a sinister and secret company that stopped at nothing, including murder. Dink thought about it as he hiked back to the wagon yard. Twisting mountain breezes lowered smoke one moment, only to whisk it away the next. Sometimes this windy day Skeleton Gulch wasn't obscured, but Dink's future was.

He reached the quiet yard, noted his nag dozing in the sun, and turned to the office of John Starr. He found the man staring out the window, his face contemplative, that hawkish profile so familiar, stamped in those oil portraits and the face of the woman who had turned Skeleton Gulch into hell.

Starr turned. "Drago?"

"Have time for some questions?"

Starr nodded and motioned Dink to a wooden chair.

"Vanishing Jack," Dink said.

"You want me to tell you what I know about Vanishing Jack?"

"No, I want you to explain why."

Starr looked blank.

"And where you get the ore."

A seven-day clock on a table ticked steadily. Jack eyed Dink, obviously sizing him up.

"And what purpose it serves. And what the family connection is. And why you wrote General Cook."

Starr stared into the sun-bright window, saying nothing.

"And what you want from me," Dink added.

"I suppose I should say I don't know what you're talking about, Drago."

"You can say it, but that would disappoint me."

Starr rose, checked the empty wagon yard, and returned to his swivel chair, which complained as he turned.

"The Yellow Rose is my aunt."

"I thought so. You're a generation younger."

"Consuela Estrella-Cooper, of Galveston and New Orleans. My father was Juan Estrella-Cooper, brother of the Yellow Rose. She is unaware that I am here and if you betray me you will seal my death. They were named by their Mexican mother, my grandmother. Their father was a Scot engaged in privateering."

"Your father lives?"

"No, he was murdered."

"Any others living?"

"Two sisters of mine, whom I have had to hide from her."

"What happened?"

"My aunt and my father were to share equally in the Victor Mine, which was then one of five independent mines here. My grandfather, the privateer, had invested in the Victor and owned a large part of the shares. Some stock in the others too. And when he died those were to be divided. But my aunt was not content to be moderately rich. Gold bewitched her. The very thought of gold unloosed some sort of madness in her. You can guess the rest."

"No, I can't."

"My father died suddenly."

"Of what?"

"The death was ascribed to a seizure."

"And you inherited?"

"No, this happened hours before my grandfather died. What did that mean? She inherited everything."

"Two murders?"

"My grandfather was slowly dying of heart failure. The process was, shall we say, hastened as soon as my father was dead."

"Is there proof?"

"Only a pattern. The owners of the other mines in Skeleton Gulch found that their holdings were fatal."

"What killed them?"

"Chloral hydrate. Mickey Finns."

"The weapon of choice here, it seems."

"It and the rats."

"Have you evidence?"

"None whatsoever. Only a pattern and hunches."

"How many deaths here?"

Starr shrugged. "That's unknown. If you count every traveler who vanished, every holder of wealth, every wretched girl in the cribs, every recalcitrant citizen, maybe seventy or eighty. That's a guess."

"And the authorities?"

"First, they're paid to stay away. Second, there's no evidence to be gotten from a pile of bones. So far as anyone knows, it's just sickness, plague. This is a plague city as far as anyone in Helena knows. The bureaucrats are calling it mountain fever."

"You are telling me a story so filled with horror I can barely absorb it."

Starr stared, letting his silence confirm Dink's impression.

"How did she get the other mines?"

"That's a mystery. Since their owners are dead, no one knows. But I suspect she used her charms."

"Why did she become a madam after she was rich?"

Starr smiled grimly. "To abuse herself. To prove she was as evil as her conscience told her she was. To flaunt it. You see, Drago, she was convent-educated. There's a certain order in New Orleans that engages in female instruction. She was there. She left the convent with those beliefs guiding her. That meant that everything she did here had a price. Every murder, every cruelty, was recorded in the ledger of her heart and still is. That ledger grows heavy, the list grows long, the spirit grows burdened, so then what does she do? She wrestles with a hatred of herself. No woman on earth despises herself as much."

Dink remembered his first encounters with the Yellow Rose. "I invited her on a picnic. She accepted. We drove up into the mountains. There was an alpine meadow bursting with wildflowers below that glacier. She walked through that meadow, touching flowers, as if each petal were a miracle. And then the moment passed."

"You were lucky she didn't leave your body there."

Dink sighed. "I suppose, for a few minutes she was the convent girl."

Starr smiled. "For a few moments her soul betrayed her."

"Why did she start a parlor house? She was rich. She didn't need to make a living that way."

"My aunt went hunting for darkness. In the end, it was a goal she lusted after even more than gold."

"She went looking for it, for sin?"

"For sin. For every debasement known to the human race."

"You believe that?"

Starr had a way of staring out the window, and now he did, as if communing with blue sky. "There is a legend in the family that the Estrellas, the Mexican branch, are the devil's children, bright and perverse and beyond the solace of the sacraments. That is the story around San Luis Potosi even to this day."

"Not your grandfather, the privateer?"

"No, he was never accused of that. He was a rough man who made a violent living, but he lived by his own code, and that code was, in its way, honorable. He regarded himself as a soldier of fortune. No, my grandmother's family is the one that was whispered about throughout Central Mexico. Maybe the Yellow Rose simply inherited the bad seed."

"It must be a burden to live with. Do you fear it lives in you?"

"Not in the blood, Drago. Not some original sin passed down in the blood. But I search myself for signs of darkness in my soul."

"And have you discovered any signs?"

"I've discovered the evil that is in me, and maybe in all of us."

"You wrote the Rocky Mountain Detective Agency?"

"And paid General Cook too. I am one man. My aunt commands an army, not of soldiers but of thugs. There needs to be a reckoning. The Territory turns a blind eye. I chose private means, at least as a first step."

"Collecting the evidence."

"Yes. But the detectives were lost, betrayed by someone."

"Yes, they were. I know who it was, and he won't betray me."

"Who, Drago?"

"A repentant man, Mr. Starr. Let it go."

Starr struggled with that, and nodded.

"Why Vanishing Jack?"

Starr smiled. The smile was so rare, so richly embedded in his craggy features, that it changed the light in his face.

"Guerrilla warfare," he said. "Eventually, she's going to find my gold mine and kill me."

"Then why not keep it secret?"

"I can't. It's right there."

He pointed out his window. A powder magazine nestled against the rocky bluff.

"Eventually, because she can't abide an independent business in Skeleton Gulch, she'll steal this freight business and kill me. Then she'll find the mine. It's a rich one, with the best ores anywhere in the region. I found it by accident while clearing away talus to build a powder magazine there. It's part of the same formation as the mines above, but a lower stratum, exposed here. Maybe they've already dug this far down. I don't know. What that company does is so secret that no one knows. They could run out of ore and it would take years for anyone to know it."

Dink stared, amazed. The building Starr called a powder magazine nestled over a ledge or a tunnel in the bluff. It would be easy for a freight outfit to remove tailings unnoticed.

"The clock's ticking, Drago. That's why I have that clock there. To remind me that my business, my gold mine, and my life are daily and hourly in more precarious straits. I send the proceeds to my sisters. There are teamsters sniffing around here, looking for work, and I know who sent them.

"Look across the road there. A new saloon going in. It's more than a saloon. It's the work of the Yellow Rose, for whom all blooms must be plucked. It will draw my teamsters and hired hands. It will be the beginning of the end for me."

"And Vanishing Jack?"

"A way to cash some of that ore, Drago. A way to get out what I can, while I can. They still think the mine's off in the wild somewhere, and that suits me fine. I can shake those pugs that chase after me."

"You had fun."

For once Starr's face lit up. "There are not many ways to defeat the Yellow Rose. But Vanishing Jack succeeded."

"For the moment."

"You have it exactly right, Drago."

Chapter 33

Starr led Drago through the quiet wagon yard, past battered freight wagons sagging on their worn wheels, past old axles and discarded iron tires caught in weeds.

"There's hardly anyone around here most of the time. I hire a slow boy to feed morning and evening. He understands it well enough," Starr said. "When the yard's full of teamsters, I put in a kitchen crew."

Some mules and oxen stood quietly in a distant pen, their tails lashing flies.

"Mules for fast hauling, oxen for the heavy work," Starr said. "Skeleton Gulch doesn't export anything; we deadhead to the railroads and mostly haul one way. The Bitterroot and Utah Stage Line handles gold and passengers."

They climbed a rocky grade and reached the powder magazine, which had a large brass padlock sealing its plank door. It had been built of mortared mine rubble, had a rusted metal roof, and was snugged into the tan granite of the cliff. A black-lettered sign, painted on rusting sheet metal, announced that it was a magazine and fire was prohibited. DANGER! it said. The sign was enough to evoke caution in even the worst of fools. And it kept people at a distance.

Starr paused, studied the surrounding country, the sleepy yard, the distant crew shingling the new saloon across the road. Then he pulled an iron key from his britches and unlocked.

Drago stepped into an gloomy interior, lit only by the light from the opened door. It was cool. There were no rats.

The powder magazine had been built against the cliff, its walls mortared into the granite. Before Dink was a hollowed area in the cliff, perhaps seven or eight feet wide, ten feet deep, but only three feet high, that glowed faintly from the light in the doorway.

"That's the seam. It's weathered quartz. I can't fire a shot in here; it'd blow out the magazine walls. So I've had to pry out the quartz by hand. I'm getting into harder stuff now; I can't just pry it out anymore. So you see, Drago, the clock's ticking."

Dink picked up a piece of the milky quartz lying on the ground, and held it up to the light. He didn't see the gold he expected to see in flecks and wires running through it.

"It's rich ore, Drago. The best ore in the gulch by far. It's probably connected to the strata in those mines above, but who knows? They haven't dug down far enough to reach this seam. I can carry two mule-loads to the mill and walk away with five hundred dollars."

"They're paying you in company scrip now, I hear."

"It's part of their squeeze. They want Vanishing Jack to spend it here so they can nab him."

"Surely someone's going to recognize you someday."

"Costume, Drago. In town I'm Starr; at the mill I'm a weatherbeaten old prospector. Sometimes white-haired, sometimes black-haired, sometimes red-haired." He laughed. "I have a wardrobe and keep adding to it."

"When do you dig here?"

Starr shrugged. "Whenever I feel like it. I'm here alone most of the time. I have mules. I have a way of carrying the ore and the tailings out, freight wagons all over the yard. But there's hardly been any tailings. Just ore. I'm just gouging out the seam. I found it by accident. I started a freight company here to keep an eye on my aunt and maybe find a way to bring her to justice. And here it was. I was scouting around here, looking over the place, and quartz caught my eye."

"How rich is this?"

Starr shrugged. "You know as much as I do. It'd take some tunneling and crosscuts to find out. But rich, Drago. Maybe richer than all five mines up there put together. Real wealth!"

"If you can keep it. Have you filed a claim?"

Starr laughed easily. "A claim. I'd be dead hours after I filed a claim. Stuffed in a rat hole."

"Then someone could steal it, file on you."

"Not quite. I have preemptive rights, and plenty of proof. But a lot of good it would do me if I end up another pile of bones for Hap Kilgore to plant."

"Why don't you take the ore to another mill? You've got the freight wagons."

"There's none close. And my own teamsters don't know about this. If I started shipping ore, they'd know."

"Why dig at all? Keep this place secret."

"Not possible. The mines will reach this seam someday soon. Even if I bury this hole and hide the mine, it'll all be found and mined. There's nothing like gold to inspire hard work and diligent prospecting. This is three hundred fifty feet below the mine heads on the ridge, and their shafts are now running three hundred feet. That's not far from this seam—if it stretches this direction. And I believe it does."

Drago had a sense that the world was closing in on John Starr. "What'll you do?"

"The question is, what'll you do, Drago? I'm one man. You're one man."

"And the Yellow Rose is one woman. She's the sole owner, is she not? Everyone's on a salary?"

"If you're saying the whole evil empire would collapse if we were to nab her somehow, I doubt it. There's too much at stake. There's a hundred more who'd gladly steal the mines and the bordellos. And kill us if they could."

"What did you have in mind when you wrote the detective agency?"

"Evidence. Cook's man would get the goods. Then we could give it to federal marshals. The Territory's no place to go with it."

"What evidence?" Dink said. "I know what's happening here. I know who's doing it. I know the names of a few of her henchmen. But I can't prove a single murder. I can't prove she stole anything."

"Then we'll need to get some evidence."

Drago laughed. It sounded so easy.

Starr ushered Drago out of the building and snapped the padlock shut.

"Witnesses," Drago said. "I'll need to find some witnesses. I need to turn someone around. Get him to give state's evidence. I know a girl in that parlor house. She hates the place. She's seen a lot. She's scared. I want to spirit her out of there and get her to a safe place and then see if she'll talk."

"Good luck," Starr said wryly.

He had the feeling that they were engaging in fantasy. There they were, bravely standing in the silent wagon yard in a bright sun, laying plans to topple an evil empire. And all they held was some deuces.

He bridled the ribby old nag, threw a collar on, and tightened the surcingle. Then he backed the nag and hooked up the tugs. The nag looked pleased, and bared yellow-stained teeth cheerfully.

He headed through a lazy morning toward Hap Kilgore's establishment. He parked in front, pulled some wire traps out of the back, and walked in.

Silence greeted him.

"Kilgore!"

He found no one there. Gently he pulled aside the somber drapes and headed into the rear, smelling chemicals and rats. A male body in underdrawers lay on the tin-topped table. The man was middle-aged, jowly, dissipated, with a veinous nose. Rats careened in all directions and vanished. The man was rat-bitten, but not enough to kill him. It was no one Dink had ever seen before. No wounds, no punctures, no limbs missing. Maybe a natural death, a rarity equal to a solar eclipse in Skeleton Gulch.

"Kilgore," Dink bellowed.

This time he heard a grunt, and Kilgore appeared, tucking his shirt and pulling up suspenders.

"A man can't go to the outhouse without being harassed," Kilgore growled. "You shouldn't be back here."

"Who is he?"

"None of your business, rat catcher."

"How did he die?"

Kilgore's glance was sly. "I picked him up at the Yellow Rose's. They said he had died in the saddle, courtesy of Lulu. Overtaxed himself. Heh, heh."

"Married?"

"Drago, there aren't twenty married people in the gulch."

"Why are there only men in the cemetery?"

"Because it's a mining town, Drago. There aren't but a few women."

"Is it because the women end up bones in those barrels?"

Kilgore pursed his lips. "You'd better leave."

"I'm going to catch your rats. I'll do it for nothing. I'll just set up some traps here."

"Don't!"

Dink paused.

"They perform certain services, but I won't say what."

"They save you an embalming."

"Yes, and other valuable things. A coffin. Barrels, Drago, barrels sometimes cost nothing at all. Then I can profit a little. I can put ten skeletons into a big wine cask and two or three into a beer keg."

"Who pays you?"

Hap Kilgore drew himself up with dignity. "The relatives of the deceased, of course."

"Who pays for unknown women?"

"The city."

"You mean the Yellow Rose."

"Drago, she is the city."

"How many women have you buried?"

"You know, Drago, I don't keep track."

"How much do you get?"

"That's not your business, but it's twenty-five, just between us."

"Plus any gold in the teeth, the usable clothing, anything left by accident on a finger. Let's see, a used cask costs two dollars. You have your rats, so there's no preparation cost. I'd say you make a good profit."

"It's a sacred business, sir. I perform a sacred and needed service."

"How long have you been here?"

"Three years, two months, and ten days, Drago."

"How many people have you buried?"

"Hardly any. There's not much trade. I should head for a larger town."

"Do you have any friends?"

Hap Kilgore glared. "Mighty personal, I'd say. I don't make friends because I don't want to bury them."

"No one in Skeleton Gulch has any friends. It's odd. There never was a lonelier town. I just thought I'd ask. Anyone you drink with? Play poker with? Go hunting with? Have over for dinner?"

Kilgore shook his head.

"Maybe you've stuffed a hundred people in barrels. Is that a good guess?"

"Not that many, Drago. Sometimes I am called upon to clean out noxious places, bone by bone. Not just the alleys. But the rat holes. Many have perished here, God save their souls. I like to give each and every soul a fine sendoff, with dignity, with a dirge, with a clergyman, except there aren't any, and with words from the Good Book. Yes, I'll stake my reputation on it. Mr. Prescott here, why, he'll have as fine a sendoff as the presidents of the United States."

"Did all those bones in barrels you planted out there in the cemetery get a sendoff?"

"Oh, no, Drago. Those were vagrants."

"I'll set up some rat traps in here."

"And catch my rats? Pox on you, Drago."

Chapter 34

Sweet lascivious Cherry. Dink was determined to get Cherry out of there. Maybe, far away from Skeleton Gulch, Cherry would open up and tell lawmen what she knew, and she knew plenty. But there was so much more to it. He remembered her terror, her vulnerability, her ritual seduction of him, her nervous glances at the shadowed entryways from whence pain and grief might rise. He remembered her still-young body, which was visible under the gauzy gown she wore. It was how she lured customers to her bosom, this girl of the night.

She had been delegated to off-hours duty obviously. She was there at the door for the stray male who wandered in at dawn while the whole parlor house and saloon slumbered. He would see her again, and this time spirit her away before she could protest, before terror froze her to that place. And if not, he could at least give her more waxen packets of rat's-bane, a weapon against the Yellow Rose's terror. He would not give her any of the strychnine-laced barley for fear that she would use it to destroy herself.

He spent that night restlessly awaiting the wee small hours, the silent time when each mortal is alone with the stars and conscience and love and regret. He studied the rotation of the Dipper around Polaris, and when the time seemed ripe, he roused himself from his bedroll in frigid air, dressed, wrapped a blanket around his shoulders against the sharp cold, perked some Java over a small campfire in the wagon yard, being a man who scarcely functioned until he got a shot of the stimulant running through his veins, and then harnessed the old nag. The ribby old thing was faintly shocked at being put to toil at such an hour, and yawned lazily.

Then he wiped the icy dew off the wagon seat and hawed the horse out of the yard and into Middle Street, and up the steady grade toward the Yellow Rose's parlor house, which dominated Skeleton Gulch like a medieval castle lording over a French village. Not a lamp glowed. At one point a footpad tried to grab the bridle, but a crack of Dink's whip shot the horse past trouble and up the steep hill. He reached the flat where the dark and sinister building stood, turned the wagon around so it faced downslope for a quick getaway, and stepped down into a chill night.

He hoped Cherry would be on duty as she had in the past. If not, he would have to find excuses, bluff his way to a drink. He couldn't afford a girl, not that he was averse to that. It was just that he had more urgent plans, the rescue of Cherry topping them.

There was something evil about that building, something that wrought a shudder in him. But he had been in grim places before, so he stepped to the massive door and knocked, a quick, sharp rap he hoped wouldn't awaken anyone.

When the door slowly creaked open, he found himself staring not at Cherry, dressed in gauze, but at the Yellow Rose herself, in her silken robe. She towered over him.

"Why, it's Drago. Do come in, sweetheart. I suppose you've come to see Cherry."

"No, not particularly. I thought I'd have a drink."

"Yes, she set up a drink for you, didn't she? I can do that too, come in, come in."

Dink stood at the door, half inclined to escape while he could, not knowing what awaited him in that place, that dawn, that hour. He stepped in.

"You'd like to see Cherry, I'm sure. What a lovely child she is. Her name is really Emma. Emma Holstein. A milk cow, you might say. But that was the name of her husband before an accident killed him. He fell into the shaft of the Victor Mine and perished, and poor Emma had no way to survive until I offered her a position here. Poor things. I extend my charity, you see. I give them a life. What an innocent girl she is. She's done nothing to deserve her cruel fate. All she wants is her liberty. Should I give it to her, Drago?"

"Yes."

She smiled. "Come back to the kitchen. We've rather expected you. Cherry will be eager to see you."

Alarms were ringing within Dink's head. "I think I'll come some other time," he said.

Too late. Out of the shadows one of her thugs materialized, caught Dink in his meaty hands, and lightly manhandled Dink toward the kitchen.

"There now, Drago. You'll get to see Cherry. We've been keeping her for you. You're the newest of the gents sent to our little town by General Cook. What a nice ploy. A rat catcher, a tradesman making an honest living. You can run around, crawl into dark corners, catch rats, and who would know? What will you tell them about Skeleton Gulch? Will you say the Yellow Rose owns the town? Owns the souls of everyone in it? Owns Cherry? Well, I do."

They reached an ordinary kitchen at the back of the building. A high window looked upslope toward the ridge with the mines. A large cookstove and counters and cabinets lined its walls. A table with wooden chairs awaited diners. A peculiar odor rose from the room, not the odor of cooked or rotted food. Something else, something faintly foul. Rats, yes. This building was infested with rats. Years of dealing with them had given him a sixth sense. He could sense the presence of rats even when he couldn't smell or see them, and now that sense was clamoring within him.

The grayest of dawn light filled the window, which was set too high for anyone to look in. Within the kitchen lay deepest gloom, but no one had lit a lamp.

Dink felt powerful hands clasping his arms and knew he was outweighed by maybe even a hundred pounds. He did not know whether he would live to see another sunrise. For the moment, he must be quiet. He could run fast. There would be a moment when he might break away.

He heard the moaning before he saw Cherry. Someone large was manhandling her through dark corridors. Then suddenly she was pushed into the kitchen. She wore nothing. An animal groan rose out of her. She staggered there, righted herself, and cowered, sheer terror afflicting her.

"Oh, don't, please don't," she whispered, and then gagged on her own siliva, gasping and choking.

"Why, Cherry, here's your friend Mr. Drago," said the Yellow Rose.

But Cherry was sobbing.

A third thug, this one skinny and short and bald, pulled aside a small rug, revealing a trapdoor, and Dink knew at once what would happen and what he would witness.

The light at the window quickened. Dawn had arrived, the beginning of a bright new day in Skeleton Gulch.

The skinny one pulled a ring up and lifted the trapdoor. A ghastly odor enveloped the room. Not rats, not garbage, but death.

"Look in there, Drago."

The goon manhandled him forward until Dink thought he'd be thrown in. There was light. The rat hole had a passage out to grass. A seething mass of rats scurried about. At the bottom was a pile of what? Bones perhaps.

"Our garbage pit, Drago."

The goon pulled him back. His pulse catapulted into trip-hammer speeds.

"Cherry, my dear, enjoy yourself," said the Yellow Rose.

"Oh, God, oh, God," she wailed.

The goon dragged her to the brink and then kicked her feet out from under her. She screamed, dropped into the pit, screeched, and then they slid the heavy trapdoor over her.

Dink struggled violently, but he was no match for the giant who pinned him in place.

"This is murder!" he cried.

"Why, Drago, how could you think such a thing?"

He heard screeching and sobs and gasping and howling now. He heard thumping and thrashing. He heard sobs and howls, a wail that shivered straight through his very being.

"Let her out! Let her out!" he snapped, feeling helpless in those massive arms that pinned him tight.

The screeching reached a climax and held there, howls and groans, and then swiftly the sounds ebbed. The thumping ceased. He heard a fit of coughing, dreadful gasping, and then one or two more thumps.

Then nothing. The nothingness stretched out. The silence of a peaceful dawn returned. It was as if none of it had happened.

"There, you see? You got to visit with Cherry," said the Yellow Rose. "She was innocent, poor thing. Entirely innocent. She didn't know you're a detective. All she wanted was to stay alive, get away. Who can blame her for that?

Poor Cherry. Now I have one less sweetheart to offer my clients."

Dink was beyond replying. The grip of the goon never relaxed.

"Too bad the rats are all sated, Drago. It will be a few days before they're hungry again. I could put you in there and let you wait for them to start in, but I won't. We keep them there with garbage, you know."

"What are you saying?"

"Why, my dear, you have seen the Yellow Rose in all her glory. There is nothing in the Yellow Rose that restrains her. Nothing of pity. Nothing of remorse. Nothing of kindness. Nothing of mercy. Nothing at all but darkness."

"Why?" Dink asked.

"Why? So that you might see the Yellow Rose firsthand. See just the sort of woman she is. See that she is beyond redemption."

Drago was too nauseated to care. He had witnessed murder. They had made him a witness. They were toying with him still. He scarcely knew what his fate would be. He stared at her and found that he couldn't see her face. It was there before him, her rough and oddly handsome visage, and yet he couldn't see her. It was as if a dark veil cloistered her; as if she had glass eyes, and no one could see in or see the person she was.

Then she settled his fate for him.

"Come see me again, Drago. Be sure and tell General Cook."

They dragged him to the door. She opened it. The thug released him. He stood there, suddenly freed, fearful that with his first step toward his dray, a bullet would fell him.

But it didn't. He staggered toward the wagon. He heard an odd laugh behind him, and the door swung shut. He tumbled into his wagon, and the nag trotted away even before Dink could sit. Away, away.

Chapter 35

A tremor ran through Dink's body, shaking him like an aspen leaf. He sprawled in his wagon seat. The nag craned its head back, studied Dink, and headed off at a smart trot.

Dink didn't care where to; just away, away.

The eastern horizon was turning blue. The rest of the world was black. The nag trotted down the grade, stepping high, and headed into town. Dink realized he didn't even have the lines in his hand. It didn't matter. Away, away.

The nag slowed when it reached Middle Street, peered about, and then took off again, having decided in its own way where to take Dink and the wagon. The old plug didn't stop until he reached Doc Cutler's place, which slumbered quietly in the early twilight. Another tremor rocked through Dink.

The nag stopped, turned around, and studied Dink. Had the horse read his mind? Dink and the nag had been teamed up for a decade and a half. Dink slumped in the wagon seat, too paralyzed to get down. The nag snorted.

Dink slowly slid to earth and felt another tremor wrack him. He stumbled toward Doc's rear door, found it open, and yelled.

"It's you, Drago. Who else would howl at five in the morning?"

Dink careened into the gloomy interior, past the silent kitchen to Doc's parlor, where Doc, as usual, slumped in his ratty robe and decrepit slippers.

And that was as far as Dink got. He felt another tremor and toppled. When he managed to right himself and start to stand, he found Doc kneeling beside him.

"Whoa, Drago," Doc said.

Cutler's hands were busy; one on Dink's forehead hunting for fever. The other was looking for pulse, and eventually Doc's hand clamped over Dink's wrist.

Doc grunted. "Close to fibrillation."

He rose, lumbered into his office, and returned with a brown glass bottle, from which he extracted a white pill.

"I'll get some water. Wash it down."

"What is it?"

"Dover's Powder. It'll quiet you."

Dink groaned. His heart was tripping too fast. He swallowed Doc's pill and downed some water, which he almost heaved up, but then lay back. It took a while, but then Dink grew aware that he was calmer, his heart was slowing, its beat was steadying.

Doc plainly wanted to know everything, but was making himself wait.

After another few minutes, while Dink stared at the ceiling, hearing Cherry's screams, Doc nodded, and Dink sat up.

"Talk?" Doc said.

"I can't."

"Well, let me see. You've been at the Yellow Rose's."

"How do you know . . ."

"Where else?"

Dink closed his eyes, seeing in his mind's eye the thug

knocking the feet out from under Cherry, and shoving her screaming into the rat hole.

"I can't," Dink said.

"That is quite understandable."

Dink felt his heart quiet. But he still was hearing Cherry's muffled screams and feeling the iron grip of the man who held him there, forcing him to witness.

"I'll never be the same again," Dink said.

"Neither will I, Drago."

Dink slid into a torpor, hardly aware of the world around him. When at last he did recover his wits, he found himself on the floor, a blanket thrown over him, and Doc Cutler slouched uneasily in his chair, eyeing Dink intently.

"You're all right now, Drago," Doc said.

"No, I'll never be all right."

Doc sat there, unshaven, unwashed, but not uncaring. He reached for a fat cigar, scratched a lucifer, and sucked smoke.

Dink struggled to his feet, tumbled into the sole unoccupied chair, and drew his blanket around him, while Doc watched shrewdly.

"Don't say a word, Drago. No sense in it. Some things aren't fit to spend words upon."

Dink was grateful. He didn't want to speak of any of it, and doubted he ever would be able to tell Doc or anyone else what he had witnessed.

"She's toying with you, Drago. She's showing you her worst. She knows who you are because I ratted on you before I got so sick of myself. So aren't we a pair?"

Drago listened. Doc wasn't pumping him for the story, and Dink knew he couldn't tell it anyway.

"Now why would she toy with you? Why not get rid of you, same as she got rid of the other agents sent by Cook? That's what I've been worrying around. And I'm going to try a theory on you, and see what you think.

"I think the Yellow Rose is crying for help. She's showing you her worst and every time she does it, she's saying, 'Stop me, stop me.' Why didn't she just kill you, Drago? This morning, why didn't she? She had her chance, I imagine. But she didn't. She showed you her worst, forced you to witness the unspeakable, and I take the word literally. Unspeakable. You can't speak it. And then released you. That sounds to me like a lady who's begging you for something."

Dink listened. Doc was making sense.

"Now the way I see it, Drago, she's teetering on a knife edge and she could go either way: kill you like she did the others, or hope you'll stop her. Right now she's desperate to be stopped, wants to be stopped, wants it so much she . . . whatever she did that left you sitting there wrapped in a blanket."

"I want to destroy every rat in Skeleton Gulch," Dink said.

Doc sucked on his cigar and exhaled, swirling pungent smoke through the shadowed parlor. It was full day now.

"Now, if a woman's begging to be stopped, she's in a bad way. If one crime doesn't shock, then try a worse crime, and worse and worse, until someone slays the monster in her. That's how I see it anyway. You want me to start some Java, Drago?"

"I just want to sit."

"Your nag all right?"

"He's suffered my neglect before," Dink snapped.

Doc studied his guest. "If I saw something bad and didn't stop it, I guess I'd feel like I failed, like I'm to blame. If only I'd acted, did something, somehow."

Dink remembered the iron grip of the big thug and how he writhed against it, how he'd thrown his hundred-some pounds this way and that, how he'd yelled at the Yellow Rose, commanded her to stop, and how it did no good,

and how just by witnessing what happened he felt he had
failed.

"I see that in medicine," Doc said. "Half the time,
when something bad happens and I can't help the victim,
I hate myself. We're trained to keep our distance, but who
can? So you hate yourself, I hate myself . . . but not as
much as the Yellow Rose hates herself."

Doc slipped into silence again. Cigar smoke filtered
through the gloomy parlor, curled past the light pouring
through window drapes.

"If she's crying for help, Drago, then we should do
something."

"Such as?"

"Walk in and take her."

"Like that."

Doc wheezed, a smile on his face for the first time in
days. "How else?"

It was madness. Dink sank back into his blanket and
relived the ordeal of the kitchen.

"I've lost you," Doc said. "Drago, there's something worrying me. Sometimes something is so bad that a person
retreats, quits the real world, heads into some private
chamber of the soul and never comes out. I don't want
you to go there."

Dink nodded but said nothing.

"Here's what I'll do, Drago. I'll borrow a revolver somewhere, hide it on my commodious carcass, walk in there,
and shoot her down, all six bullets, and make sure she returns to the hole she crawled out of."

"You'd do that, Doc?"

Doc nodded and sucked hard on the cigar, turning the
lit end bright orange.

"You'd die," Dink said.

"That would be the idea, Drago. Now what are you
going to do? She's waiting. She's hurting more than life

itself is worth. If you don't stop her, you know how she'll feel? Disappointed in you. She's decided you're the man to stop her. You're the anointed one."

"Stop that."

Oddly, Doc smiled. "If you don't save her from herself, she'll kill you."

"What if I walked away?"

"You wouldn't get a mile down the road. She has eyes and ears everywhere. It's your fate, Drago. She's begging to be stopped. And you're the person to do it. It's your destiny."

"Doc, you've read too much mythology."

Doc sucked on his cigar until it crackled, and shot a blue plume into the room.

"I went to see Cherry. That's one of her girls. Was. She was the girl on duty when everyone else slept. We'd talked a few times. All I wanted was to spirit her out of there. Then, this time, the Yellow Rose opened the door. She was waiting for me. And this time . . . I saw what has only been a whisper in Skeleton Gulch and I will never get the screams out of my ears, Doc, never."

Doc didn't reply, but nodded and smoked his cigar, and rubbed the stubble on his jowls.

"There's one other person in this town who knows who I am. Maybe he'll help. That'd make three."

Doc waited, alert.

"Vanishing Jack," Dink said.

Chapter 36

The jangle of a bell announced the arrival of a patient. Doc cussed softly, excused himself, and headed into his public chambers, still wrapped in his dingy robe and ratty slippers. He now had a week's gray stubble decorating his jowls and an unkempt mat of white-streaked hair drifting off in all directions.

Dink wondered if the man was going to live in that robe the rest of his life.

"Oh, you're not up," someone said.

"I'm as up as I'll get," Doc growled.

"But . . . you haven't completed your toilet."

"I can look at your tonsils just as well or better," doc retorted. "Now what's the trouble?"

"Cancer of the sacroiliac," the man replied. "I think I am dying."

"I see. A backache. And it's no wonder. Your skull is too large for your backbone. You are carrying too much weight above your shoulders. Solid bone too. You need to shed twenty pounds. I suggest we cut off your head."

"I'll come back after you've had your Java," the man said.

"I drink straight bourbon for breakfast and Java before retiring. As you can see, it's an improvement on the conventional wisdom. Now, let's see about your sacroiliac. Right there? That's not your sacroiliac. That's your Last Will and Testament."

Dink thought he had heard enough. The Dover's Powder had done its work and quieted him. He cast aside the blanket and slipped out the rear door, discovering that the sun had barely started its journey this bleak day. It was still early.

The nag yawned, bared yellow teeth, and whickered. Dink absently stroked its neck. Faithful old beast. Dink clambered up and the nag instantly headed for the wagon yard, trotting briskly through a quickening town. It was going to be another smoky day, with the trick currents of the mountains lowering yellow smoke over Skeleton Gulch. The nag coughed and headed for the yard where the air was better.

Dink sat numbly, uncaring. He heard only Cherry's screams.

He turned into Starr's wagon yard and found turmoil. A large freight train had rolled in and now burly teamsters were unhooking weary oxen from their tugs and driving them toward the pens. Others were lifting the heavy oxbows off the beasts' shoulders and checking them for chafing. Others, sweating in the early sun, were unloading crates and barrels off the tailgates of the freight wagons into carts and light wagons that would haul the goods to outlying places. Starr paced through the chaos, a clipboard in hand, noting what had arrived.

It was not a time to be visiting, and Dink didn't want to visit anyway. Starr had tons of goods to deliver or store, and scores of animals to see to. He had his hair drawn into a queue again, which somehow made him look all the more like his family. Dink found a peaceful corner of the yard, unharnessed the nag, led it to the pen, and pulled off the bridle. The nag butted him and trotted off, happy to court the oxen and bite at flies.

There was something Dink had to do, maybe the most important thing he had ever done, and this day he would prepare, and this night he would do it. He dug an iron bucket out of his wagon, filled it with barley, pulled on India rubber gloves, and then carefully mixed two ounces of arsenic trioxide from a small canister into two quarts of water and poured it over the barley. He stirred with a wooden paddle, making sure that every grain of barley was well saturated with the arsenic. He stirred until his arms were numb, but didn't notice. He stirred until he knew that every grain would kill a rat. Then he poured the wet grain onto an ancient canvas he kept for the occasion, keeping a wary eye out for any living thing, from oxen to birds. Twice he chased off crows. While the sun did its work, Dink diluted the remaining solution with as much fresh water as he could add to the bucket, and carried it well away from the wagon yard. In a gulch below the yard, he dug a hole with a small spade, poured out the lethal water, and shoveled dirt over it until he was satisfied that no creature would suffer.

He had a gallon of the poisonous barley. He spread it over his canvas to finish the drying, then poured it into a metal canister and pressed its top down tightly. He poured buckets of water over the canvas and let it dry in the warm sun.

He was very tired. Sometimes he heard Cherry's screams. Other times he felt her spirit hovering next to him, watching him, her big hurt eyes seeing his every act.

Then, prepared, he didn't do anything. He didn't feel like lunch. Starr was busy, which was good. Dink didn't feel the need for company. He clambered into his wagon and tumbled into his bedroll and immediately slept. When he finally stirred, the day had passed by, wood smoke from kitchen fires hung in the evening air, and the fierce mountain light had dwindled.

He was not hungry. He wondered if he would ever be hungry again. Dark came slowly, with blue twilight lingering over the western mountains. He needed full dark. He dug in his trunk and found black britches and a black sweater and a black watch cap, and put them on. He checked his tools. He didn't know what he would need. Then, around ten when it was almost black, he slipped a bridle into the mouth of the nag, harnessed up, and steered his wagon quietly into the night. He was going to do what he had to do and nothing would stop him. Nothing.

He steered up Middle Street, the quiet clop of hooves echoing off the wooden stores. Middle Street was mostly dark; over on Yellow Rose Street every saloon hung lanterns, and every double door emitted raucous noise, or fiddle music, or piano music, into the summer night.

He did not tackle the grade up to the Yellow Rose's parlor house. Instead, he circled the base of the hill until he found a remote area at the end of an alley, perhaps fifty yards from the building above. The Yellow Rose was doing a fine business. Light spilled from almost every window. It was the shank of the evening and the girls were all busy. Except for Cherry.

Dink waited. When the last of the twilight turned into blackness, he reconnoitered, slipping upslope to the rear of the building, his black attire keeping him more or less invisible. He looked for the housemen and saw none. He reached the rubblestone foundation and began hunting for something, he didn't quite know what, but it would be near the kitchen. The rat smell caught his nostrils.

Then he found it, a tile drainpipe poking out of the foundation at the level of the grade. So many rats had come and gone that no weed or grass survived there for yards around. From now on, he would have to guess, have to remember. The rat hole was close to the wall. The drainpipe ran perhaps three feet, but probably less. He probed it with a stick, and found no barrier. Then he slipped down to his wagon and waited for thicker dark, quieter times, sleepy times. He didn't mind the wait. He was going to kill every rat, every son and grandson of every rat in that hole. This was the beginning of the end for the Yellow Rose, even if she didn't know it. This was the first rat hole on his list. Tomorrow night he would tackle one of the others on Yellow Rose Street.

Around midnight he carried the evil grain up to the rat hole, the canister wrapped in a dark towel so it would not glint in starlight. He saw no one. Rats scurried away as he approached the drain tile.

He carried with him a broomstick with a spoon on the end, a device he used to drop rat poison in areas he could not reach. Carefully, he slid open the canister, filled the spoon, and probed into the drainpipe. He encountered no obstacle. At the last, he dumped the spoonload and then repeated, over and over, driven by something almost berserk. And then, because rats are canny and reject foods they learn are harmful, he added the West African rat's-bane, and then some strychnine-laced barley for good measure. Obsessively he jammed the rat poisons into that murderous place, heaping up more than needed, enough to kill a thousand rats. Then, suddenly, he quit. A sob caught in his throat.

He withdrew the spoon on a stick, scattered still more seed close to the hole, and hoped birds or other creatures wouldn't get to it. He doubted they would. The rat smell was so powerful that no small animal would venture there. Then, feeling a savage pleasure in what he had achieved, he retreated down the hill to his wagon, loaded his gear, quietly hawed the nag to life, and let it clop its way back. But this time he steered into Rat Alley, behind the saloons on Yellow Rose Street, and artfully dropped more rat poison along the way, selecting the rat's-bane for fear of harming dogs or other creatures. Then he covered Death Alley on the other side, threw West African rat's-bane along the path. By the time he was done, he had only a few packets of the rat's-bane left. But he knew the rat population of Skeleton Gulch would shrink.

He eyed the bordellos along that stretch, looking for rat holes, but it was too dark and too late. That was something to do in broad daylight.

He would by God clean up Skeleton Gulch. He would kill the rats. He would free it from darkness and misery. He would drive away every saloonman who ever made a Mickey Finn. Every pickpocket and footpad who ever stalked the sporting district. He would clean out the richer pirates whose homes nestled in that secluded gulch.

He rattled into the wagon yard, unharnessed the old nag, who sighed, caved to the earth, and rolled happily. Then Drago fell into his bedroll. He had fought back with the weapons at his command, and would keep on fighting, and would never stop until he had driven the devil out of Skeleton Gulch.

Chapter 37

Was he in Hell? Smoke, flame, scorching heat. Dink awakened, chased the fog of sleep away, and discovered that his wagon was engulfed in crackling flame. He couldn't breathe the furnace air. His face was blistered. Embers dropped into his hair. All that spared the rest of him was his bedroll. Above him fire raced up the canvas and caught the wooden bows.

He yanked the bedroll around him and clawed toward the front, only to face a wall of flame. The rear of the wagon was ablaze. He coughed, desperate for air.

Trapped.

He jumped over the side, through fire, and landed hard on the clay of the wagon yard, hurting his shoulder, banging his head. He heard shouts. His wagon burned furiously. He rolled away from the heat. He smelled coal oil in the black smoke boiling into the dawn sky. His hair was singed, his cheeks and ears felt burnt. He got to his feet and staggered away, out of the circle of hell, and watched the flames consume everything he possessed. The box traps, his trunk, his tools, his clothing, his moccasins.

Someone came running with a bucket of water.

"No, let it burn," Dink yelled.

The teamster tossed the bucket on the inferno anyway. "Let it burn and stay away from the smoke."

The teamster stared at Dink as if he were daft. But then Starr appeared.

"You heard him. Stay away. Don't breathe smoke. There's poisons in there."

The teamster dropped the bucket and backed off.

Dink saw rage in the man's face.

Starr warned the other yardmen away and herded them all upwind. Dink knew that the smoke carried arsenic and strychnine in it, and that it would sicken, maybe kill, living creatures who breathed it.

The wagon took a long time to die. Fire licked its box and its axles and its spoked wheels and its springs. But in time it collapsed into a smouldering heap.

Dink found himself with nothing but the blanket he wore and some small clothes.

"Almost got you," Starr said.

"You're lucky I'm parked away from your freight wagons."

"They're next," Starr said, something fatalistic in his voice. "Coal oil."

They heard a shout. A yardman pointed at the pens.

Dink hurried that way, knowing what he would find.

The old nag lay in the dirt, its throat cut, its neck reddened. His old nag, his old friend. The horse that knew his mind better than he did.

Grief flooded through Dink. He opened the gate and knelt beside the old horse. Its eyes were open. It looked surprised. It didn't believe any mortal would do such a thing. Dink drew a hand over the old nag's mane.

He was aware that Starr stood beside him, and two yardmen, and then Starr helped him up. Off a ways, the wagon fire settled into a pile of glowing coals.

Starr issued sharp commands. "Stay away from that fire. Keep out of the smoke. Keep the stock away. Don't touch anything over there. We'll need to bury everything deep. And drag Mr. Drago's horse out to the gulch." He glanced at Drago, a question in his eyes. Dink nodded.

Starr steered Dink toward the yard's offices, lit now by the earliest gold of the rising sun. The construction crew building the saloon across the road began to arrive on the job, and they were staring.

Dink, wrapped in his brown blanket, slumped into a chair.

"Now you don't leave town so easily," Starr said. "The woman has claws."

"I don't care about the wagon and traps. But the old nag . . ."

"He was a great old horse."

Starr was trying to be kind, but Dink didn't want to talk about it anymore. Sometimes the bond between a man and an animal is too private to be understood by others.

"I haven't talked to you about yesterday," Dink said. "And how this ties in with yesterday. I'm not sure I can talk about it."

Starr waited.

"I saw a murder," Dink began. It was grievously hard to talk. He forced the words out in small timid spurts, in sharp staccato bursts, and finally in a slow sad roll of events, including his refuge at Doc Cutler's house.

"The nag took me there. The nag knew I needed Doc," Dink said. "The old nag was my friend."

"I guess we need to outfit you."

"Could you wire General Cook for some money? He's put my pay into my account in Denver. But out here, in the field as they call it, I made my living as a rat catcher."

"She'd learn about it. She pays the telegraph man for a copy of every flimsy."

"I'll have to owe you then."

"I'll send a man to the mercantile."

Dink scribbled a list of clothing and sizes. Shoes worried him the most.

"Drago, you need a revolver. I'll stake you to one."

"She would like that, wouldn't she?" Dink said. "A little man with a big gun. No . . . I'm better off without one."

"How can you even think that?"

"She has layers of toughs, every one of them skilled with weapons. No, there's a key somewhere. Doc gave me the idea. There's a key that will stop her. Something in her is crying out. I don't know what. But if I strap on a side arm I'll never find out. I've never shot one in my life. Kilgore will add my bones to one of his barrels."

Starr didn't like it. "Suicide, Drago."

But Dink didn't respond.

"If you want, I can sneak you out of Skeleton Gulch tonight. Lend you a mule. I slide in and out of here all the time. Vanishing Jack knows every trail."

"I'm not done here. I've just begun."

Starr smiled suddenly. "You're burned out and penniless. You've lost your livelihood but you're not quitting. I like that. We both have business to finish with the Yellow Rose, Drago. And there's three of us to do it. I want to talk with Cutler. His theory about her interests me. The idea that she's aching to be stopped; that she knows she's out of control. That she didn't throw you into the rat hole because something inside of her is begging you to stop her. That's all new to me, but I think it's true. That's why some madmen leave clues, leave hints, so someone else will stop them. Maybe my aunt's one of those."

"Cutler was the one who ratted on the first agents sent by General Cook. For money. He got sucked into it."

"I thought so."

"He's so stricken now I think he wonders whether to keep on living. I haven't told him your name. I told him only that I know Vanishing Jack."

"Tell him, Drago."

"I will."

"I'll send a man for your outfit. Stay here, unless you want to wander around in a blanket."

"He'll have trouble finding ready-made shoes my size. I'll take whatever this town offers. Boots, shoes, moccasins."

Starr vanished into the yard and from the office window Dink watched him instruct a yardman. The man nodded and took the list, and hiked toward town.

She had forced the issue, trying to kill him or burn him out or cut off his transportation. So it had come down to that. He had nothing but the blanket thrown over his shoulders and was facing a mob. The odd thing was, he didn't feel intimidated. He had two friends; she had none, and was not even a friend to herself.

There were some men in the kitchen, so Dink headed that way.

"Burnt out, eh? You tip over a lamp?" asked a skinny teamster.

"I don't know when or how it started," Dink said.

"You got anything left but that blanket?"

"It's Starr's blanket."

"You got nothing?"

Dink nodded.

"Me and the fellas, we'll see what we can do, eh?"

"I would be most thankful."

"Your rat poisons, they went up in smoke?"

"Yes. I'd used most of them last night, all the arsenic, but that was deadly smoke, and everything in that ash pile should be buried deep."

"You kill a few rats around here, you do the whole town some good."

Dink nodded. He sipped some Java and ate some johnnycakes and waited.

The yardman didn't return for two hours, but he had some clothing for Dink including two bib overalls, two flannel shirts, some underwear, and some stockings.

"No ready-made shoes at all, not that size. But the cobbler, Dobbins, says he'll fix up some old moccasins he's got in there. You can pick them up. He got right at it."

"Thank you. I'll dress and go there."

He found a corner and changed into the ready-mades. The denim of the bib overalls was as stiff as the flannels and he knew it would take some while to soften. But he was clad. He had a place to eat. He had a blanket to cover him in some corner of Starr's yard.

He set off for town barefoot, found Dobbins, who was as good as his word, and tried on the high-top moccasins. They fit well enough.

"I sewed some soles on and cut the toe back," the cobbler said.

"It'll be a while before I can pay."

"It's been paid," Dobbins said.

"Then I'm in debt," Dink replied.

He walked into the morning sun without the faintest idea of what to do or where to go. Or how to stop the Yellow Rose.

Chapter 38

Dink slipped into Doc Cutler's back door, and was startled to find John Starr sitting quietly in the dingy parlor. Doc had a patient and was rattling around in his front chamber.

Starr nodded. He had obviously come to introduce himself to Doc. That relieved Dink, who dreaded to reveal Starr's secret.

Voices drifted back to them.

"No, Miss Stark, you do not need to disrobe. If you had leprosy I would see it upon your extremities."

"I wouldn't mind," Miss Stark said. "Some women would mind."

"Well, first of all, you don't have leprosy. Your fingers are not falling off. You have all ten toes. Your earlobes are intact. Your mouth is just fine. Your lips are in capital shape, good for ingestion and whatever other uses you put them to."

"My ears stick out. If they stuck out, I'd want leprosy to shrink them."

"No, Miss Stark, you would not want leprosy to shrink them. You don't have the disease. It is actually very difficult to get it. And you haven't been where you might."

There was a titter. "Actually, I was less worried about leprosy than I am about having a baby."

"Now why would you think you're going to have one?"

"After every meal my stomach bloats."

"I see. So perhaps you've swallowed some little starter babies in your pudding and now they're perking up?"

"How did you know?"

"I have been a physician for longer than you've been alive. I tell you what. You just go ahead and eat what you want and make all the babies you want."

"Oh, I'd run out of names."

"That's fine, call them all Cutler."

"Oh!"

"Ah, that'll be two dollars."

"I only have fifty cents."

"That will do. Now you can lace those shoes."

There was some shuffling, and at last the door opened and closed with a jangle of bells.

Doc shuffled back into the grim parlor. He was still wearing his ratty robe and scruffy slippers. He eased into his ancient chair and studied the empty tumbler next to it.

"People catch the most fashionable diseases," he said. "That and biblical diseases. If there's a disease in Matthew, Mark, Luke, or John, I've got a patient." He eyed Dink. "I've been talking to Starr here."

"Starr's freight company yard has been my home for weeks."

"Your wagon burned," Doc said.

"Everything."

"Purely an accident," Doc said. "Spontaneous combustion."

"John here provided the clothing on my back."

"You're welcome to anything I have, including a bunk. He's also been telling me we three have a certain interest, or object, in common. For him, it's a family matter. For you, it's a professional matter. For me, it's repentance."

"There are no secrets among us," Starr said. It was a way of letting Dink know what had transpired before Dink arrived.

"None," said Doc. "I have informed this gent that I was on the take and ought not to be trusted."

"So I trusted him," Starr said. "Any man who won't get dressed after facing his conscience is a man I trust."

"Ah! Then I'll put on my striped pants and gaiters and boiled shirt! Then you'll see the sort of scoundrel I am, Starr."

Dink listened carefully to all this, unsure where this meeting was heading. But he liked what he heard. Here were two friends, and they were discovering they had a great task before them, and not a one of them had the faintest idea how to proceed against a sinister woman with brutal whims and all the powers of the world at her beck and call.

"Doc, I would like John to hear your theory about his aunt. The theory that she's crying out for help, she wants to be stopped, something in her knows she's a lost soul."

Doc settled in his old chair and pulled his robe tight. His calves rose like white celery stalks out of those foul slippers.

"It's just a notion, Drago. You need an expert, not some rogue doctor on the take."

"It's the most important theory of the Yellow Rose that I have, and I want you to explain it to John."

"It's just speculation. You need science, not fiddlesticks." Doc sighed. "I am interested in the criminal mind, because I am one."

Starr started to object, but Doc waved him off.

"The Yellow Rose embarked upon a strange trajectory. At first it was wild greed. She wanted gold and nothing would stop her. She, ah, disposed of your father, Mr. Starr. She wanted the other mines so she disposed of their owners one way or another. I don't know the whole of it, except that none of the owners or their heirs lives. She missed you and your sisters. She grew rich, but having killed, she found her soul was restless. Gold with guilt. Gold with fear of God's justice.

"That separates her from the ordinary run-of-the-mill criminal, the sort who has no conscience and has no more ethical sense than a rat. And I suspect, Drago, that rats have their own ethics."

"They do."

"What do you do when you believe you are beyond redemption? Ah, there's the key. What do you do when you are brimming with self-loathing? When nothing on earth can restore your soul to you? In some cases you withdraw from life and wear your robe and slippers."

Doc's voice quivered slightly.

"In other cases, you flaunt it. The Yellow Rose flaunted it. She was rich, she had a fortune pouring in every hour of every day from these mines that she had killed and stolen and seduced to get, and all it brought her was darkness. So what did she do? She sought ways to make herself more wicked than she already was, or felt she was. What was a whole new kingdom to conquer? Vice. She made herself a madam. What else? The Tenderloin. She bought saloons and gambling dens and opium parlors and began to bilk and kill and roll and destroy more victims. And the greater her success, the greater her lust for villainy. She didn't care who knew. She wanted it known. She would be the bad one."

"There is something of that in my family," Starr said. "Something in the blood. Something of that in me. My grandfather was a corsair, a pirate with letters of marque, and my grandmother came from the wildest stock ever to rise up in Mexico. Maybe all this is just Consuela's blood running true."

Doc shrugged. "Maybe so."

"Where is this leading us, Doc?" Dink asked. "If your theory's true, what will she do next?"

"She's already doing it. She's begging to be stopped."

"I don't see it."

"She knows who you are because I ratted on you. That was worth a lot of money, ratting on you. But she hasn't destroyed you."

"She tried this morning."

"Yes, but that's because you haven't stopped her. She wants you to stop her."

"I don't follow, Doc."

"She has had a dozen chances to kill you. She could have shot you when you went on a picnic. She could have thrown you into her rat hole any time. Instead, she preferred to horrify you, killing that poor woman before your eyes. Doesn't that tell you something?"

"Not exactly."

"It tells me she's at the end of her rope. She cannot think of any way to be more evil, to flaunt her cruelty, and you've thought of no way to stop her, to shut her down, to demolish her evil grip on this town. So she'll kill you. You failed her."

"I failed her?"

Doc was laughing and coughing and snarling. "Get out of here, Drago. I'm done with you."

"Doc, what should I do?"

"How should I know? Walk in and drill her with a forty-five-caliber pill."

"But if there's a pattern, a compulsion, she'll do something you can foresee?"

"Foresee? Do you think this is science? That I've read

this in my medical texts? Ha! You're an idiot, Drago. You need a dose of salts. Your mental bowels are clogged."

"Take a guess."

"I'll make that guess," Starr said. "There's only one thing she still wants: Vanishing Jack and his mine. I think you could lure her out of her house by telling her you know where to find me."

They hashed out ideas for an hour, but in fact no one could say what might gain them anything. Who were they? A cranky doctor who lived in his bathrobe and slippers, a successful freight operator related to the Yellow Rose, and an out-of-business rat catcher. Against them was an organization with ears and appetites and powers beyond anything known in the West.

"Well, maybe we'll think of something tomorrow, if tomorrow ever comes," Starr said. "I have a freight outfit due late today, if all goes well, and I'd better head back."

"Leave separately, one at a time," Doc said.

It was good advice.

Dink slipped out first, cut across rear yards until he was on Victor Street, and then wandered. He felt oddly lonely but he had been lonely all his life, and couldn't really explain why. Here he was with two new friends, strong and gifted friends in their own way, trying to help him, offering what resources they could. And yet that somehow made him feel all the more lonely. Nothing helped.

So much for theories, he thought. He had hoped that maybe Doc would have some plan, some understanding of Yellow Rose's nature that would allow Dink to pull a thread and her world would collapse and he would haul her off to the authorities.

Instead he had nothing. And he knew, somehow, that as helpful as Doc and Starr had been, he would have to confront the Yellow Rose by himself and somehow bring her to her Armageddon.

Chapter 39

Dink stood in the warm sun. This was one of those rare days when the boiler smoke climbed straight up instead of lowering over town. There were still patches of white on the mountains and the glacier glistened in its distant valley. The breezes hinted of alpine cool and pine and juniper. There was no evil up there in that clean world; only here.

He was used to feeling alone, but this time it was worse. Feeling alone among friends is somehow sad. Gathered around him were two gifted and able men, both supporting him to the hilt, offering whatever they could, and yet he felt isolated and could not say why. There was John Starr, awaiting a chance to recover what had been stolen from him and his family; and Doc Cutler, a man of such intuitive power that he had a plausible explanation for the Yellow Rose.

She owed Dink a wagon and traps and tools and a nag and his clothing. He stood there uncertainly, well aware of what he was about to do. But he didn't chasten himself or suppose he was being reckless. He would just do it.

He walked slowly upslope, past the mercantiles on Middle Street, past housewives buying bread from the Hohenzollerns' bakery, past husbands sitting patiently in wagons or collecting to talk wherever it was shady. He walked up the hill into the late morning, and then up the long grade to that sinister rectangle that lorded over the town, and stood outside it. The place had no beauty. Why did the Yellow Rose, with all her fortune, settle for that?

The parlor house would be stirring now. She might well be up. He opened the massive door and entered, aware that he was leaving the world of liberty and life and sunlight and penetrating a darker place. Oddly, no one approached. The barroom was empty. No nymph awaited customers in the red-draped room to the other side. One could almost imagine it was just like a thousand other houses that catered to the vices. But it was nothing like that. This place was different. He had the sense that this place was sucking him into itself, almost as if this visit were preordained.

No one appeared. He headed toward her office, the one handsome room in the building, the place where her ancestors gazed out from gilded oval frames. He found her there at her desk, dressed in gauze, all of her visible through the filmy white fabric, faint yellow roses embroidered over it.

"This is perfect, Drago," she said. "You can hop aboard and bounce around before I dispose of you. What a way to die."

She did stir him. Her coarsely powerful body radiated something he could put no word to. It lured him. He was ready, and she was smiling, and then he stopped cold.

"You owe me," he said. "A wagon, a good dray horse, a lot of rat traps, a lot of tools and gear, and my personal things. It comes to fifteen hundred."

"Why, Drago, this is entertaining. I could pay you. Yes indeed, I think I will. Give me an itemized list. If you lack one, sit down there and write it. Then I'll give you pure gold for your wagon. That would be a treat for me, seeing you thrown to the rats with a bag full of double eagles."

"It was a botched job, Consuela. If they had used another gallon of coal oil, I wouldn't be here."

"Yes, and they'll pay. I used a pair of pugs from the saloons. I should have employed someone with brains. They won't be around here for long."

"There's no way you can ever replace my old nag. He knew me better than I knew myself. There is no price tag for grief, and for that reason you can never pay me what you owe me. Can you think of a way?"

"That's the whole point, Drago. I do what can never be remedied. There is no restitution. You see?"

"No, explain it to me."

"I can destroy love, Drago. You loved that nag and now it's dead, a butcher knife across its throat. I can destroy much more than material things. I destroy lives."

"Why?"

"So that people like you can come and feel superior to me before they croak."

She drew apart the gauze of the robe and smiled. Her buxom chest was alluring.

He stared at her lovely figure and went cold. "You really have a long way to go, Consuela. You've never killed anyone yourself. You really won't reach your goal of perfect evil until you do it. You can't rely on thugs to do all of that for you and still believe you're the devil's child."

She darkened a moment. "Well, I can change that, can't I?"

"No, you can't. You don't have the courage. You can only command others to do your dirty work."

He watched her darken, some rage boiling up like lava through her.

"You could have one of your hooligans dispatch me, but it wouldn't do you any good, Consuela. You would still know, and I would know, that you didn't do it yourself. So if you really plan on killing me, you'll need to do it all

by yourself. You can, you know. You're two feet higher and
seventy pounds heavier, and probably could manhandle
me with one hand."

She laughed.

"But you won't. You just aren't very evil, Consuela.
You'll dig into your desk there for gold and pay me.
Fifteen hundred should do it. That's as much gold as I
can carry, but I'll carry it away."

"I burned you out. Why don't you go to the authorities?"

"It's between you and me, Consuela. And you didn't
burn me out. Your pugs did."

"I sent them."

"That's because you have no stomach for violence. It's
always someone else, on your orders."

"I'll show you what my orders can do!" She pulled a
cord and a bald thug materialized instantly.

"Kill him."

"You afraid to do it, Consuela? Haven't the heart?"

"Take him away."

The bald pug clamped Dink's shoulders with his huge
hands and dragged Dink off. Dink found himself being propelled toward the kitchen, toward the rat hole. Another big
lout was lifting the cover from that sinister rectangular slot.
Dink smelled rotting garbage that had been thrown into
that foul place.

Behind him, the Yellow Rose followed, trailing her diaphanous robe. She was happy.

"See, Drago, you're in my power."

"No, I'm in this pug's power. You're not the one who'll
toss me to the rats. I think you should do it."

She laughed. "You're a card, Drago."

"Consuela, you're just a convent girl trying hard to be
bad."

She stopped cold. "Where did you hear that?"

"From Vanishing Jack."

She turned to the goons. "Pound him until he tells me who Vanishing Jack is. And how I can get him."

"No need, Consuela. He's your nephew. Your dead brother's son."

She stopped, waved off the pugs, and approached Dink. She walked around him, studying him, clearly unsettled.

"Go ahead, Consuela Estrella-Cooper. Push me in yourself."

"All right, I will," she said, and shoved. But not hard enough. Dink teetered on the edge of that foul pit. A rank odor drifted into the kitchen.

"You didn't push very hard, Consuela."

"Where is he?"

"If you kill me, you won't find out."

"We have plenty of ways of finding out and by the time you scream out what you know, you'll be sorry you tempted me."

Dink said nothing. The Yellow Rose circled him again and again. Then she pushed. Hard.

Dink staggered. He found himself tumbling into that dark, dank hole, falling past the floor, past light, into hell. He landed on a heap of soft slimy stuff, unspeakable. The trapdoor rattled into place over him and snuffed the light. But a small glow remained from the tile drainpipe. He gagged on the smell, the foulness under his fingers, the slime soaking through his new bib overalls. She had done it, shoved him in, overcome whatever barriers lay within her. This time she had killed all by herself.

He searched wildly for rats, for the swarms of dark hungry creatures pouring out of every cranny. He smelled death and rot and wondered how long he could breathe. The very air was lethal. No rats. He studied the dark recesses, strained his eyes trying to see, and saw no rats, no armies of the night lined up to attack. His rat poisons, dumped so liberally here earlier, had taken their toll. He might escape.

It occurred to him to scream. He screamed. He yelled. He bellowed. He kept it up for a minute or two. Above, he heard muffled laughter. Then he fell into silence, wondering how long it would be before some rats did emerge from the crannies, rats not killed by all the rat's-bane he threw in. But if there were rats, he saw none. Nothing bit. He heard the pad of feet above, and then nothing. It would be a long wait until dark, until the evening's revelries ceased, a long wait before he could push that trap-door up and crawl out. He tried to breathe and thought he might perish from the foul air, and decided he could not wait. Rats might not kill him, but air like that could.

It was still morning. He listened and heard only quiet. The house had returned to its morning torpor. He clambered to his knees, repelled by the squishy hell under him, and pushed gently on that trapdoor. It lifted. He pushed higher, and found that a rug covered it. He couldn't see, but heard no shout. The girls were still asleep. The pugs and the Yellow Rose were probably celebrating.

He slid the cover aside and climbed out, utterly repelled by the stinking liquids that permeated his new clothing. Tiny white worms crawled all over him. No one came. He quietly slid the trapdoor back, settling it in place as gingerly as he could, and replaced the old piece of carpet over it. Then he walked through the silent house and out the front door, taking pains to slip it open and closed as quietly as the hinges permitted. It creaked, and his pulse lifted. But no one checked.

And then he walked into the sun. He had failed, but he was alive. He had come out of the rat hole and lived.

Chapter 40

Never had sunshine seemed so sweet. He stared at his clothing, horrified by the hundreds of tiny, writhing white worms over it. He felt them in his hair, in his moccasins. His pulse lifted. He trotted through the fresh morning, knowing only that he needed a horse trough.

The Howdy Livery Barn had one. He raced there, past early shoppers, past sleepy storefronts, until he found the black cavern of the livery barn, with its high double doors. He headed straight into the yard and the trough, and splashed in, diving under the surface, wallowing in the cold water, slapping and rolling and soaking. Then he surfaced, and saw the little worms swimming everywhere.

"Hey!" yelled that hostler. "What you doin'?"

"Having a bath."

"Get out of there."

Dink did, water rivering off him. He stepped down to earth.

"You, is it? I should charge you."

"Thank you for the bath. I needed it. You may want to change the water."

Dink walked off, feeling water squish around in his moccasins. He felt better. Maybe the Chinamen could get the new clothes clean. He abandoned the livery barn and walked down the long slope to Starr's wagon yard, dripping water all the way.

Starr saw him and started laughing.

"Fell into the creek, did you?"

"Fell into the Yellow Rose's rat hole."

John Starr listened, mouth agape, as Dink recounted the rest of his morning.

"Why weren't you eaten alive?" he asked.

"I went up there the night after she'd destroyed Cherry. I had a long spoon I use, and I loaded most of the rat poisons I had left into that hole from outside. I threw so much poison in there I killed them off, and all their cousins. It saved my life. But meanwhile, the garbage and refuse was piling up in there, uneaten by rats, the feast of worms. When I got out of there, I was covered with hundreds, maybe thousands, of little white worms. I headed for the horse trough at the livery stable."

"You went there alone? You confronted her alone?"

"I thought Doc's theory about her might have something to it. It does."

"But she pushed you in."

"Only after I drove her to it. I taunted her. I told her she was just a convent girl trying to be bad. I was wrong."

Starr laughed suddenly, but it was a sharp, pained laugh that veneered the hurt within him.

"She doesn't know you escaped?"

"She thinks I'm dead, eaten alive. I remembered to yell and scream for a while. When I pushed that trapdoor open, no one stopped me. The place was still quiet."

"I'd like to see her face when you show up again."

"If I show up. I've run out of courage, John. There are other rat holes and they're still full of rats."

"Just walking in there alone and unarmed was more than I could manage," Starr said.

"I need to clean up and change," Dink said.

"Sure, and let's talk after you get squared away."

Never was any mortal so glad to get out of something he wore. Dink scrubbed himself furiously at the horse trough, poured water over his head, and finally toweled himself dry and stepped into the other set of clothes. There was no help for the moccasins, and he put them on knowing they would dry tight around his feet. He headed into sunlight, let the zephyrs dry his hair and draw the water from his moccasins.

She thought she had killed him. She was willing to try. But he had driven her to do it with his taunts. For some reason, he thought Doc was right. She was pushing herself farther and farther into blackness and begging to be stopped.

He had no money for the Chinamen, so he build a fire in Starr's stove, found a kettle, and boiled his clothing until he was confident that everything was clean. Then he rinsed the duds and hung them to dry in the bright light. They looked none the worse for wear. They had survived the pit, just as he had.

He found Starr hard at work over his ledgers.

"I want to try again. I want to take her out on a picnic."

"You're a brave man."

"No, not really. She'll be so rattled at the sight of me that I'll have an advantage. What I want is to borrow your trap and a horse, and maybe put together a lunch from your stores."

"It's yours. But Drago . . . Are you sure?"

"No, I'm not sure. I'm never sure. But I'm on the brink of it, right on the edge of something. That last picnic, she fell into being the girl she was, just for a while."

"After what happened this morning, you'd try that? Drago, you have more courage than I do. Or is it a wish to die?"

"I can't quit now."

Starr stared out the window. "Do you think it'd help if Vanishing Jack showed up at your picnic?"

The idea stunned Dink. "Vanishing Jack?"

"Sure. One look at me and she'd know who I am. Do you think that'd tip her over?"

"John, if I'm not back here in an hour with your trap, I'm off on a picnic. Last time, we drove up the gulch above the mines and kept on going until we got to high country near the glacier. Maybe I'll see you there."

"Unless I find the trap parked at the Yellow Rose's and you're nowhere in sight."

It was something to consider. Dink nodded. They both knew they were playing with giant powder.

As fast as he could, Dink harnessed a black horse, found some fragrant fresh bread and a wheel of Swiss cheese and some bottled sarsaparilla, and set off for the parlor house.

The place was alive now.

He dropped a carriage weight and hiked to the door. A momentary fear clutched him. That sinister place exuded violence and terror. But when she set eyes upon him, the terror would be hers, not his.

He pulled the door open and walked in. The saloon side had a few customers, afternooners in black broadcloth suits. Two or three nymphs occupied the red-draped parlor on the other side, dressed to seduce. The Yellow Rose was nowhere in sight.

He boldly hiked down the dark hallway to her office, but she wasn't there. He pushed onward, into the forbidden precincts of her private apartment, opened a door, and found her lying on her vast silken bed in dishabille. She sat up with a start.

"Oh . . ." she said, unable to comprehend the man standing there in bib overalls.

"No," she said, her voice rising. "No, no."

"I'm here, and I'm inviting you to go with me. We'll drive up to the high country and have a picnic."

"Who are you?"

"Drago, same as before."

"But how . . ."

She stared at him as at a specter. "No, not you."

"Consuela, it is time for you to get dressed."

"I've a headache. I've been in bed ever since . . ."

"Pushed me into the rat hole. Now get ready. We're going on a picnic."

She couldn't cease staring. She stared unblinking, her face masking everything. Did she believe her eyes? Dink couldn't say.

As if in a trance, she arose, not bothering to conceal her flesh from Dink, and slowly slid into a cream silk dress. She combed her dark hair, and then she turned to him.

"You have power over me," she said.

Dink thought about that. If she thought she was seeing a specter, some horrible ghost from the other side of the great divide, then let her think it.

"You liked the high country the last time. We'll go there."

At last she was ready. She reached for a tasseled red Chinese shawl, and then they walked out of her quarters, through her office, through the foyer and out. Eyes watched them. Men stared. The nymphs held their breath.

Outside, in late afternoon, he helped her into the trap, and then he picked up the carriage weight and joined her on the quilted leather seat. He flicked the lines, and the well-trained harness horse took off at a smart walk.

"Why am I doing this?" she asked.

"Because I invited you."

She stared at him, somehow passive and mute, not at all the harsh and sinister woman whom he had encountered several times. She sat there with a blank expression.

"You . . . Are you alive or dead?" she asked suddenly as they passed the mines on the bench.

"I'd killed your rats," he said.

She stared, and then reached for something on her calf. He grabbed her arm. It would have been no contest, that six-foot woman against Dink, but she subsided.

"I'll take that," he said. With his free hand he found the stiletto and pitched it into the grass.

She submitted passively. Doc was right. Something in her wanted to be stopped, ached desperately for Dink to control her.

But he knew she was still dangerous, still unstable, still likely to lean over and strangle him with her bare hands.

They drove slowly upslope. The horse was working now, dragging that trap up an endless grade. They passed the stumps of a woodland long since denuded by the woodcutters, passed from the sight of the mines and the town, passed into silent country, passed away from the mill and mine smoke into a land not yet spoiled. They crossed a virgin meadow laced with rills. He saw the eagle circling far above.

And still Dink drove. They climbed a slope and reached the plateau where alpine flowers formed a purple carpet. He drove onward, toward that wall of ice, the front of a glacier and the source of a dozen rivulets. The air had chilled.

She drew her red scarf around her.

They reached an aspen grove, and he halted.

"I have bread and cheese and some sarsaparilla," he said.

She didn't respond, but sat in the trap, her gaze upon the breathtaking and bright world they had penetrated.

Chapter 41

High above, the glacier filled the valley and it fed the rivulets that laced this plateau. The summer's wildflowers carpeted the meadow with purple and blue. Chill air from above occasionally eddied upon them, and then the Yellow Rose drew her red shawl close.

They didn't speak, but somehow he knew her moods. There were times when she was sullen and explosive and dangerous, when she might have wrapped her fingers around his neck and strangled him. But there were other times when she subsided into a desolation, when she mutely absorbed the innocence of the world they were piercing.

Dink stepped down, unhooked the tugs, and led the horse to a rivulet and let it drink. She watched, but did not leave her seat. He wondered if anywhere within her was a kindness or a courtesy toward animals.

This time she refused to leave the wagon, refused to step into the purple and blue carpet of flowers as she had done the other time. This time it was late in the afternoon and the sun hovered not far above the western peaks.

He picketed the horse and dug around in the trap for his picnic. He pulled out the crusty loaf and the golden wheel of cheese.

"No," she said.

He nibbled on cheese and said nothing. In his scheme of things, she would step out, wander through the lupine, return to the innocent girlhood that lay within, and slide into remorse that would end in great sobs and sorrow. But it was not like that. She sat there as hard as granite, her soul resisting the sweetness of the mountain meadow, fighting the innocence of nature with all of its bitter strength. Some fierce and deadly pride possessed her still.

"That is a big glacier," she said at last. "Do you suppose one could walk to it?"

Dink surveyed the steep slopes and found no reason a person could not. "From here it looks possible," he said.

"Would it be dangerous to walk out on it?"

"Yes, very."

That was all she wished to say. The ridges above cast long blue shadows that were crawling across the alpine meadow, and he thought that soon it would be cold, and they would need to hurry back. This had failed. This woman who commanded the legions of darkness had only managed to bring her darkness here. Maybe Doc was all wrong about her.

Dink finished a piece of cheese while the Yellow Rose sat inertly. He wished he had those special graces by which one mortal reaches into the heart of another, until all barriers fall away and souls commune with one another in perfect liberty. But he had no such gifts.

He thought to hook the horse to the tugs when he beheld, half a mile away, a horseman and a laden mule following behind. The horseman wore buckskins; that was all he could make out. And the mule bore two heavy panniers on a packsaddle.

She saw him too, and recognition bloomed in her. She sat rigidly in the trap, her mouth a slit, her gaze hooded. It could be only one person.

Vanishing Jack stopped some yards distant, surveying them as they sat silently in the trap. Then he touched heels to his horse and rode the last yards. He pulled off his broad-brimmed slouch hat so she might see that craggy and angled face, the face stamped with the harsh lines of his forebears—and hers.

She gasped.

"Aunt Consuela," he said.

"You!" She flew into a fury. "You!"

He nodded.

"Stealing from me," she yelled.

He did not nod, but simply waited.

"You're going to kill me," she said.

"You killed yourself long ago," he replied. "What's left to kill?"

"Where are your sisters?"

"Where you'll never find them."

"I will find them. I will destroy you."

He sat quietly, subtly reining the restless horse under him. Her threat did not faze him.

"What's in those packs?" she asked.

He dismounted leisurely, opened one pannier, and extracted a fist-sized chunk of quartz. He studied it a moment. The amber light of the late sun made the quartz glow.

"The native gold is visible," he said, and handed it to her.

"I will rattle your teeth until you tell me where it comes from," she said.

"I have it milled and I send the money to my sisters," he said. "They have so little. You took everything that my father possessed."

"And I'll take this! You think you can hide from me but you can't. I have eyes everywhere."

"Yes, and they look into your heart too, Consuela."

She threw the quartz at him. It hit the withers of his horse and bounced away.

She turned suddenly on Dink. "You knew he was coming here."

"We arranged it, yes."

"A picnic. Some picnic."

Starr gazed somberly at her. "You killed my father."

"He was in the way."

"The way of what?"

"Of my intentions."

"And are you happy now?"

"I'll kill you too. You can't escape. There's a reward for you. I'll double it now that I know who you are. I'll tell the world you look like . . . me."

"You'll throw me into a rat hole, I suppose."

She fell suddenly silent.

"Will you do it yourself? The way you shoved Drago here into the hole, into death?"

"Yes, I will."

"And what will it gain you?"

"I will be one step further toward my goal."

"Which is?"

"To be the last of my family."

"And what will happen to your fortune when you die? The mines, the buildings, the businesses, the parlor house?"

She stared into the setting sun. "They will die with me."

"Is that what you want? Aunt Consuela?"

She wouldn't look at her nephew. "I am the bad seed," she said. "I am the one with the bad blood, the Estrella curse. All the bad seed of ten generations gathered in me and made me what I am. I am the devil's child. I am walking death. I am the one who poisoned hope and life. I drugged him and threw him to the rats, just as I'll drug you and throw you to the rats."

She was raving now. Dink watched, transfixed by the spectacle of the Yellow Rose coughing up the bile and darkness from some black well of the soul.

"I am evil. I love the gold, not the life it can give. I have sold my body, I am a whoremonger. I have spread the nets of darkness through Skeleton Gulch. I have paid hundreds to do evil. The bones pile up and I pay Kilgore to get rid of them, and there are more bones than he can bury. I have the bad seed, and when I die, so will my family die. I will not die until you are dead, you and your sisters, and then I will be the last, and then I will die."

"You're already dead, Aunt Consuela," Starr said.

Now the sun was sliding behind the peaks, and the sky turned gold.

She slumped on her seat in the trap. Dink looked into her face and saw ruin there, and pathos, and darkness.

"I suppose you'll take me to the authorities," she said. "There's no evil I haven't done, nothing I would not do in the future."

This was important. Dink was hearing the voice of a woman who could discern good and evil. The voice of a woman who could not, in the end, escape her conscience. It was even as Doc had surmised.

"Because of me, men die, their widows are turned into my whores. And who can prove anything? The bones are all that are left. I cannot be convicted of anything. There is no case to be made against me. It's the plague. I laugh at them anyway. They are bought with trifles."

"You can tell them what you tell us, and make your own case against yourself," Dink said. "The evidence is yours to give."

She growled, some odd, strangled snarl that rose up in

her and burst out so suddenly that Dink started, and nearly abandoned the trap.

"They will never lay a hand on me! They will never put a hood over my head and the noose around my neck. I will not let them. They will never hear a shred of evidence from me. They will never convict me of the smallest crime."

She calmed suddenly.

"That glacier," she said. "It's almost as cold as I am. But I am colder. I am colder than anything on earth. I am colder than arctic ice, I am colder than anything ever recorded on a thermometer. Feel me!"

Dink pressed a hand on her arm and was shocked. It was as if he had touched ice.

"I will make my home in the glacier. Maybe in a thousand years it will discharge me upon these meadows and then the birds will pluck my thawed flesh."

She turned to glare at John Starr.

"Vanishing Jack. Vanishing Consuela."

And she stepped down from the trap and began hiking toward that slope with its wall of ice.

Chapter 42

They watched. The Yellow Rose hiked slowly upward, plainly weary, and yet determined. She reached the foot of the glacier and then headed left, struggling up a steep rocky slope until she stood at last beside the glacier.

A trick of light made her red shawl glow. She stood there a long time, catching her breath, surveying the surface of the glacier, which spread across a half mile and rose toward the distant peaks for several miles.

The valley grew lighter, as horizontal sunlight bounced from its steep walls. She walked out on the ice, and they could follow her easily, the red shawl a beacon. She walked slowly, wrestling with ledges and rough patches, her footing treacherous. She slipped and wobbled but would not stop.

Neither Dink nor John Starr spoke. The air was hushed. Soon twilight would fall. For another ten minutes Consuela struggled across the pale blue glacier, somehow avoiding a tumble.

And then she stopped. She stood for a long moment. The reflected light caught and lit her. She turned to face them. She wanted them to see her. Then she stepped into nothingness and vanished. One moment she was there, the next she was gone.

She had stepped into a crevasse and that would be her grave. A warm breeze eddied about Dink and Starr. It was as if the coldest thing on earth had been swallowed up. They stared upward. Starr pulled off his slouch hat. They waited as dusk thickened, but she was gone and they knew she would never be seen again.

"Amen," said Starr.

Dink felt a shiver run through his frame. He felt strangely lonely, and wondered how a person could be lonely at a moment like this.

He returned to the trap. Above the mountain meadow the eagle circled patiently.

Starr led the way, and all Dink had to do was follow behind the pack mule as the darkness engulfed the land. He soon was riding through night, not knowing where he was going, but the steady clop of Starr's horse and mule took them down and down, past the denuded woods, and finally to an overlook where they could see Skeleton Gulch below.

"I'll leave you here," Starr said.

"We need to talk," Dink replied.

"Doc Cutler's in an hour."

Vanishing Jack vanished. Dink carefully steered his horse toward the bench where the mill and mines pumped yellow smoke into the starlit night, and on down the long slope. He stared uneasily at the well-lit parlor house, entertaining its first customers of the evening. Nothing had changed and maybe that was the problem.

He unharnessed the horse in Starr's wagon yard, brushed it, and put it in the pens. It whickered and trotted off to be with friends.

Dink walked slowly into town, his mind dwelling on the moment when the Yellow Rose paused and then deliberately, carefully stepped into a crevasse. Soon the snows would enfold her and she would be trapped there for aeons of time.

He reached Cutler's darkened house, opened the rear door, and yelled.

"Drago, you are the least civil man in the universe," Cutler bellowed.

Doc was sitting in utter darkness, still in his ratty slippers and ancient bathrobe.

"You mind if I light the lamp?" Dink asked.

"Walk into a man's house, yell, and light his lamp. I was enjoying my solitude until you ruined it."

Dink scratched a kitchen match, lifted the glass chimney, touched the wick, and settled the glass. The flame faltered and then flared. Doc stared at him. The room was full of bobbing shadows.

"She's gone," Dink said. "Gone forever."

That certainly caught Doc's attention. Dink wasted no time telling Doc the whole story, the picnic, the appearance of Vanishing Jack, the teetering soul of the Yellow Rose, and then the long, lonely, fateful walk up the glacier.

"You were right, Doc. She wanted someone to stop her," he concluded.

Cutler rubbed the bristly stubble on his cheeks. "Some people can never shake their conscience," he said.

Starr knocked and was invited in. Miraculously, Vanishing Jack had vanished, and here was the head of a local freight company in denims and flannels.

"So it is done," Cutler said. "This creature whose ability was to destroy everyone and everything is gone. We should rejoice, but I see no happiness here."

"I won't be dancing on her grave," Starr said. "She was my aunt. Once she was lovely."

Cutler laughed unkindly. "You choose your words too carefully."

Starr frowned. "What next? That's what Drago and I are here for."

"What am I, some sort of oracle? Go figure it out yourselves."

"You're the man who might have some idea. We don't," Starr said.

Cutler slouched in his chair. In the yellow light of the single lamp, his white calves poking down from his robe seemed to collect light.

"What is it you want? I have no advice to give you."

"There's an army of the night and no one to lead it," Drago said. "There's men skilled at mayhem and murder; men capable of every cruelty. Men devoid of conscience or restraint. Men so rapacious they would kill for a dime. Corrupted women, desperate women. Secrets, undercurrents, agreements and alliances unknown."

"She left no will and no heir?"

"She walked up the glacier and vanished."

"But there might be a will in her safe?"

No one could answer that.

"There won't be," Doc said. "It is not in that sort of person to think beyond herself."

Starr nodded.

"So now there is a headless monster. An army of thugs with no leader. A platoon of killers, battalion of enforcers and petty crooks and grifters. Expert mixers of Mickey Finns. A gaggle of snitches who are the eyes and ears and antennae of the mob. Thugs in the mines who kill grumbling miners and leave their bones in the bottom of shafts. Suave executives, all of them on a paycheck. Every one of these grafters are looking out for himself. Every one of them is capable of killing you, Starr. It's yours, you know. You're the sole heir."

"No, most of it should be returned. I need to find the true heirs. Not mine at all."

"I know one thing, Starr. You wouldn't last an hour if you walked into her office and said you're taking over."

Starr stared into the lamp. "I've waited for this moment for years, planned for it, thought what I would do to bring her to justice. Well, here it is and I don't know what to do. Or whether I should do anything."

Cutler growled, raised phlegm, and spat into a coffee can he had next to his chair. The can was full of cigar butts.

"What's going to happen?" Doc said. "I imagine for a day or two nothing at all. They'll be waiting for the Yellow Rose to return, to walk in. To resume. The parlor house bosses will collect money and leave it on her desk. The mine and mill bosses will bring gold and receipts. The poor girls will pander and seduce. Then they'll begin to wonder. Where did the Yellow Rose go? If she's gone, what is there to steal from her? And if they're caught stealing, why worry? Who's there to punish them?

"I suppose, what I'm saying is that as the minutes and hours tick by, crime-fevered minds will set to work. The iron lady is gone; the spoils will go to the most ruthless. It will be the war of all against all."

"We can't allow that; we need to notify the Territory."

Doc's cruel cackle seemed to Dink answer enough.

"I don't know how long we can wait," Dink said. "She has a vault and there's millions in that vault, and when it's clear she's not returning, there's going to be a fight for that gold."

Doc acknowledged it with a nod. "Let them," he said. "Let them fight over it, steal it."

"But Doc!"

"I'll get my share patching up bullet wounds," Doc said, and laughed darkly.

Dink didn't like it. "Doc, we can't just sit here. She's gone, and we've got to take over and put everything into John's hands."

Doc laughed nastily. "You've read too many trashy novels, Drago. Someone comes along and wins the day. Maybe you, eh? That your secret dream, Drago? One small man plays the white knight, conquers an empire, and turns over the spoils to the rightful heir?"

That was exactly what Dink was dreaming of, damn that doc.

"Yes, and I will."

Doc wheezed and spat into his makeshift spittoon.

Dink wanted to finish it.

"I'm going to go up there to that parlor house and tell them they're going to leave the territory."

"All by yourself!"

Dink nodded.

"Drago," Starr said, "Doc's right. You wouldn't last two minutes. They're all greedy, and they'll destroy each other, and that's the best justice of all. Then I can pick up the pieces."

"I'm going."

"Unarmed?"

"That's the only way."

Dink felt their stares on his back, and stepped into the warm night. The whole town was warmer. It was as if the Yellow Rose had frosted the very air.

From Doc's house it was seven blocks to the parlor house. Dink set out, not knowing how it would end.

Chapter 43

Dink stepped in and was greeted with that musky, acrid smell he knew so well. There were still rats in the building. It was obviously a normal evening. Men in black broadcloth lined the bar of the saloon on the left; on the right, haunted women in gauze awaited their customers in a chamber lined with red velvet drapes. The hum of conversation rose from the saloon. The usual deep silence filled the spaces of the ladies' reception room.

He paused.

"Come right in, sweetheart," said one of the girls he had never before seen.

If the Yellow Rose's pugs were around, they were being discreet. He scarcely knew where to go, whether to talk to those mining men in the saloon or the girls, or go elsewhere. He decided first to head for her office, and walked unimpeded back through a gloomy corridor, faintly lit, to her private rooms. There he found one of the pugs, the bald thick one who had watched when the Yellow Rose shoved Dink into the rat hole.

"You," the pug said, scarcely believing his eyes. "Where is she?"

"She's dead."

"What?"

"By her own hand. You won't ever see her again."

"What is this? You can't walk in here and say that."

"I'm here."

"Why should I believe you?"

"You'll believe me with every tick of the clock, every sunrise and sunset. She hiked out upon that glacier high above this place, and threw herself into a crevasse."

The pug moved in, grabbed a fistful of Dink's bib overalls. "That's crap."

Dink didn't respond, and the pug loosened his grip.

"Who knows this?"

"You're the first person here that I've told."

"Who owns this now? Maybe I'll kill him."

"Did she leave a will?" Dink asked.

"How the hell should I know?"

"You could look."

The pug glanced fearfully at the door, as if expecting the Yellow Rose to walk in any second. And then he began hunting through cabinets, yanking out drawers. He found nothing. Not even ledgers. The Yellow Rose had kept her business inside her head. Dink marveled. She ran an empire, mines, houses, stores, saloons. She paid an army. But the pug found nothing.

"Maybe in that safe," Dink said.

"She'd kill me."

They stared at a small black safe with cherubs painted on it and a combination lock on its enameled door. The door was ajar. The Yellow Rose had left it that way.

The pug piled into it. Within was a metal box filled with eagles and double eagles. Nothing else. It was probably the cash she used to pay her snitches and errand boys and killers, maybe pay tradesmen.

He hesitated, shoved the heavy money box back, and headed for her bedchamber. He knocked politely, got no response, and walked in. He lit a lamp with a lucifer, while Dink watched. He pushed and probed fiercely, pawed through her lingerie, felt the bottoms of drawers.

"If she died with no will, and no heirs show up, then the Territory gets it all," Dink said.

The pug cursed, turned down the wick, and stormed out.

"Who's in charge?" Dink asked.

"No one. Maybe I am."

"Then do what you will," Dink said.

"How do I know this isn't some trap of yours? And hers?"

Dink shrugged. "I'm leaving shortly. You can sit here and wait for her. Sun rises at five, sets at ten."

The pug stood there, paralyzed with indecision. Then suddenly he loomed over Dink, a foot higher and fifty pounds heavier. He grabbed Dink by the bib again. "You're not telling anyone. If you tell anyone I'll kill you."

"You're too late. Other people know."

"Who?"

Drago felt himself pulled upward. "One of the heirs knows."

"Who?"

"Vanishing Jack."

The pug dropped Dink suddenly and stared.

"What's your name, fella?" Dink asked.

"Doe, John Doe."

"Very well, Mr. Doe, I'll leave you here. Do what you will."

The pug let him go. Dink drifted back to the lamplight of the foyer, and turned into the red room. Three girls instantly stood up and smiled.

"Ladies, the Yellow Rose is dead. You're free to live your lives as you choose."

That evoked only strange titters and giggles.

"She's not here and won't be coming back. By tomorrow that'll be obvious."

"Hey, fella, you're a great loverboy," said one.

Dink retreated to the saloon. Some of those faces were familiar, tough mining bosses in black broadcloth. It didn't matter which one he chose. But somehow this would be riskier.

He edged toward the bar and interrupted a conversation between two black suits.

"The Yellow Rose is dead," he said. "She killed herself."

They stared at him, took in his bib overalls, and laughed.

"Get this. She's croaked," one said.

That was good for a chuckle.

"She went on a picnic, walked out on the glacier, and threw herself into a crevasse," Dink said.

"Hey, peanut, that's a dangerous joke."

"Have you seen her tonight?"

The black suits peered about uneasily.

"What're you doing in here?" asked one.

"Spreading the word."

"Spreading manure."

"By tomorrow it'll be plain. Why don't you go find her?"

The pair looked amused and turned back to their conversation. They were discussing the assay values in the last load of ore from the bottom level of the Victor. And those values had declined sharply. Dink listened, saying nothing, and then drifted off.

He stood quietly to one side, watching all the black suits talk. But then the fatter one set down his tumbler and headed into the foyer, looked around, and headed down the dark hall toward the Yellow Rose's private chambers. A minute later he returned, shook his head, and resumed drinking.

"She's upstairs with a customer," he told his drinking pal.

They chuckled again.

The bald pug who called himself John Doe quietly slid

through the foyer carrying a heavy metal box, and vanished out the door. There went a thousand dollars or so.

The black suit turned to the barkeep. "Hey, where's the lady tonight?"

The keep shook his head. "I haven't seen her."

"Upstairs, I guess." It was a question.

"She doesn't entertain upstairs."

The black suit abandoned his drink and began touring the building. Dink watched quietly. He saw a frightened but determined blond girl in street clothes slide into the night, carrying a small case. One free; many others still slaves.

The black suit returned and began whispering to his friend. Then they spotted Dink watching them, and immediately hemmed him in.

"Tell it again," the fatter one said.

"She died by her own hand at twilight. Vanishing Jack and I watched her. If there's no will, this place has no owner. The mines have no owner. You don't work for anyone. If there are no heirs, the Territory gets this, all of it."

"Who are you?"

"Dink Drago, rat catcher. I've caught my rat."

"You've made a good joke, pal, now get out."

Dink nodded. He was done there anyway. He quietly walked to the massive door, opened it, slipped into the dark, and heard the muffled sound of revelry within. It had gone about as he figured. News travels slowly, and news like that runs up against walls. It would take a day or two.

He stood there, staring at that sinister rectangle of a building. But somehow it seemed less ominous now, less evil, with her far away, swiftly turning to ice. He slipped around to the rear, where he might see what there was to see. Light spilled from the window in her office, and through the soft curtain he saw all sorts of people frantically tearing it apart, and some of them were dressed in black. They had obviously cased the whole place and found no Yellow Rose.

The carrion birds were feasting.

He heard a muffled shot, and the black bulk of a fat man slumped slowly to the floor. Once again, Dink had witnessed murder in that house. He thought of poor Cherry, whose feet were knocked from under her and who perished from loss of blood a few minutes later, eaten alive.

It sickened him. He circled around to the front, and now saw black suits racing into the night, rats abandoning a sinking ship. He heard a muffled scream. Then more. The pugs were doing something to the girls. He pitied them. A half-dressed customer fled into the night, carrying his polished high-top shoes. A girl wearing nothing but a gauzy robe raced out the door, sobbing.

"Whoa up, you're safe," he said, but she only ran harder.

He heard the tinkle of shattering glass, and laughter in the saloon. He edged toward that window, and saw two black suits circling each other. One had a broken whiskey bottle in hand.

Then John Starr materialized beside him.

"I'd like to get those oil portraits of my grandparents," he said.

Dink nodded. They walked in, steered past knots of people, headed for the office, found it crowded with relentless treasure-seekers, lifted the handsome ovals off the wall without being challenged, and walked away.

"Thanks, Drago," Starr said as they slipped into the safety of the night.

Chapter 44

There was no vault in the parlor house. No mountain of gold ingots. That was all legend.

Doc, properly dressed at last, and John Estrella-Cooper, still using the name of Starr, and Dink Drago probed every corner of the forlorn building, looking for secret chambers, hidden walls, unexplained bulk. But there was nothing. Only the small office safe, which was empty.

Doc wore striped pants, boiled white shirt, black tie, cutaway, cummerbund, white gloves, and silk stovepipe top hat. He said that clothing performed ceremonial purposes and nothing could be more consequential than burying the evil empire. So it was a black-tie event as far as he was concerned.

Where the gold from the mines went remained a mystery, and the managers could not or would not explain it. The mines and mill had shut down, there being no way to run them until their ownership was established. Most of the miners and managers had drifted off, unpaid, some of them carrying anything of value. The gallows frames stood as silent sentries along the bench, and no smoke from the stacks lowered over Skeleton Gulch or blotted out the blue of heaven.

The poor wretched women of the cribs and parlor

houses had escaped. Some preferred the life, but others wept at finding their liberty and it didn't matter that their reputations were ruined and they had little or nothing. They would make their way somehow. Most of the saloons closed too. Starr had immediately fired everyone in the Traveler's Rest, the worst of the death traps. Whether he had the power to do so was questionable, but he did it anyway just by walking in and doing it.

Most of the rats of all descriptions had left town. The ball was over. The Golden Hind closed its doors and the tinhorns folded up their green oilcloth layouts and headed for other mining camps. Hap Kilgore shut down his mortuary and fled, afraid of an inquiry. To get properly buried these days in Skeleton Gulch, one had to wire Missoula where Hugo and Sons laid out the dead.

The Territory made only a few perfunctory inquiries. So far as it knew, the owner of the mines and other properties had vanished, was presumed dead, and had died intestate. All the rest was rumor. If there were dark secrets, they resided in the heads of well-greased officials, who lost interest anyway as soon as it had become clear that the Yellow Rose had vanished and was presumed dead. The Territory might find itself with unclaimed properties.

One evening, over dinner at Doc's house, Starr confessed that he wasn't going to claim the inheritance.

"It's too fouled. It's built on human bones, destroyed lives and dreams, murder and vice and corruption. Neither my sisters nor I want anything to do with any of it. We'll share equally in my own mine and let Aunt Consuela's properties go. They would soil us if we owned them."

"A sound decision," Doc opined.

So he filed no claim upon the estate, but did file a mining claim that would cover his bonanza, and put his sisters' names to it. Skeleton Gulch would have a new bonanza mine.

Then one day, when Starr was poking through the few papers the Yellow Rose left behind, he found some curious receipts from Wells Brothers, a San Francisco financial and transfer company that specialized in moving wealth of all sorts from one place to another in complete safety. There were two sets of receipts; one acknowledged the receipt of gold bullion at their San Francisco bank. These receipts were for large sums, and probably recorded most of the output of the Victor Mining Company mines. There were, in all, receipts for over three million dollars in bullion.

But it was the other receipts that fascinated Starr. These affirmed the safe delivery of hundreds of thousands of Mexican pesos to a certain bank in San Luis Potosi, on behalf of a foundling home called the Little Sisters of Santa Rita. He knew, suddenly, where the vast treasure from the Victor mines had gone. San Luis Potosi was the original home of the Estrellas, his grandmother's family. The connection with the foundling home was unclear. But the meaning of his discovery was clear enough: The Yellow Rose had diverted the fruits of her dark life into something sweet and innocent and good.

As soon as he had figured it all out, he corralled Drago and Doc and showed them the receipts.

"It figures," Doc said. "What would a woman who cannot escape her conscience do? She would expiate her sins in just such a manner. And the worse she behaved, the more desperately she shipped her bloodstained gold and wealth to this orphanage, if that's what it is."

That made sense to Dink. He had one last task, which was to figure out just what had happened in Skeleton Gulch and then report it all to General Cook. The general was a martinet when it came to facts, to completeness, to tracking down the loose ends so that every question might be well and truly answered. So in the days following the demise of the Yellow Rose, Dink had set to work, recording what he knew, what he surmised, and in what ways that cancer had been blotted from the Territory.

Human pack rats had made off with all the furnishings of the parlor house. There was not so much as a bar towel left. The buildings along Yellow Rose Street that had contained cribs and dens were likewise as empty and hollow. John Starr hired a powderman from the mine to set some charges and blow to rubble that sinister building, where so many had perished and others had been enslaved. One morning, with spectators kept well back, the powderman fired his charge and the grim fortress lifted up and then crumbled into a heap of rock. And as the dust settled, a change came over Skeleton Gulch. It was as if a cruel, cold darkness had lifted from it, grim memories had been burned out of it, and the future would be bright and warm.

Doc watched, dressed once again in his striped pants and cutaway and boiled shirt because this was an important occasion.

As the rubble settled and the dust blew away, he ventured his opinion.

"I'll be treating fewer injuries," he said. "And seeing less melancholia."

Starr nodded. "You'd better be perfect, because there's no undertaker left in Skeleton Gulch."

Doc smiled.

John Starr busied himself with mining engineers and the beginning of a mine head and a shaft. And even while that was under way, he was hiring good hardrock miners.

"I like it better this way," he said. "I came to reclaim an inheritance stolen from me; I'm here now to create my own wealth."

That appealed to Drago too.

Dink wired General Cook, briefly reporting on events

and promising a full report shortly. He billed Cook fifteen hundred dollars for a new wagon, traps, dray horse, and personal goods lost in the holocaust. And he requested rail fare back to Denver.

But Cook had other ideas.

"Request denied," he wired. "Loss of wagon and traps not our agency responsibility. Charge it to your rat business. Rail fare to Denver approved. See stationmaster, Helena."

Cook was behaving true to form.

Drago thought that there were rats in Denver too.

THE LAST GUNFIGHTER SERIES BY
WILLIAM W. JOHNSTONE